OPEN YOUR EYES

HEATHER J. FITT

*To Irene
Happy Reading!
Heather J Fitt*

BLOODHOUND
— BOOKS —

For my wonderful husband, Stuart.
My best friend, my soulmate and my number one cheerleader.

INTRODUCTION

incel

noun

1. a member of an online community of young men who consider themselves unable to attract women sexually, typically associated with views that are hostile towards women and men who are sexually active.

feminism

noun

1. the advocacy of women's rights on the ground of the equality of the sexes.

femoid ("foid")

noun

1. term used to describe women. Usually "female humanoid (organism)", sometimes "female android".

Regardless, it's used to indicate that women aren't fully human, and are either sub-human or "other". Often used in conjunction with the pronoun "it" to further dehumanise women.

truecel

noun

1. True incel. Reflecting debates around authenticity and the purity of the incel label, this is used to denote someone who is *really* incel. This might mean that they have never kissed/touched a woman, or that they genuinely could not have sex even if they tried.

Stacy

noun

1. Used to denote a woman who has sex with a lot of men and is stereotypically air-headed, unintelligent, beautiful and promiscuous. As with other terms used to describe women, Stacy homogenises and demeans them.

Becky

noun

1. Beckys are the majority of the female population and are subordinate to Stacys. They are "average" looking and have lower social status.

PROLOGUE

He was standing in the bushes at the entrance to the tunnel, out of sight of anyone in the Tesco car park; not that there was anyone to see him. He pulled off his gloves, worn to protect his hands against the biting Edinburgh winter, and sparked up a cigarette. He took a long, deep draw on the smoke and exhaled into the frigid night air. The smoke mingled with the condensation of his breath and hung for a second before disappearing.

From where he stood, he could see anyone walking along the path, making their way into the tunnel. During the day, they would probably have been able to see him too, but the moonless sky and his black clothing ensured he blended seamlessly with the shadows. Someone walking up the path would only be able to see the gentle orange glow from the tip of his cigarette. As soon as anyone came along he would extinguish it, crushing it beneath his boot. He could imagine them questioning whether they had seen it at all. He imagined them peering into the inky blackness wondering if anyone was there. He imagined the uptick in their heart rate, their breathing becoming shallower and their mouth drying. He smiled and he felt his own heart thump with excitement.

He finished his cigarette and pulled out a hip flask. A little nip to keep him warm. It wouldn't be long, she'd be here shortly. Her Tesco shift ended soon and he knew she'd take the shortcut through the tunnel and across the park. He knew because he had watched her do it several times before he decided she would be the one.

She had caught his attention a few weeks before when she'd scanned his shopping through the checkout; it soon became apparent this was a regular shift. She was pretty, confident and feisty – he'd soon knock that out of her. He followed her home that first night and was delighted when she took the route through the park. Had she no concern for her own safety? Tut, tut.

He'd noted with interest that she picked up her pace as soon as she entered the tunnel. It was unsurprising really, it was long and stank of piss. The walls were covered in graffiti and despite the strip lights down the middle, only half of them were working and you couldn't see clearly to the other end. People hurried through it during the *day*, desperate to be outside and in the clean air again.

Once she realised she was being followed she checked behind her. He kept far enough back that she wouldn't be able to recognise him, but when she sped up, so did he. He laughed quietly to himself when she took out her phone and spoke.

'Hello, yeah, I'm in the park. I'll be home in ten.'

As she reached the exit to the tunnel, she started jogging; slowly her speed increased. By the time he made it into the park itself, she was running full pelt. Pleased to see her running up the ramp at the far end of the park, he didn't go after her. He needed her to keep using the tunnel and if he made it obvious he really was following her, she never would again.

After observing her from afar and watching her take the same route several nights in a row, he had decided tonight was the night. To be fair, she had to be expecting it. No woman walks on their own through an inky black park, with questionable lighting, who isn't secretly asking for it. Anyone who truly *wanted* to be safe would go the long way round.

The still night was broken with the sound of footsteps to his left. Confident footsteps, making a noise; not for hiding this one. It had to be her. He'd rarely seen anyone else at this time of night.

He waited until she was most of the way through the tunnel, before emerging from his hiding place, and followed her. He didn't want to spook her, not yet anyway and if she ran it would ruin everything. The constant wind rushing the length of the tunnel disguised the sound of his footsteps and he was able to catch up with her a bit.

She was absorbed by whatever was on her phone, and hadn't noticed there was anyone else in the tunnel with her. As expected, she took the path past The Yard and the children's slide built into the earth on the side of the park. He was close, any second she was going to realise there was someone behind her, someone she hadn't noticed before. She would get a fright and she would start to wonder, was he a harmless man passing her in the night, or was he an aggressor out to do her harm? The thought thrilled him to his core and excitement coursed through his body.

There! She'd heard him and spun her head round so quickly he thought her neck might snap. The surprise and shock on her face delighted him. He smiled at her and carried on walking; he wasn't doing anything wrong, just walking through the park, the same as she was. She put away her phone. Silly girl, *now* was the time she was going to need it.

Her pace increased and he knew he had to make his move.

It was perfect, they were approaching the bottom of the ramp and the trees down the side would give him the cover he needed.

He pounced. Grabbing her from behind, he clamped one hand over her mouth before she could even think about screaming. Pulling her backwards so she was off balance, he dragged her into the trees.

He threw her to the ground and smiled as she scrabbled backwards towards the graffiti-covered ten-foot concrete wall. She wouldn't escape that way, he thought, standing between her and any semblance of safety. He was pleased to see fear had paralysed her vocal cords, but he knew that wouldn't last long and pulled the black-handled hunting knife from his pocket. Serrated on one side and razor sharp on the other, he'd never actually had to use it on flesh, the fear it inspired on the little slappers was enough.

He stepped forward and knelt on the ground, grabbing her jacket, he slowly cut it open. Horrified, she watched him gradually slide the knife through the material. She whimpered so he leaned in close and held the tip of the knife to her cheekbone, just below her eye. 'Make another sound and you'll lose it.' She nodded frantically, but said nothing; her face glistening with snot and tears. 'There's a good little whore, I knew you wanted it.'

He climbed on top of her and cut off the rest of her clothing. She lay perfectly still and turned her head to one side, eyes closed. She made no sound and made no attempt to get away, clearly she was enjoying it. If she wasn't, she would have fought, wouldn't she?

Afterwards, he ordered her to lick his penis clean, promising to cut off her nipple if she refused. He then zipped up his trousers and walked away. She'd be fine, she was only ten minutes from home after all.

CHAPTER ONE

'Frankie! Get in here!'

Frankie's head popped up from behind her computer screen where she'd been hiding, hoping Sid wouldn't notice her, but he'd already disappeared back into his office. She quickly tapped out a final few words on the document she'd been working on and pressed save.

'What's up with him today?' Amy whispered from the other side of the desk.

'No idea, I've tried to stay well out of his way,' groaned Frankie. She hauled herself to her feet, and picked up her pad and pencil. 'I'd better go and see what he wants.'

'If you're not out in ten minutes, I'll interrupt with a "phone call".'

Frankie smiled at her friend and strode across the open-plan office of the *Edinburgh Chronicle*, trying to ignore the blatant stares from her colleagues.

She tapped on the office door and opened it, poking her head through the gap to make sure Sid wasn't on a call.

He looked up from the sheaf of papers in his hand. 'Come

in, come in. It's bloody freezing out there, you'll let all the heat out.' Grumpy was Sid's resting mood.

Frankie slipped past the door, closing it behind her, and took a seat opposite him. He tossed the papers on the desk, leaned back in his chair and rested his hands on his ever-expanding stomach. 'I've read your Valentine's Day article.' He gestured towards the printed copy in front of him.

A whirl of thoughts flashed through Frankie's mind, trying to figure out exactly what was wrong with her article. It was standard Valentine's Day fare: an article about famous couples whose marriages had stood the test of time.

Of course, it wasn't the kind of reporting she wanted to be doing. No, Frankie had her eyes firmly set on proper news-reporting journalism. She wanted to write stories that truly mattered to people, not some Z-list article that next to nobody would want to read. However, she knew working her way up through the ranks was the only way to get there and she had accepted it a long time ago.

'Is there something wrong with it?'

'Not as such. I mean it's good writing, as always, but don't you think it's a bit... safe?'

'I mean... I suppose so, but this is the kind of thing people who care about Valentine's Day want to read. Isn't it?' Frankie had thought the article was a solid piece, but her confidence was wavering. Where was Sid going with this?

'I think you could do better. I don't mean your writing is bad,' said Sid quickly, seeing the look on Frankie's face. 'I mean, I think the subject matter could be stronger, more... *significant*.'

'I know I'd definitely like to write more serious articles.' Frankie was warming to the conversation and imagining her name on the front page of the newspaper.

Sid held up a hand. 'Let's not get too far ahead of ourselves. Do you think you can do another Valentine's Day article that's less... *saccharine*? I mean, we'll still use this, but I have space for another 500 words or so, if you're up to it?'

Another article? It was the day before Valentine's Day and that would mean producing something in an afternoon. Frankie liked to take her time over her articles, allowing herself a few days to write and edit and re-edit. She would often have several on the go, so that her time between stages was never wasted.

Sid interrupted her thoughts. 'Think of it this way, it's good practice for you if you're serious about reporting crime. This is the kind of turnaround time you'll have to stick to when you're playing with the big boys.'

What Sid said was true, writing articles days in advance was not the same as reporting crime which evolved and changed on a daily, sometimes hourly, basis.

'Okay, I'll do it. Put my name down for that space.'

'Excellent! Consider it done.' Sid looked at her expectantly. 'What are you waiting for? Bugger off out of my office and write.'

Frankie didn't need to be told twice. She made her way back to her desk and flumped into her chair, rubbing her forehead while she tried to think of an appropriate Valentine's Day piece she could deliver before the end of the day.

Amy arrived back with two cups of tea, she passed one over to Frankie before sitting down on her side of the desk. 'What did he want?'

'He thought my Valentine's Day article was too safe and he wants me to write another piece.'

'Another piece? What about?'

'Still Valentine's Day, but something not quite so hearts and flowers.'

'What are you going to write about?' Amy sounded as bewildered as Frankie felt.

'No idea. I don't have much time to do any real research. I

mean, what's Valentine's Day if not hearts and flowers?' Frankie was beginning to regret her earlier enthusiasm. 'Maybe I should tell him I can't do it.'

'No, you can't do that. He's giving you a chance and you need to show him what you're capable of.'

'I know he's giving me a chance, but I'm not sure I *am* capable.'

'Okay, let's think logically. You need something easily researchable and quick.' Amy was ignoring Frankie's look. She swept her long red hair over her shoulder and typed furiously, her eyes fixed on the screen. Frankie watched on, trying desperately to think of a good topic that wouldn't come across as pink and fluffy.

'Bingo!' exclaimed Amy, still reading the text on her screen.

'What?' Frankie made her way round to Amy's side of the desk. On the monitor was a picture of a stained-glass window depicting a man dressed in religious clothing, holding a staff in one hand and a fern in the other.

'You want me to write about stained-glass windows?'

'No, don't be daft. I want you to write about how there were – are – several St Valentines,' replied Amy triumphantly.

Frankie took over control of Amy's mouse, clicked on the article alongside the picture and started reading.

After a minute or so, Amy gave her a nudge and shooed her back to her own side of the desk. 'I'll send you the link. I've got my own stuff to be getting on with.'

Frankie spent the next couple of hours researching as much as she could about the various St Valentines and it grew on her how much more there was to the day than she realised. The saints in question were often patron saints of various things, and the day itself had started off as a pagan holiday called Lupercalia.

Amy had interrupted by placing yet another cup of tea on the coaster next to her keyboard.

'Thanks, mate.' Frankie took a sip and checked her watch. Shit! She had become so engrossed in her research she had lost track of time. She only had ninety minutes to pull it all together and submit it for publishing.

For over an hour Frankie typed at a furious pace, determined to make the deadline Sid had given her.

With five minutes to spare, Frankie sat back in her seat and breathed out heavily. 'Right, I think that's it. I'm emailing it over to you – two sets of eyes and all that.'

Frankie's eyes moved back and forth across her screen as she read the words she had only just written. She hated doing a final read through so soon after finishing but needs must.

'This looks good to me. There'll be at least another two people read it before it goes to print anyway,' said Amy after a couple of minutes of silence.

Frankie tapped a few keys and then clicked her mouse with a flourish. 'It's gone.'

The following day was Valentine's Day itself. The day both of Frankie's articles were due to be published in the paper. These days it didn't only appear in print form, but was also posted on the newspaper website, as well as Twitter, Facebook and Instagram. Frankie often set up notifications so she could gauge reaction to her features, and today she wanted to compare the reactions between her two contrasting stories.

While she researched a few different ones she had in the pipeline, Frankie's mind wandered to the romantic evening she was looking forward to with her boyfriend, Todd. This year he had promised to organise everything. It wasn't that Frankie constantly needed hearts and flowers and date nights, but a girl does like to be made to feel special on occasion, and recently she had felt Todd was taking her for granted.

It had all blown up a week or so earlier during a blazing row which had started because Todd hadn't bothered to wash the dishes even though he'd been at home all day. She'd walked in and immediately spotted the unwashed dishes strewn across the kitchen side. Todd was playing on his Xbox in the room. Frankie's temper snapped after a difficult day at work.

'Are you fucking joking?'

'What?'

'You've been at home all day and you've not even done the dishes? You and your bloody Xbox!'

'I've only been on for a wee while, I was going to do them later.'

'Do I have to do everything around here?' Frankie slammed the door behind her and marched into the kitchen to make a start.

Todd followed and the row continued as she ran water into the sink.

Frankie blurted out how she was sick and tired of being the one who always made the effort and maybe Todd didn't love her at all. Maybe he just found her convenient because she rarely complained, was easy to live with, and not bad in the sack.

Todd had responded by pointing out if she wasn't so worried about being an 'independent woman' – the voice he used and the air quotes angering Frankie even more – then maybe he would do nice things more often. Frankie had enquired as to what, precisely, was wrong with being an independent woman. From there the argument had escalated to epic proportions.

It raged on for some time, exhausting both of them. Once they had calmed down to a simmer, Todd had cracked open two beers and handed one to Frankie. They had apologised to each other and had an open and honest conversation. Frankie promised to actually talk to Todd more, and in turn, Todd promised he would take sole responsibility for Valentine's Day this year. He drew the line at paying extortionate restaurant prices though, he would arrange everything in the flat.

Todd had instructed her not to arrive home before 6pm. He was working his shift at the gym until just after lunch and he said he needed time to prepare.

Frankie was excited, four hours of preparation could mean all sorts of things. She wasn't fussed about presents or cards or flowers, but she did hope there would be fizz and some really good food. A nice meal and a bottle of bubbly would be absolute heaven.

She and Todd had met at the gym where Todd worked. She had decided one Saturday, after having a hissy fit at not being able to get into her favourite dress, that it was time to do something about her wobbly belly that definitely wasn't getting smaller.

When she'd arrived for her induction, Frankie had been faced with a man nothing like she had expected. He wasn't a muscle-bound behemoth, instead he looked toned and taut, comfortable in his own skin. His dark chocolate brown eyes had twinkled as he introduced himself and when he gave her a lopsided smile her stomach flipped.

And that was that. They had been together for a little over five years and had moved in together eighteen months after their first official date. It just kind of happened; they spent most of their time together anyway. After a while it made no sense to be paying two lots of rent, bills and grocery shopping.

The one thing that really wound Frankie up though, was Todd's laziness. He was often in at odd times because of the way his shifts worked, but he never thought to give the place a hoover, or clean the toilet, or replace the milk they'd run out of. He would do it if he was asked, but he never did it just because. Frankie hated leaving him a list of things to do. Consequently, she ended up doing a lot of it herself and quietly fuming.

'Frankie, have you seen these comments?' Amy's voice pulled Frankie from her daydreaming.

'No, what comments?'

'On your Valentine's Day articles.'

'Not yet. Haven't had the chance to look.'

'You need to read them.' Amy rushed round to Frankie's side of the desk and pushed her out of the way, taking over her keyboard. She switched to Twitter and showed Frankie the screen. 'Look.' She pointed at the monitor.

Frankie pulled herself closer to the desk and leaned in to read the Twitter comments under her Celebrity Marriage article on the screen.

@MrsKircaldy1980

I am so sick of reading this nonsense on Valentine's Day. Does @EdinburghChronicle not realise we're bored of all this crap? #RealValentinesDay

@Feminist101

Yawn! More vacuous crap from @EdinburghChronicle. You're a newspaper, not a teenage magazine, sort it out! #RealValentinesDay

Frankie switched to her other Valentine's Day report and continued to read.

. . .

12

@MarkWhite
  This is so cool! I never knew any of this stuff!

@DanDan
  Finally! A newspaper reporting something interesting and factual about St Valentine!

'Oh my God.' Frankie scrolled down the replies, flicking between the reports; each reply was a variation on a theme. But it was clear, the readers of the *Edinburgh Chronicle* had spoken and they wanted solid factual reporting. And they *loved* Frankie's serious writing.

'This is amazing!' Amy was practically squealing.

'This is... unbelievable.' Frankie switched over to Instagram and then Facebook, the majority of the comments were all the same. She looked up at Amy, bewildered.

Amy beamed at Frankie, her eyes shining. 'You know what this means, don't you? It means Sid was right and he'll have to give you more of the serious stuff.'

'You know what Sid's like. I don't know...'

Sid roared from his office door, 'Frankie! Get in here!'

CHAPTER TWO

L iam hurled himself through the front door of his house and slammed it shut behind him. He could hear his mum yelling at him from the kitchen, telling him off for all the noise as he pounded up the stairs and into his bedroom. He slammed his bedroom door, not caring what she had to say about it.

Liam shrugged off his coat and dumped it in the corner along with his school bag before flinging himself face down on his bed. He could feel tears pricking at his eyes and drew in a long, deep shuddering breath. He would not cry, he was seventeen for fuck sake, what would his mates think if they found out he'd let something like this upset him? Cancel that, what would his mates think if they found out he'd cried?

He sat up on his bed and scrubbed the tears from his eyes. He could hear his mum coming up the stairs and he didn't want *her* to know he'd been crying either. He pulled out his phone and logged on to the Facebook app; anything to make him look untroubled.

Liam's mum knocked on his door and he called for her to come in. He liked that she would always knock first, it meant she respected his space.

'You all right, son?'

'Fine,' he grumbled.

'You don't sound fine. It's not like you to slam doors and stomp up the stairs.'

'Mum, I said I'm fine! Just leave me alone, will you?'

She looked hurt, he was usually pretty calm and she obviously didn't know what else to say.

'Okay,' she said after a few seconds. 'I'll leave you be. I'll shout you when dinner's ready.'

'Thanks, Mum.' He offered her a small smile by way of apology and she smiled back, quietly closing the door behind her.

He felt terrible for being rude, but there was no way he could speak to her about what was bothering him. He couldn't speak to anyone. His mates would laugh at him, it wasn't like he had any brothers, and his dad had disappeared a long time ago. So long ago, in fact, Liam wasn't even sure what he looked like.

He'd been desperately hoping, and under the impression, that Kirsty Boyd was not only going to give him a Valentine's Day card, but that she was also going to ask him out. He'd have asked her out himself, but he was nervous, and Paul had told him she didn't like it when boys came on too strong; she liked to be the one to do the asking, be in control of the situation.

Paul had told him he'd heard from Kirsty's mate, Helen, she was definitely giving him a card, and who knew what else after the date she was definitely going to ask him out on. And Paul would know about these things seeing as he'd been having his end away with Helen for a few weeks.

Only it hadn't turned out that way. Liam had spent the whole day trying to appear casual and not at all like he was waiting for a girl to hand him a card or ask him out. He'd wandered past Kirsty's usual hangout spots at break and lunch, trying hard to make it look like he happened to be there for no apparent reason, but she hadn't so much as glanced at him, let alone spoken to him.

Liam figured maybe she was waiting to catch him after school, so he hung about at the gates chatting to Paul and a bunch of his other mates. Paul, with a smirk on his face, asked him if he'd spoken to Kirsty. Anger swelled up from his stomach, spreading through him. Paul knew full well he hadn't and bringing it up in front of everyone else was purely an effort to embarrass him. Some mate!

The rest of the lads started taking the piss and Liam was ready to either punch Paul or stomp off home. He heaved his rucksack onto his shoulder and turned to tell them all to fuck off when he noticed Kirsty and Helen and the rest of their gang coming towards them. Paul gave him a nudge and said this could be it.

When the girls arrived, they paired off with the boys, including Kirsty who had walked over to a boy called Scott and proceeded to shove her tongue down his throat. They broke apart after a minute or two and Kirsty looked over at him, smirking.

Liam was mortified, he didn't think he'd ever been so embarrassed. He turned and marched towards home, the jeers and taunts of his so-called mates echoing in his ears. Worse than that, he could hear the girls giggling at his expense and he felt utterly worthless.

His anger had simmered all the way home, his marching pace doing little to dissipate the rage he felt inside. Slamming the doors and stomping up the stairs had helped a little and his fury had damped down to be replaced with misery.

He was never going to lose his virginity. He was already behind the other lads and he had been humiliated in front of almost everyone in his class. What girl was going to want him now? He'd lied to his mates when he said he'd done it loads of times; he'd figured once his date with Kirsty had happened it wouldn't be a lie anymore, so who cared?

His anger built again as he thought of Kirsty and that nasty little smirk on her face. Liam knew he wasn't ugly, he was no film star, but he wasn't ugly. He was definitely no worse looking than that spotty twat Scott who she'd played tonsil hockey with right in front of him.

She was nothing but a skanky little slapper who liked to put it about. But not with him apparently. She'd regret that. The tears returned and this time Liam didn't bother to stop them.

CHAPTER THREE

Todd glanced up at the clock on the gym wall, he had fifteen minutes left of his shift. He loved his job, but the day had seemed to drag on forever. All he wanted to do was get home, take a shower and start getting organised for his and Frankie's big Valentine's Day date.

Normally Frankie took charge of their date nights, and he'd let her get on with it because he had thought that's what she wanted. Even if he did have an idea, she never thought it was a good one, so he stopped trying and left her to it.

Except, during a row Frankie had screamed at him how sick and tired she was of being the only one who ever organised anything. When he screamed back that he never knew if he was doing the right thing because she was so bloody independent, the argument had blown up.

Once they had calmed down, their blazing row had led to an open and honest conversation about how they both felt. He would rather there had been no confrontation in the first place, it wasn't his style, but at least something good had come of it.

'How... much... longer...?'

Todd was dragged back to the present day by his client who

was puffing away on the treadmill. He checked the time and realised she'd been on there for far longer than he'd intended. He'd been so lost in his daze, he'd forgotten all about her. 'Right! That's enough for today, Mel. Cracking workout. Make sure you cool down and I'll see you next time. Do we have a session already booked in?'

Mel looked up at him from where she stood with her hands on her knees, gasping for breath. 'Yeah, next week.'

Todd was already halfway across the gym floor when he turned and gave her the thumbs-up. 'Awesome, see you then,' he said as he hurried out the door.

He made his way down the corridor to the staff changing room and went inside to retrieve his bag from the locker. His colleague, Ryan, was already in there pulling on his trainers.

'Todd, my man!' Ryan was *always* effusive and *always* wanted to chat. Todd had neither the time nor the inclination. He had things to do.

'Hi, Ryan. Sorry, can't stop.'

'You not bought Frankie's Valentine's Day present yet?' Ryan smirked.

'As it happens, I have. But I'm organising our date tonight, so I need to get going,' he replied while punching in the combination on his locker.

'What? She's letting you organise Valentine's Day?'

Todd turned in time to see Ryan swoon in a pretend faint. 'Very funny.'

'I hope you've got something special planned. That woman of yours has high standards. God knows what she sees in you.' Ryan chuckled at his own joke.

'Yeah, cheers for that.'

'Ah, man, I'm only messing with you. I'm sure your Frankie will be grateful whatever you have planned.' Ryan's eyebrows lifted and he gave Todd a knowing look.

'Whatever. At least I have a date.' Todd left, leaving a speechless Ryan behind him.

On the bus home, Todd ran through a mental checklist of things he needed to do when he got back to the flat. First on his list was 'clean'. Frankie had informed him in no uncertain terms, it would be nice if the place was clean without any input from her once in a while. After that, a quick shower and then he could turn his mind to making dinner and setting the table. He was rubbish at cooking, Frankie knew this, so he'd ordered a selection of their favourite junk food to be delivered from Asda before she finished work; stuff he could shove in the oven and not worry about too much.

He'd settle Frankie on the sofa with a glass of her favourite Prosecco while he cooked everything. All she had to do was relax. He'd even ordered candles, flowers and a card to go on the table, which he planned to lay as if they were eating at a fancy restaurant.

Then to complete the evening they would watch whichever cheesy chick-flick Frankie wanted. It would be her choice entirely and he vowed he would not even so much as quirk an eyebrow if he didn't fancy it.

Todd's phone pinged as he opened the front door to the flat. He pulled his phone from his pocket and read the message.

You home from work yet? Quick game of FIFA before you embark on your elaborate date-night plan?

It was Craig, they'd been mates since school and he was very good at distracting Todd.

Todd smiled to himself and responded.

Not today mate. Stuff to do, shit to organise!

He loved Frankie more than anything and he was determined the evening would be a success.

Moving further into the flat, he looked around and decided to tackle the bedroom first. You never know, if he played his cards right it might see some action later.

He was piling dirty clothes from where they covered every available inch of carpet space into the laundry hamper when his phone beeped again.

Come on! Half an hour? You hardly ever play these days – exactly how under the thumb are you? It's the least you can do for a mate who's been single since granny was a boy.

Craig was right. Compared to the days before he met Frankie, he hardly ever played on his Xbox anymore. When he did, Frankie rarely voiced her complaint, but would tut and roll her eyes, telling him she was going for a walk, or to keep the noise down because she wanted to watch a film. Regardless, her message always got through, and now Todd usually only played when Frankie was out.

He looked at the time on his phone screen. He still had at least three hours before Frankie was due home. The flat wasn't really *that* messy, and if he had to, he could always forgo cleaning the toilet.

She would never know.

Fuck it! You win!

Todd was right in the middle of giving Craig the arse-kicking of his life on FIFA and he was relishing every minute of it.

His phone beeped from where it lay on the carpet beside him, distracting him for a few seconds. Frankie's name flashed up on the screen and he thought he'd better check what it said.

He paused the game and told Craig to hang on for a minute while he checked the message.

'*Come on, Todd, my man! Now's not the time for phone checking*,' Craig called through his headset.

'Two seconds.' Todd was somewhat distracted as he swiped the screen of his phone to read Frankie's message.

On my way home, I should be there in about 45 mins. Really looking forward to our evening together. I can't wait to see what you've got planned for us. I love you. Xoxoxo

'Shit!' Todd checked his watch and realised he'd been playing for a lot longer than half an hour. He only had fifteen minutes until the shopping was due to arrive and he hadn't so much as thought about cleaning since he'd switched on his games console.

'*What's up?*'

'I've got to go! Look at the time.' He wrenched his headset from his head and turned off the Xbox, not even waiting for Craig to reply.

He dragged his fingers through his spiky hair, tugging at the ends. Panic was starting to set in, the furthest he'd got was to bundle the dirty washing into the hamper. Wasting no more time, Todd set about hoovering carpets, plumping cushions and wiping down the sides in the kitchen. A quick squirt of bleach down the loo would have to suffice.

The shopping arrived soon after, which Todd put away with

lightning speed. Thank God he hadn't decided to cook anything complicated.

He checked his watch. He had about twenty-five minutes before Frankie said she'd be home. He opened the fridge again and pulled out a bottle of the Prosecco, which he then wedged into the freezer.

All that was left to do was set the table and have a shower. He grinned, he might just be able to swing this.

CHAPTER FOUR

F rankie flashed her pass at the driver and made her way to the back of the bus. She slumped down into a seat and closed her eyes. She was exhausted, but in a good way. Tired or not though, her mind was still whirling at what had transpired during the course of the day.

Sid had called her into his office, in his usual crabby manner, bellowing her name from his door before retreating inside.

Once inside, she took a seat and he wasted no time in getting to the point.

'Your Valentine's Day articles seem to have caused quite a stir online.'

'Yeah... I was just reading the comments with Amy...' Frankie trailed off, not quite knowing where Sid was going with the conversation.

He cleared his throat. 'Well, between your articles today and a couple of others recently, it's become abundantly clear this is the style of journalism the readers of the *Edinburgh Chronicle* want to read,' Sid said with a pointed look.

'This is true. So... what now?' She still had no idea what this might have to do with her and hoped he would get to the point quicker.

'I had a conversation with Mick earlier, he likes your stuff and wants me to give you a go at writing proper news, as well as a few more serious articles.'

'What? Mick liked it?' Mick was the top boss at the *Edinburgh Chronicle*, and he liked her writing? This was all a bit surreal.

'He did. He also mentioned there's some big women's day coming up and—'

'International Women's Day?' Frankie's heart sank a little.

'That's the one. Anyway, he wants you to write an article for it. Reckons you'd be the right man, eh... woman, for the job.'

Frankie knew this was a great opportunity and if Mick had specifically asked her to write the piece she should be bursting to get started, but she couldn't help feeling a little disheartened. She knew feminism and International Women's Day were important, hell she wanted equality as much as the next woman, but she didn't want to be put in a box at this stage of her career: particularly a feminist box. Once she was pigeon-holed, it would be hard to extricate herself and she would be left open to being labelled a bra burner. Like it or not, print journalism was still a male dominated environment.

She voiced her concerns to Sid, who nodded sagely, appearing to understand her worries. 'I hear you, but it's one article and Mick wants you to write it. We're not asking you to turn into a hardcore feminist. It's quite a straight-forward piece, I promise.'

'What's the piece?'

'He wants something around the history of the day. Who invented it, how it started. That sort of thing.'

That didn't sound too bad. It wasn't like they were asking her to beat a drum and write about how evil men were.

After making sure it was clear that she would *not* become the *Chronicle's* feminist writer, she agreed.

'You have a couple of weeks, so you'll need to be working on your other assignments too.'

'Sure.'

She had left Sid's office and sat down at her desk. The more she thought about it, the more excited she became. She was going to write proper, serious articles. This was the next step on her journey to becoming a bona fide crime reporter. It really didn't matter what the subject was, surely?

As long as she wrote across a range of themes, she could easily avoid being stuck with a feminist label. And, to be fair, she didn't want to be stuck with *any* label, she had nothing against feminism, she just wanted to keep her options firmly open.

A blaring horn pulled Frankie from her reverie. Startled, she peered out of the bus window, trying and failing to recognise the scenery around her.

Shit! She'd been so absorbed in thinking about her meeting with Sid, she'd totally missed her stop. She pressed the button and alighted as soon as she was able.

She stood with her back against the wall of the nearest building and considered her options. Should she jump on the next bus going back the other way? Or walk?

Frankie checked her phone and realised she had plenty of time before Todd was expecting her. It was a clear, crisp, winter's day in Edinburgh, the likes of which the city didn't often see, so she decided she would enjoy it and walk back.

She texted Todd to let him know she was on her way home and how much she was looking forward to their special evening together. Feeling lighter and happier than she had for a while, she started walking.

Walking had seemed like a great idea at the time, but the temperature had plummeted halfway home and she was bloody freezing. As Frankie hurried up the steps towards the front door of the flat, she hoped to God Todd had the heating up full whack.

In the hallway, she sent up a silent thanks that her prayers had been answered while she removed her layers of clothing. She called through as she hung up her coat on the hook and slipped off her boots. 'Todd, I'm home.'

'Hiya, I'm in here.'

Frankie made her way up the hall and into the open-plan kitchen/lounge area, where she found Todd in the middle of lighting candles on the small dining room table. She looked around the expansive room with a smile, eager to see what Todd had been planning all afternoon.

Her eyes swept over the room twice before her smile faltered. Forcing it back onto her face, she hoped Todd hadn't seen her disappointment. She couldn't see anything particularly special or different.

He'd clearly tried to position the cushions on the sofa, but it looked all wrong. And he'd only hoovered half the carpet, she could still see some dust in the corner. Todd snuck up and slipped his arms around her waist, kissing her behind the ear.

'I know the cushions aren't quite right, but I can never get them just how you like them. I did try.'

She turned and gave him a kiss. 'I know you did. Maybe I'll send you a picture for next time.' She was only half joking. 'What time are we eating?' she asked looking over at the remarkably clean and tidy kitchen area.

'We can eat whenever you want, babe. Dinner will take no more than half an hour to heat up. I've bought in all our favourite junk food, so we can sit and munch away on that and then you can choose any film you like and I promise I won't say a word.'

Heat up? Munch away? This wasn't anything like what she had been expecting. She had envisioned coming home to see ingredients for something delicious covering every surface of the kitchen. Or maybe even something already cooking away in the oven, making the whole flat smell amazing. Maybe a bowl of olives to nibble on and a nice aperitif while Todd put the finishing touches to a delectable Italian dish; he knew Italian was her favourite.

Frankie closed her eyes and shook her disappointment away. 'Sounds good,' she replied trying to affect an airy tone. 'I'm going to get changed and then I have news.' This time the smile was for real.

In the bedroom, Frankie sat on the edge of the bed and rubbed at her temples. Todd had made an effort and done what he thought was right, she must remember that. On the other hand, he had promised her a wonderful Valentine's evening, but the flat still needed a bloody good clean, and he intended to *heat up* junk food for them to eat – where had the hours of planning gone? It was then Frankie spotted the Xbox controller and headset abandoned under the television stand in the corner. *That explains it! Lazy sod!*

She looked up as Todd pushed the door open. 'A glass of fizz for Madame?' he enquired in a dodgy French accent. 'I have her very favourite,' he teased.

'That would be fabulous, thanks, babe. I'll be through in a second.'

Once he was gone, Frankie gave herself a good talking to. Todd had clearly made an effort, and she was being an ungrateful cow. She didn't love him because he was perfect, she loved him for him, faults and all. He might've only spread the bed covers instead of making the bed, and he'd only semi-hoovered, but he had tried and, for Todd, that was something.

He'd made sure to buy her favourite fizz and was pouring her a glass. He'd bought their favourite foods and given her control of the telly for the night. It was the small things that mattered and she could see he really had put some thought into the evening.

CHAPTER FIVE

Todd poured Frankie some Prosecco, remembering to use the tall thin-stemmed champagne glasses she liked. *Flutes*, he thought, smiling, they were champagne flutes as Frankie had told him a hundred times before.

While he waited for her to get changed, he put the finishing touches to the dining table. The candles were lit, the cutlery was laid out exactly as instructed by Fred Sireix via Google and Todd had placed one of their 'good' plates at each of the settings. He wondered about the water glasses and side plates as Fred had also suggested, but decided against it. The table was already looking cluttered and he was worried about accidentally breaking his champagne flute which already looked incredibly fragile in his large hand.

Todd had hoped his anxiety would disappear once Frankie got home, but if anything he was even more worried now. Had he done the right thing in making it a casual evening? Should he have organised a posh restaurant, or at least posh food, and got dressed up? Even though she'd tried to hide it, he'd seen Frankie's face when she walked into the lounge, she'd definitely been expecting more. *Why* had he agreed to play FIFA with Craig?

'Is this for me?'

He turned to see Frankie hovering in the kitchen next to her glass of Prosecco. 'Yep, I've got mine here.' He waggled his flute at her.

'You're drinking Prosecco? And you've used the champagne flutes.' She made her way over to him, glass in hand. 'Monsieur, you are spoiling me,' she said, using the same fake French accent as Todd had earlier.

Todd pulled her into him and kissed her, murmuring against her lips, 'But of course, Madame.'

He relaxed, feeling as though he'd done something right amidst all the half-heartedness that he blamed Craig for entirely.

Todd picked up the stereo remote and pointed it at the sound system in the corner of the room. Their favourite song sounded true and clear from the speakers. Todd pulled Frankie in tight and danced with her around the room. She giggled and rolled her eyes a little, but there was no mistaking her smile as she joined in.

After the song was finished, he broke away and pulled Frankie into the kitchen. 'Come and see what I bought for us to eat.'

A short time later, Todd was feeling much more chilled. His relaxation was, in part, assisted by a couple of glasses of Prosecco, but it was mainly because Frankie seemed to be enjoying their evening.

With a flourish he deposited a platter of food in the middle of the table and took his seat opposite her. 'Enjoy.'

'This looks lush, but I'm pretty sure there's enough here to feed the five thousand.'

'Meh, so I'll take some for lunch tomorrow. Hey, didn't you say something earlier about some good news?'

Frankie's sea-green eyes lit up. 'Yes! You're never going to believe what happened at work today...'

Todd sat back in his seat and listened to Frankie's story. He loved her enthusiasm and realised how long it had been since he'd seen her this way. He knew she had goals and ambitions, and although she was happy to work her way steadily towards them, it was about time she was given a push. He might be biased, but he thought her talents were wasted writing pop culture articles.

'I'm so pleased for you, babe.' Todd covered her hand with his. 'It's about time your talent was recognised.'

'I know, but do you not think it's maybe too soon?'

'Too soon? You've been there writing those filler articles for years. You should be pushing yourself forward, especially since they've started noticing it themselves.'

'You know I'm not very good at that. What if I put my hand up for something then I can't write it?'

Todd gave her a hard look. 'You and I both know that's never going to happen. I wish you could see what I see when I read your pieces. You have such a skill with words and you absolutely deserve to be reporting crime. You only need to read the comments under your St Valentine post to see how much people like what you're writing.'

'I suppose you're right, but it all feels a little bit surreal.' Frankie dunked a chicken dipper in a pot of houmous and took a bite. 'Anyway, how was your day?'

'Yeah, it was good, I had a couple of one-to-ones, so that means some extra money this month.'

'That's great! Although, you know if I do get promoted, I'll get a pay rise and you won't have to do that anymore?'

'I like working at the gym, it's fun,' he said with a shrug.

'I know, but you could be so much more, babe. I just want the best for you.'

His heart sank a little. It wasn't the first time Frankie had hinted she didn't approve of his job. Did Frankie think he stood around all day flexing his muscles in the mirror? She seemed to forget all the training and studying in anatomy and nutrition he'd had to complete.

Not wanting to spoil the evening by getting into an argument, he decided to change the subject. 'Have you chosen a film to watch yet?'

CHAPTER SIX

L iam had seriously considered chucking a sicky and skiving off school for the day. The very thought of facing his, so-called, mates and the bitches who'd mocked him the previous day made him flush hot with embarrassment. He'd been too scared to even log on to Facebook. He knew there'd be no let-up for days; why couldn't it have happened on a Friday? At least then he would have had the weekend break in the way.

As he'd lain in bed that morning considering what made-up illness he might be able to get away with telling his mum, he realised how it would look if he didn't turn up. That lot would take his absence as some sort of sign they'd succeeded in humiliating him; that they'd won. They *had* humiliated him, but he wasn't going to give them the satisfaction of knowing that.

No, he thought as he rolled out of bed, *I'm not giving them any more ammunition.*

He took extra care getting himself ready, ensuring his dark hair was side-parted just so. No need to hand them another stick to beat him with.

Liam arrived at his tutor group classroom seconds before the bell rang. He'd had to hunt for his spare tie after he dropped egg on the first one. He stood outside the door for a second and took a deep breath before he walked in.

He took his usual seat at the table with Paul and Scott, and glanced around the classroom. He saw Kirsty and Helen smirking at him and whispering to each other, so he gave them what he hoped was a withering look and stuck his middle finger up.

Paul smirked. 'Bit harsh, mate. You still sore about yesterday?'

'Whatever. I haven't got time for wee slappers like them.'

'Oh aye, birds suddenly fallin' over themselves to shag you, are they?'

Scott guffawed from the other side of the table and Liam shot him a look of pure hatred. 'You can shut the fuck up, *virgin.*'

The smile slid from Scott's face, he'd not been quite so clever at making up stories about who he was having sex with and had actually confessed to Paul and Liam he'd barely even kissed a girl. Liam felt bad for using it against him, but his temper was too near the surface for him to care. It was every man for himself as far as Liam was concerned.

The bell rang and Mrs Purves called for them all to be quiet, putting an end to the verbal sparring around the table.

***

Paul and Scott were already in the dining hall when Liam arrived at lunchtime. He made his way over to their usual table in the far corner, only noticing when he was halfway there that Kirsty and Helen were also sitting there. He groaned inwardly, hoping nothing of what he felt showed on his face.

Dumping his bag on the floor, Liam scanned the table, pretending to ignore what seemed like the ever-present smirk on

Helen's face. 'I'm going to get something to eat, anybody want anything?'

After a chorus of 'no' and 'no, I'm all right', Liam headed toward the queue for some hot food. He really fancied a scotch pie, chips and beans.

As he paid for his lunch, Liam became aware of people watching him. He pocketed his change and looked around the room. It seemed like everyone was sniggering at something and he was the only one not in on the joke.

Voices rang out across the room, loud and clear, punctuated by raucous laughter from the rest of the students.

How many times did you make her cum, Wallace?

Did you have to pick her tits up off the floor?

Did she take her teeth out when she sucked you off?

He tried to ignore them but when he arrived back at the table he was shaking slightly. As he sat down he caught a sympathetic look from Scott, and he could tell Paul was trying desperately not to laugh.

'What the fuck's going on?' Liam hissed.

The girls, who were already giggling, started howling with laughter and even Paul had given up. Scott handed Liam a piece of paper with an image printed on it. Looking around, Liam could see similar pieces of paper spread across all the tables. He looked down at the A4 sheet in his hand and tried to make sense of what he was seeing.

The image was of an old flabby woman. She was on all fours with a lewd expression on her face, and wearing fire-engine red lingerie that would have looked tacky on the prettiest of girls. Behind her was a man clearly shagging her, doggy-style. Liam's face burned as it dawned on him that someone had super-imposed his picture over the man's face, making it look like he was the one banging the old crone.

Humiliated, he looked to his friends for help. Paul was

laughing uncontrollably and Scott could only offer him a sympathetic shrug. The whole dining room was laughing having seen Liam's entire range of emotions play out on his face.

'You can all fuck off!' he shouted, grabbing his bag. Burning with embarrassment and not caring about anything other than escaping the stares and laughter of half the school, Liam barged through the fire exit. Once he was out of sight of the dining room, and with the fire alarm blaring in his ears, he ran, aiming to put as much distance between himself and his humiliation as possible.

———

Liam refused to go to school for the rest of the week.

His mum had tried to find out what was wrong with him, but gave up quickly when she realised she wasn't getting anywhere.

Paul and Scott had texted him when he didn't turn up for school. Paul was typically unsympathetic, whereas Scott tried to be supportive.

Liam was pissed off with Paul. He was supposed to be his best mate, but all he'd done recently was laugh at his misery. What kind of mate did that? Even if he hadn't publicly stood up for him, he didn't expect him to be so cruel in private.

Scott's message might've been supportive, but he didn't want his pity. Scott was even further down the food chain than Liam. Mind you, that was before someone spread pictures of him shagging a toothless old granny.

The week after he refused to go to school was half-term, which meant there was even more time for Liam to recover from the social hand grenade that had been lobbed in his direction. He spent all his time in his room playing video games – where he set his status to 'offline' – and avoiding social media. He didn't want to talk to anyone and ignored the messages he received.

After a few days, he grew bored of playing video games by himself and his curiosity as to whether anything had been said about him on social media. Tentatively, he logged back into Facebook and checked his notifications – he didn't appear to have been tagged in anything at least.

He spent the next few hours scrolling through his timeline and checking the profiles of the people most likely to want to add to his mortification. He relaxed and relief flooded through him as he realised there was nothing to see. It occurred to him that even if someone had shared the picture, it was likely Facebook would have taken it down pretty quickly; nudes were a quick way to find yourself in Facebook jail too.

Feeling better, Liam shared a few memes and stopped hiding his presence online.

He was trying to decide if a particular meme would land him in trouble with his mum – she'd given him no choice but to add her as a friend – when he received a notification telling him he had a DM. The anxious feeling returned in his belly as he clicked on the icon to see who it was from.

Wanted to see if you were okay after what happened at school last week. I know you haven't been in and I haven't seen you online, that's all. X

It was from Kirsty. She was probably the last person Liam expected to receive a message from. She'd made it clear on Valentine's Day she wasn't interested, and she'd been laughing just as much as everyone else in the dining hall.

Like you care, you were laughing along with the rest of them.

He owed her nothing, he definitely didn't need to be nice to her.

I know and I'm sorry. I was just going along with everyone else, but I could see when you ran out the door how upset you were. X

I didn't run. I stormed, there's a difference.

Okay, but I wanted you to know I'm sorry and make sure you're okay. x

Liam didn't know how to reply. He was still pissed off with her, twice she'd been involved in his embarrassment, but she was hot and he couldn't help but fancy her.

He was pondering over what to say when another message came through.

Listen, what are you up to tonight? Fancy meeting? I could make it up to you... x

Liam's eyes widened. Was she really saying what he thought she was? Could this be his chance to finally stop making a liar out of himself?

What about Scott? I thought you were seeing him now.

There was no way Liam was putting himself out there without checking the facts. Mind you, what did he care if she was still seeing him? This was every man for himself and if Scott couldn't keep his bird happy, how was that Liam's fault?

Nah, he's a shit kisser. x

He thought it over for no longer than a minute before he made a decision.

Okay, where? What time? X

Meet me in the park – half an hour? x

Liam looked at his watch. Half an hour meant he would be able to have a quick shower, change his clothes and get to the park in time.

I'll meet you by the swings, see you in half an hour. X

Liam burst into action and twenty minutes later he was heading out the front door. Hearing his mum calling behind him he pinged her a text to say he was meeting his mates and not to worry.

The park was made up of a large grassy field and a play area off to one side. The only illumination came from street lights that ran along the path circumnavigating the whole field. It meant the majority of the play park, and particularly the swings, were in darkness. If he really was going to pop his cherry with Kirsty, there was no way he wanted there to be any chance of an audience.

In the distance he could hear the cars on the nearby roads, but he had yet to encounter anyone since he turned off the path and made his way over to the playground. Perching on the edge of one of the swings he stuffed his cold hands in his pocket and felt the serrated edge of the condom wrapper; he'd brought it along, just in case.

Nerves and the cold started to kick in as he waited for Kirsty to arrive. His thoughts slid to whether or not the plummeting temperature would affect his 'performance' and he wished he'd thought things through some more. It was too late though, if he chickened out it would be spread round the school that he'd turned down sex on a plate and that would be his reputation ruined irreparably.

Liam checked his watch, Kirsty was five minutes late. How long was he going to wait? What if it was all a joke and they were watching him from the bushes to see how long he hung around for a shag that wasn't going to happen?

His spiralling thoughts only served to wind him up and he was on the brink of leaving when he heard footsteps coming from behind him. He whirled round and peered into the darkness.

'Liam?' a voice whispered.

Liam huffed out a relieved breath, it was Kirsty. 'I'm here, sat on the swings.'

He heard the footsteps coming closer and when she was a few metres away he could see her shadowed in the darkness.

'Hi,' she said, smiling shyly.

'Hi,' he replied, wishing he sounded more confident.

They smiled at each other, neither one of them knowing what to do next. Liam decided to take charge.

'Shall we sit on that bench? Be easier to talk.'

'Sure.'

Once they were both seated, Kirsty leaned into him a little, and taking it as a sign, Liam put his arm around her.

'I'm really sorry about taking the piss out of you, by the way,' she said, glancing up at him.

He pulled her in tighter as she looked away. 'It's okay.' He wasn't about to ruin his chances by telling her what a little cow she'd been over the last couple of weeks.

'Really? You forgive me then?' she said, looking up at him again.

Their faces were inches from each other.

'Really,' he murmured, lowering his face until his lips met hers.

The kiss was soft, tentative at first, he was nervous, but when he felt her respond positively his urgency grew. Before he knew it, she had her hand down his trousers and was encouraging his hard-on with firm strokes. He groaned and grabbed at her breasts with his free hand, not entirely sure of what he was doing, but knowing he felt good.

After a couple of minutes Kirsty pulled away; they were both panting heavily and Liam hoped to God she hadn't changed her mind, not now they were getting to the good stuff. She stood up and gently pulled him to his feet.

'What are—?'

She put her finger to her lips and shushed him silently. He obeyed and watched as she undid his belt and jeans. She slid slowly to her knees and yanked down his trousers and underwear, exposing him entirely from the waist down, his raging boner standing proud. *Dear God, she's going to suck me off!*

Liam's excitement was short-lived when he heard Kirsty shout, 'Now!'

Before he knew what had happened, there were lights dazzling him.

Smile for the camera, Wallace!

It's like a dick, only smaller!

And the laughter; the mocking laughter drilled into the centre of his brain.

He didn't know how many people were there, but they all appeared to have the torches on their phones pointing at him and he could hear the clicks of the cameras as they took picture after picture.

Liam wrenched up his underwear and trousers and ran, holding them up with one hand. He didn't stop to fasten them until the laughter had faded in his ears and all he could hear above the noise of the traffic were his own sobs as tears coursed down his cheeks.

INTERNATIONAL WOMEN'S DAY: A HISTORY

FRANKIE CURRINGTON

By now, most of you will probably have heard of International Women's Day, and you may even know a bit about what it's for – HINT: The clue is in the title! – but do you know how it all got started?

International Women's Day (IWD) as we know it started in 1975 when it was celebrated for the first time by the United Nations. Two years later the General Assembly adopted a resolution proclaiming a United Nations Day for Women's Rights and International Peace to be observed on any day of the year by each of the member states. The date of 8th March actually originates from a strike by Russian Women in 1914.

But the history of IWD goes back to 1910, when the idea was proposed by Clara Zetkin at the annual International Conference of Working Women. Unsurprisingly, the idea was met with much enthusiasm.

Clara was active in the Social Democratic Party of Germany for a number of years. She was the editor of their newspaper for women, 'Die Gleichheit' (Equality) for 25 years and became leader of their women's office in 1907. Her idea for International Women's Day was first recognised on 19th March 1911 by over a million women in Austria, Denmark, Germany and Switzerland.

Since 1996 International Women's Day has had an annual theme. The first was 'Celebrating the Past, Planning for the Future', with the most recent being, 'Choose to Challenge'. IWD also has its own colours which pay homage to the women's suffrage movement from the early 20th century. Purple stands for justice and dignity; green stands for hope; and white stands for purity. The latter has attracted some controversy due to its associations with virginity.

Many people will question the relevance of IWD in the 21st century, but according to the World Economic Forum none of us will see gender parity in our lifetime, and neither will our children. They estimate it could take 100 years.

Oh... and if you're reading this and asking, 'But when is International Men's Day?', the answer is 19th November.

CHAPTER SEVEN

Frankie turned round and pushed her way through the crowds of people trying to get to the bar. They were in The Albanach on the Royal Mile, one of her and Amy's favourite pubs. The carved wooden bar ran most of the length of one side of the space and the walls behind, from the counter up, were crammed full of bottles; whisky everywhere. It was Friday night and pub-goers stood shoulder to shoulder.

She spotted Amy waving at her frantically from the other side of the pub, having found them a table. *Thank God.* Frankie's feet were killing her and standing up all evening would have put a downer on her good mood.

After sliding sideways around a group of teenagers who had no intention of making room to let her past, Frankie placed the wine cooler on the table.

Amy plucked the champagne flutes from the bucket. 'Oo! Moët, we really are celebrating.'

'Why not? Sid's promised to give me similar assignments in the future and I say that calls for a celebration.'

'That's the best news I've heard all day.' Amy offered Frankie the bottle. 'You want to do the honours?'

Frankie beamed and took the bottle from her friend, raising it into the air she pressed her thumbs against the cork. It released with a crack and soared through the air and into the crowd. A cheer went up from the throng of people crammed into the bar, and Frankie and Amy giggled as they watched a young boy's eyes open wide in shock as the cork shot passed his ear.

Frankie poured two glasses and passed one over to Amy, who raised it aloft and proposed a toast.

'To you, Frankie. You're going to change the world with your writing.'

'I don't know about the world, but I'll settle for Edinburgh. Cheers!'

'Cheers!'

Frankie took a mouthful of the delicious apple-tasting champagne and closed her eyes while she savoured the sensation of the bubbles fizzing on her tongue. She opened her eyes and gave the glass full of deliciousness an appraising look. 'Now that is some good stuff.'

'It really is. So, is Sid going to let you choose your assignments, or make suggestions?'

Frankie shook her head. 'I'm really not sure. I have these ideas swirling around and I want to do them all *now*. I'm supposed to have a meeting with him on Monday, so I guess I'll find out then. I do know I'm not going to be railroaded into being their go-to reporter for all things feminism.'

'God no. The last thing you want is to be stuck with that tag.'

'Exactly!'

Frankie dug out her phone to check if she had any messages from Todd. She'd rung him earlier, but he hadn't answered, so she'd left him a message letting him know she was going out to celebrate and asking if he wanted to come along.

'Have you heard from him?' asked Amy.

'No, but then he has been working this afternoon. I'm sure his shift should've finished by now though.'

Amy lifted an eyebrow. 'You don't know when his shift finishes?'

'Not exactly. It's hard to keep track, they keep changing all the time.' Frankie ought to know when her boyfriend's shifts were, but they'd never really been that sort of couple. They did their own thing a lot of the time and if Todd wasn't in when she got home from work, it was never a problem.

'You *have* had a lot on your mind recently.' Amy poured them each another glass of champagne, letting Frankie off the hook.

Frankie's boyfriend swooped in planting a kiss smack on her lips. 'Hello, ladies.'

'Todd!'

'Hey, where's mine?' Amy asked playfully.

Todd grinned at her and winked. 'On the good stuff, I see. Are we celebrating?'

'My International Women's Day article was published today and it was really well received.' Frankie gave Amy a look as if to say, *See, it's not only me who forgets things.*

'That's amazing, babe,' he said giving Frankie another kiss. 'I'm going to get a pint, you two need anything while I'm at the bar?'

Ten minutes later Todd was back at the table, pint in one hand, phone in the other and a frown on his face.

'Everything okay?' asked Frankie.

'Babe, have you looked at the comments on your article recently? I hadn't had a chance, so thought I'd read it while I was waiting at the bar.'

'I looked before I left work, most were good.' Frankie didn't feel so sure now though, there was a real look of concern on Todd's face. She pulled out her phone and called up her article.

'Jesus.' Amy, who was one step ahead, gasped.

Frankie scrolled through the comments, which as she remembered were really positive, until she reached the later ones. Her hand flew to her mouth, there under her article were screeds of nasty, vile, horrible comments.

Careful, your misandry is showing!

Anyone got a picture of Franke? What's the bet she's fugly?

Get back in the kitchen and leave the journalism to the men who know what they're doing.

Sounds to me like Frankie needs a good fuck – whether she wants it or not!

'Oh my God.' Tears filled Frankie's eyes. 'They're just... horrible.'

'What a bunch of wankers,' Amy fumed. 'It's not even as though what you wrote is anti-men.'

Frankie shook her head. 'This is the sort of thing I was worried about. Why are people so horrible?'

'They're trolls,' said Amy gently. 'Ignore them and concentrate on all the good comments.'

'I can't ignore them. That last one sounds like a rape threat.' The tremor in Frankie's voice was unmistakable.

'Bastards! Absolute bastards!' Todd had continued reading the comments and tapped furiously on the screen.

'What are you doing?'

'Giving these bastards a piece of my mind.'

'No!' Frankie pushed Todd's hand and phone down. 'You can't feed them.'

'What am I supposed to do then? Let them carry on saying all that stuff about you?'

'I love that you're trying to protect me and stand up for me, but squaring up to them only makes things worse. We'll take some screenshots and I'll report it to the police. I don't know what they can do, but at least they'll have a record.'

'How are you not more angry about this?'

'Oh, I'm angry! I'm furious, especially as it doesn't even mention men, but I know no good can come of engaging with them. Please, babe, for me?'

Todd sighed, deflated. 'Fine, but only because you've asked me to, and you have to promise to go to the police about it.'

'I promise.' Frankie picked up her glass of champagne and downed it in one, no longer caring for the luxurious taste, but needing the hit of alcohol to soothe her.

Amy got the point straight away. 'I'll get us some shots and a couple of gins, shall I?' Frankie nodded mutely and Amy headed for the bar.

Frankie dropped her head into her hands. 'What the fuck?'

CHAPTER EIGHT

'Frankie! Get in here!'

Plenty of things had changed for Frankie in the last year, but the one thing she could count on to remain the same was Sid. Despite her graduated, but decisive, move towards crime writing and therefore increased seniority, Sid still summonsed her to his office in exactly the same way as he always had.

She walked into his office, notepad in hand and made to sit down ready for whatever assignment he had for her next. Their discussions always followed the same path: he gave her an assignment, they talked over what angle she should take and then she went off to do the research required and write the piece.

He held up a hand halting her. 'No time for that, you won't be here long.'

'What's up?'

'You heard about the attack on the girl in the park the other night?'

Of course. Everyone had heard about it, it was the third rape in as many months and the police had nothing to go on. All they knew was they occurred in parks and the perpetrator used a hunting knife. Frankie couldn't believe there was a woman left in Edinburgh prepared to walk across any of the parks at night. Especially considering none of the victims had been able to give a proper description, such was their trauma.

Even the few details they had been able to give were inconsistent. One woman had said the man was tall and dark-skinned, another agreed with the height, but said the man was pale and his hands were freckled. Frankie had learned from her fellow reporters, the contradictory descriptions were driving the detectives, tasked with finding the man, to distraction.

'Fenton Caldwell is giving a press conference and I want you down there. It starts in half an hour, so you need to get going.'

Frankie blinked and took a second to process Sid's words. 'You want me to go down to City Chambers and report on Fenton Caldwell's press conference? What about Andrew? That's his beat.'

'That's what I said, and Andrew is otherwise engaged.' Sid looked at his watch. 'If you don't get a move on you'll be late.'

'But, I...'

Sid was throwing her in at the deep end and she didn't feel ready.

'Out! Go. Now. Come back and write your story after, I want it for the morning edition.'

He ushered Frankie out of his office, closing the door very firmly behind her.

The sound of his door slamming jolted her to life. There was no time to stop and think, she would have to do that on the way to the Edinburgh Council's offices on the Royal Mile.

When she arrived at the City Chambers, the sheer number of journalists and cameras gave Frankie pause for thought; these were the big boys. Her eyes swept the room, taking in the details: the TV reporters dressed immaculately, not a hair out of place; the print journalists fiddling with their audio recorders. They were all so relaxed and comfortable with their surroundings. Frankie felt small and inconsequential amongst the sea of national newspaper reporters and TV news presenters. They were chatting away as if they were best of friends.

A couple of them were eyeing her up and down with smirks on their faces. Did she have *Rookie* tattooed on her forehead?

Rookie? No, this may be her first press conference of this magnitude, but Frankie was no rookie. She'd lived in this city her whole life and had been writing about its citizens and their lives for years. None of these national reporters could compete with her where local knowledge was concerned.

She raised her chin and confidently made her way to the front of the room, looking for an empty chair. She would not be one of those small-time newspaper reporters who meekly took their seat at the back and waited for the bigwigs to ask all the questions and garner all the attention.

Although not full, each seat in the front row had a coat or a bag, or sometimes just a notepad on it. Frankie swore: if she wanted to get a question answered she needed to be right up at the front. Clearly she had been the last to hear about that afternoon's press conference.

She spotted an empty seat in the middle of the second row and shuffled and apologised her way towards it. After a few glares and pursed lips from people she'd had to push past, Frankie sat down in the empty seat and began noting the questions she'd thought of to ask Councillor Caldwell, should she get the opportunity.

'Excuse me.'

Frankie looked up to see a tall slim man, dressed in a well-tailored suit, staring down at her. 'Can I help you?'

'I think you're in my seat.' He gestured towards it unnecessarily.

'Oh!' Frankie checked to make sure she hadn't sat on something and that there wasn't a coat or a bag underneath the chair. 'Sorry, there wasn't a jacket or anything holding it so I assumed it was free.' She stood.

'No problem, that's just where I sit during press conferences.'

Frankie hesitated and sat back down. 'So you hadn't saved it?'

'No, like I say, this is just my seat. Everyone knows, which is why it was free.'

Frankie glanced around the room. The other reporters were taking their seats and if she gave up this one she'd end up having to stand at the back; there would be no chance to ask her questions from there.

The stage in front of them was filling up, the press conference was about to start. She made a decision. 'Looks like you should've got here earlier,' she said with a sardonic smile; inside though her heart was pounding.

The man glared at her, outraged and shuffled his way out of the row as the PR person on the stage made the introductions and set out the structure of the briefing. She watched him exit the line of seats and lean up against the wall, his eyes catching hers with a glare.

Fenton Caldwell stood and approached the bank of microphones. Too late, Frankie realised her voice recorder should be in amongst all the others. She switched it on anyway, hoping she would be able to catch some of what was said.

'I'd like to thank you all for being here. I'll read a statement and then answer a few questions.' Councillor Caldwell shuffled some papers in his hand and cleared his throat, before looking up and starting his speech. He talked with empathy about the victims and urged women to take their safety seriously. He encouraged them not to walk alone, or take shortcuts through the park. He suggested they not listen to music and make sure someone knew where they were and when they were likely to arrive at their destination. He finished by asking for anyone with any information to come forward and speak to the police, no matter how insignificant it may seem.

All at once and somewhat unexpectedly, the reporters around Frankie leapt to their feet and began talking at the same time, yelling questions in Fenton Caldwell's direction. Frankie stood up too and raised her hand as Caldwell gestured for calm.

'Come on, I can't answer you all at the same time. Molly, you go first.' He pointed at a small woman with red curly hair in the front row.

'You talked about three victims, but isn't it true there have in fact been five rapes in recent months, and that you only started giving press conferences and warning women to be on the lookout once it was established these recent victims weren't prostitutes?'

Frankie's head swivelled towards the woman. *Five?* Could that possibly be true? How had she missed the first four? She winced, what kind of journalist did that make her? She tried to console herself by remembering this wasn't her beat and she was only filling in. Still, she knew if she wanted to be the *Edinburgh Chronicle*'s go-to crime reporter, she needed to keep her finger on the pulse.

The smile dropped from Councillor Caldwell's face. 'That's not strictly true, Molly. We called press conferences when there was an uptick in the attacks. The occupation of the women had nothing to do with it.' He was trying for a light tone, but his eyes were pure steel.

Frankie's brain was going into overdrive. Her reporter's instinct tickled at her brain – there was something in this, she knew it. She jotted down a few lines to serve as a reminder later and turned her attention back to Caldwell. He'd moved on from Molly's question and was clearly not going back to it. The next few reporters he called on were all men and it appeared he was much more comfortable answering their 'appropriate' questions.

The press conference was coming to an end and Frankie still hadn't asked anything. She'd barely had time to formulate a question, so intent was she on noting down Caldwell's answers.

'Right, I think we have time for one more.'

The lady beside Frankie practically jumped out of her seat with eagerness, her hand straight up in the air like the teacher's pet at school.

'Yes, the lady with the black jumper.'

'Councillor Caldwell, you have gone to great lengths to advise the women of Edinburgh how to look after themselves and how to ensure their personal safety, but I'm curious as to what advice you're going to give the men of the city?'

What an odd thing to ask, thought Frankie.

Caldwell frowned. 'I'm sorry, I'm not sure I understand what you mean?'

'You're asking the victims to stop themselves from being attacked. But you haven't asked men to stop going out at night, to help women to feel safer. Nor have you asked the man to stop attacking women.'

There was absolute silence in the room. No one breathed and all eyes were on Frankie's seat neighbour, including Frankie's. Slowly their gazes turned back to the front, their pens poised to record Caldwell's answer.

'I think it goes without saying that we want this man to stop attacking women, but I don't really think it's fair to expect all men to stay in at night, because of one bad egg. Right, that's all we have time for, thank you everyone.' Fenton Caldwell's tone was smooth, but the flint had returned in his eyes and his face was almost purple with the strain of trying to remain polite.

Frankie sat back, her brain ticking over everything she had seen and heard in the last thirty minutes.

CHAPTER NINE

There was a soft bong from the laptop's speakers as Liam powered it to life. He checked his watch – 11am – later than he would normally be online when he didn't have school, but his mother had insisted he go shopping with her to 'get him out of the house' and help her to carry the bags home.

He tapped his fingers impatiently on the sides of the keyboard waiting for the operating system to load. He wondered what news there would be. The previous day had been slow and they had all become bored and resorted to teasing the new guy. He'd come round to their way of thinking eventually and joined in with the banter.

Liam had found this safe little corner of the internet the previous year after being humiliated at the hands of Kirsty Boyd. The pictures of him stood in the park with his trousers round his ankles, his penis hard and obvious, had hit the internet before he'd even arrived home.

Mortified he had refused to leave his room, or speak to his mum for days. It was only when the school had got in contact with her that she'd any idea what had happened. She had been torn between trying to console him and being so consumed with her own anger that she had marched down to the school and demanded to speak to the head teacher. Demanded that he do *something*. *Anything*. But Liam had refused to tell them who was responsible. It was bad enough that they had played such an awful trick on him, but there was no way he was going to be known as a snitch too.

Slowly the embarrassment had given way to anger. Encouraged by his new friends, after they had heard what Liam had been through, he had made some video diaries explaining how he had been made to feel. He talked about the abject humiliation he had been subjected to at the hands of a little bitch who had used her sexuality against him. How dare that jumped-up little hingoot set him up like that? The comments below his videos confirmed he was not alone.

He would get his own back on the whore when the time was right.

For months he had no idea when that might be, or how that might happen. His school mates were merciless in their mocking of him. Kirsty had told everyone he was a shit kisser and that he hadn't even felt her up right. Said it was clear he was a virgin no matter what he'd said in the past. Someone started the rumour he must be gay if he didn't even know how to finger a lassie.

It got to the stage where Liam spoke to no one at all during the day, barely even answering his teachers' questions. He arrived at school as late as possible and disappeared home as soon as the bell went for the end of the day. He wouldn't have bothered going at all, but he was determined to go to university and get away from this shithole of a city – it was the only thing that kept him going.

He felt the anger and humiliation course through his body once more as he remembered how excruciating those first few weeks back at school had been. He closed his eyes and reminded himself he had a plan; it wouldn't be long before Kirsty Boyd got exactly what was coming to her.

He'd come up with the idea with the help of his new online mates. He'd found them in those dark months when he wondered if he might always burn with shame at the thought of those photos appearing online. Liam could not believe that he was the only teenage boy to have ever felt like this, to have ever had something like this happen to him. He knew nude pictures of girls appeared online all the time, but that was because they were stupid enough to send them to their boyfriends. It was different for Liam, he'd had no choice in the matter; he'd been tricked.

When Liam had googled *male revenge porn* the results hadn't been exactly what he'd been looking for. Faced with an array of pictures of naked men, he'd quickly refined his search. *Victims of male revenge porn* had turned up some more promising results. Although, not all the victims were like him, some had made the same mistake as the silly slappers who sent their boyfriends nudies.

It wasn't long before he found a forum that seemed to reflect the thoughts he was having. It was called Black Knight and Black Pills. He was desperate to have sex, yet it seemed no women wanted to have sex with him. He knew it wasn't his fault, he was a nice guy and it wasn't like he was horrifically ugly, or that he had terrible acne, it was that the girls were too picky. The more he read the posts and comments in the forum, the more he had realised he really wasn't alone. There were thousands of men like him all over the world and there were even some in Edinburgh.

Before long, Liam had signed up and become a frequent poster. He immersed himself in this group of like-minded people. He began to feel more like he belonged and less like the odd one out. His new online friends shared his frustrations and he was relieved that he could talk to them about how he felt without fear of ridicule. He had found a community and even an identity – an identity he shared with many other men. He was an Involuntary Celibate.

Liam quickly realised there was a scale, and some of the users who'd been around for a while would post images depicting exactly what they would do to a woman given half the chance. At first he thought this was a bit much, but after a while and after reading the comments he began to understand.

Liam's laptop screen blinked into life and he logged on to the forum. There were several new threads for him to catch up on and he'd also been sent a direct message. Excited, he clicked on that first. It was rare to receive a DM, it was one of the forum rules that everything should be kept to the public message boards.

Message from @beta2:
It's your turn. Are you ready?

Liam stared at the screen. It was his turn. He'd been waiting for this for months. Ever since they'd come up with the idea on the Edinburgh message board, he'd been desperate for it to be his go. He knew this was a stepping stone to his revenge on Kirsty Boyd and originally the thought had thrilled him. But now, now he wasn't so sure. Could he really go through with it?

Then he remembered the painful humiliation she had rained down on him and he allowed that anger to fire up in his belly. Remembered how everyone knew what had happened, even his mum, so he replied.

Message from @gingercel2003:
Yeah, but I'm a bit twitchy about it. Do we have details yet?

Message from @beta2:

Don't worry, we've all been there and most of us have done something similar. Awaiting instructions from previous cel. Stay online.

Message from @gingercel2003:

No problem – I'll be here.

CHAPTER TEN

Frankie barged into Sid's office without knocking. She hadn't even stopped to take off her jacket or put her bag down. Amy had called to her but she'd waved her off, focused on talking to Sid and explaining her idea to him. There was no time, she needed to get a jump on this and she needed his go-ahead immediately.

Sid was on the phone. He glared at her and tried to shoo her from his office with his free hand, mouthing the word *out*. Frankie stood her ground, refused to move, shaking her head emphatically. Sid rolled his eyes, and taking this as a good sign, Frankie sat in the spare seat and pulled her curly hair into a ponytail – she meant business. She cocked her head and stared at him, eyes wide, impatiently waiting for him to end his call.

After a minute or so he got the message and promised the person on the other end of the line he would call back soon.

'Seriously, Frankie, you can't barge—'

'Sid, listen, there's more to this story than they're saying. Apparently there's actually been five rapes. The police have only just started asking for help from the public and taking the investigation seriously because these latest ones weren't prostitutes. I think we should do some digging and speak to our guy at the station, find out what's been going on.' Frankie was sitting forward in her seat, forearms on Sid's desk, eagerly awaiting his excitement and approval.

Sid leaned back in his chair, toying with his pen, and gave Frankie an appraising look. 'Where did you hear that?'

'At the press conference. Some reporter called Molly asked Caldwell about it and he totally brushed it aside, but the look on his face said otherwise. This could be huge – police discrimination against sex workers.'

'There's nothing new in that, Frankie, it's been happening for years.'

'Yeah, but what if they're ignoring important evidence just because these women are prostitutes? Surely there's an angle there.'

'Hmmm, I'm not convinced. Why don't you write up the press conference and I'll have a think about it.'

'But... I thought you'd want something about it for the morning. That's what you said, wasn't it?' Frankie threw her hands in the air in frustration.

'I did.' Sid nodded slowly. 'I said I wanted your report of the press conference for the morning. Apart from anything else, I haven't got much space. Look, I can see you're excited, but I'm just not sure there's a story here.'

Frankie fixed him with a stare. 'I think you're wrong.'

'That's fair enough, but I've got a little bit more experience than you about these things. I tell you what, I'll put a call in to my man at the station and then I'll make a decision. How does that sound?'

Frankie bristled but recognised this was as good as she was going to get. She wouldn't get the fast start she'd wanted on the story, but perhaps it could be a longer, well-researched, piece. If that was the case, then maybe she could have all the space she needed, rather than having to condense it down into whatever inches were left in the morning edition.

She stood and picked up her bag. 'Fine. I best get started on this one. Let me know when you've spoken to your man though, yeah?'

Back at her desk, Amy leaned over to whisper to her. 'What's going on?'

Frankie cocked her head towards the kitchen and they made their way over under the guise of making a cup of tea. There was an unwritten rule in the office, if two people went in there together, everyone else left them to it. It said very loudly, 'This is a private conversation'.

Once inside, the door closed behind them, Frankie put on the kettle and explained everything that had happened, both at the press conference and in Sid's office.

'So what are you going to do?' asked Amy after Frankie had finished.

Frankie shrugged. 'Dunno, wait and see what Sid has to say after he's spoken to his informant I guess.'

'Do you really think there might be something in it?'

'Do you not think it's a bit odd? That Caldwell started holding press conferences after a nurse and a young teenage girl were attacked?'

'I suppose, but it might be because there have been so many now?'

'I would've thought after two or maybe three attacks the police would want to advise women to be on the lookout, but it was only after the fifth one, the nurse, they said anything. It doesn't sit right for me.'

'Maybe. I hadn't really thought of it that way.'

'Me neither until that woman at the press conference asked the question.' Frankie looked at her watch. 'I need to get this written up. Finish making the tea for me?'

'Hmmm?'

Frankie was sitting in her mum and dad's front room, a tray of fish and chips on her knee. She'd been listening to them talk about the news on the telly, but hadn't really heard what they'd been saying. She was still thinking about the press conference and her meeting with Sid, and hadn't realised her mum was speaking to her.

'I said, where did you say Todd was tonight?'

'Oh, sorry, Mum. I was miles away. He's working.'

'That boy always seems to be working.'

'It's not that, just odd hours, that's all.'

'It's about time we had you two round for Sunday dinner, you know.'

'It hasn't been that long, Mum, but I'll check his rota and we'll sort something out.'

They carried on eating their dinner in silence for a while when the Edinburgh & East local news came on. The lead story was that afternoon's press conference with Fenton Caldwell.

'Oh, those poor lassies. It's awful what's happened to them.'

'Shh a wee minute, Mum. I need to hear this.'

They all watched as Councillor Caldwell's statement was shown in full and then a couple of the reporters' questions were answered. Frankie noted with interest that Molly's question about when the police started taking the attacks seriously was aired, although the news anchors didn't discuss it afterwards.

'I can't believe things like that still happen,' said Frankie's mum.

Frankie turned to face her, intrigued by what she'd said. 'What do you mean, Mum?'

'It's a tale as old as time, isn't it? The law and the public treating women differently, treating different classes of women differently. They did exactly the same with the Yorkshire Ripper murders in the seventies and forty-odd years later they're making the same mistakes.'

'What happened with the Yorkshire Ripper? I don't really know anything about it.'

'Well, you wouldn't, hen, it was before you were born.'

'Your mum's right, Frankie. This is almost exactly the same as what happened back then. The only difference is these women aren't being murdered.'

'Really? That's unbelievable.'

'So much has changed, yet so little has changed. At least you won't lose your job for being pregnant though.'

'That never used to happen, surely?'

'It happened to your mum.' Frankie's dad watched his wife with a grave look on his face.

Frankie's gaze flicked back and forth between her parents. 'What happened?'

'I was going to the cashpoint...'

I hope they've bloody paid me.

Nikki forced her card into the slot and entered her PIN before selecting the option to check her balance.

She automatically glanced at the number on the screen and had pressed the button to withdraw some cash before she registered something was wrong. Convinced she had misread the screen, Nikki cancelled the transaction and made the appropriate selections to check her bank balance once more.

'That can't be right,' she whispered to herself. There was at least double, maybe even triple the amount in her account there should be. Nikki rubbed at her temple and forced herself to try to think why there might be so much extra money in her account, but nothing would come to mind.

The machine beeped at her, warning her that she had taken too much time. Flustered, Nikki quickly requested the machine give her £15 and an itemised receipt. It was more than she would normally put in the electric meter, but she did not want to have to venture out again anytime soon, and apparently she had the money to do it. She shoved the receipt into her pocket to look at later.

After walking all the way home, Nikki made it through her front door and into the bathroom in time to throw up. Was it the fourth or fifth time that day? It was getting harder to keep track.

Exhausted from walking too far in her condition and from throwing up for the last twenty minutes, she decided to make herself a cup of tea and settle on the sofa to watch the soaps.

Rubbing at her three-and-a-half-month pregnant belly contentedly she thought about what the doctor had said the previous week. Apparently throwing up most of the day and night was unusual and not every pregnant woman had to deal with it. There was even a special name for it, hyperemesis gravidarum. She had made a point of memorising the proper name so when people asked she sounded like she knew what she was talking about.

She was supposed to be resting as much as possible, and drinking as much water as she could, but it wasn't always that easy. The doctor didn't understand that, although he'd signed her off work, she still had a house to keep clean and dinners to cook. As much as John was a good man, he was in no way domesticated. He'd tried to cook bangers and mash one night, but after he burnt the sausages and boiled the potatoes to mush, he'd ended up having to go and buy them a chippy tea.

She'd finally given in and gone to see the doctor when her boss had insisted upon it. It was just over a week earlier and she'd spent an hour in the office toilet throwing up. When she returned to her desk, he had summonsed her into his office.

'Frankly, Nikki, not only am I a little worried about the amount of time you spend with your head down the toilet these days, but more that you're not doing as much work as you ought to be as a consequence. It's not fair for you to expect your colleagues to continually pick up your slack and I really must insist that you go and see a doctor immediately.'

Unwilling to confess to being pregnant so soon, Nikki agreed to make an appointment at her surgery, thinking she might be able to persuade the doctor to give her some anti-sickness pills. However, once the doctor had diagnosed her with extreme morning sickness, he insisted she be signed off from work immediately.

'You must rest as much as possible. Constant vomiting will only add to the exhaustion you already feel from your pregnancy.'

Nikki thanked him for his time and took the sick note he proffered, promising to take his advice on board.

When she arrived home she managed to persuade John to drop the sick note into her office, meaning she wouldn't have to face her boss. Not only was he going to be annoyed about the time off, he was going to be furious that she hadn't told him she was pregnant.

Nikki heard nothing from her boss, not a phone call or even a letter.

'He was like a bear with a sore head for the rest of the day after your John left his office,' said one of her colleagues, Val, when Nikki bumped into her at the supermarket.

Hearing John's key in the lock, Nikki rocked and rolled her way to her feet, pausing for a moment once she was upright. She'd learned this was the best way to avoid the waves of nausea that usually washed over her when she stood.

'Hello!' she called out to John and smiled to herself. They had greeted each other coming through the door this way for as long as she could remember.

'Hello!' he called back. 'Are you putting the kettle on? I wouldn't mind a wee cup of tea.'

'Yep, I'll put your dinner on as well.'

It wasn't until the next morning, while John was getting ready for work, that Nikki remembered the extra money in the bank account.

After she'd waved him off from the front door, she dug out the itemised receipt from her pocket and scrutinised each of the lines. One entry in particular jumped out.

Hawksby Accountancy £1,501.33

That wasn't right, her monthly wages should have been less than £500. She would phone Mr Morrison and explain there had been a mistake. It was all well and good her keeping the money, but they'd soon realise their error and expect her to return it.

What a pain to have to sort out. Hopefully the bank could transfer the money and she wouldn't have to withdraw the cash and walk around with £1,000 in her purse. It would be her luck some scrote would try to nick her bag with all that money in there, and it wasn't like she could fight back in her condition.

The phone call would have to wait though. Nikki's stomach had started to gurgle and she knew, from grisly experience, it wouldn't just pass. If she didn't move now, she'd spend all morning cleaning up vomit from the carpet.

A couple of hours later, after she had finished her morning bout of throwing up and her stomach felt calmer, she dialled her work number.

'Hello, can I speak to Mr Morrison please?' Even to her own ears she sounded exhausted.

A tinny, clipped voice asked her to hold the line and Nikki prayed he'd be unavailable, or off sick, or on holiday. Anything that would mean she could speak to someone else.

'Alisdair Morrison speaking.' No such luck.

'Good morning, Mr Morrison, it's Nikki Currington.'

'Oh... hello, Nikki.' He sounded slightly flustered. 'How can I help you?'

'Well, it seems there's been some kind of mix-up with my wages. It looks like I've been paid three times, instead of just the once.'

Mr Morrison cleared his throat. 'No, that is the correct sum for your redundancy payment.'

'My redundancy payment? But I haven't been made redundant.' Nikki was certain she had misheard the man, or he had made a mistake.

'Eh, yes, now, let me see... Aha! Here it is, you were made redundant last week, and three month's pay is your redundancy package.'

'Are you sure? I haven't received a letter or anything. I wasn't aware there were any redundancies being made.'

'Yes, yes, quite sure. It was decided that given your current disposition and your pregnancy that redundancy was the best option for you. You would have only been working for another month or so before you left to have the baby anyway, and now you can relax and get plenty of rest.'

'Decided by who? I'm a trainee accountant, I had planned

to return to work after my maternity leave ended.' Nikki's hand grasped at her throat and she felt tears prick at her eyes. She'd worked hard to get as far as she had, and now... nothing?

'There, there, my dear, don't go upsetting yourself. The management team here at Hawksby Accounting made the decision, taking into consideration your condition and what was best for the business. And once you've had the baby, you'll feel totally different about coming back to work. Women always change their minds and want to stay at home and look after the little ones.'

Nikki's head was swimming and she could feel another bout of sickness threatening. She quietly thanked Mr Morrison and placed the phone back in the cradle.

Her job, her career, was gone – poof! – just like that. Yanked away from her in the blink of an eye, or the click of fingers. Two years of studying and hard work down the drain, without her even so much as being consulted.

She struggled to her feet and made her way to the bathroom. Tears slid down her face as she braced her hands on the toilet and lowered herself onto the cold floor to retch into the toilet bowl. Each convulsion reminded her that the tiny baby in her belly was not only causing this, but was also the reason she had lost her job.

When John arrived home later that night, she did not greet him in their usual way. She couldn't even pretend.

'What's the matter, hen?' he asked, rushing to her side. 'Is the baby okay?'

'The baby's fine. It's all about the baby, isn't it?' She knew she was being scornful towards the wrong person, but she couldn't help it.

'What? I...'

Nikki pinched the bridge of her nose and closed her eyes. 'The baby's fine, but I've been made redundant. I phoned today because they'd put too much money in my account, that's how I found out.'

'That's great news! A wee bit of extra money, and then you won't have to make a decision about going back to work. You can be a full-time mum, it'll be brilliant.'

'I wanted to go back and carry on with my training though. That's what I wanted to do.'

'Aye, I know, hen, but this is good too. You're gonna be the best mum ever, you wait and see.' John pulled her into a hug. 'I'll get a chippy for tea, seeing as you're a wee bit upset.'

Nikki looked at him, searching his face for something, some glimpse of understanding. There was nothing. He was a good, kind and loving man, but he did not understand. 'Sounds good. Just chips for me though, I don't think I can face anything else.'

'You see, hen, securing a position as a trainee accountant wasn't easy and I had to work my socks off to keep ahead. All the effort, all the extra hours I spent poring over my books, sacrificing evenings out so that I, so that *we*, could have a better future, it had all been for nothing.'

Her mum had had a career? How could Frankie not know any of this stuff? Her mum had always been a stay-at-home mum. She'd looked after Frankie, took her to school, baked, made home-cooked meals and generally been the perfect wife and mother. Frankie had assumed that was what she always was, what she had always wanted.

Frankie's eyes filled with tears listening to the sadness in her mum's voice. She couldn't imagine being told she couldn't be a reporter just because she happened to be having a child. Her mum was right, how could so much, yet so little have changed?

'These days lots of things are different,' said Nikki, seeing her daughter's face, 'but you know, you were a wee feminist yourself when you were younger. When the teachers asked for big strong boys to help move stacks of chairs, you'd get the hump and do it yourself. You used to hate wearing skirts and didn't understand why you couldn't wear trousers like the boys.'

Frankie smiled. 'I'd forgotten all about that. I was there, you know, this afternoon, to report on the press conference. My article's going to be in the paper in the morning.'

'That's great, Frankie, well done!' her dad boomed.

'Thanks, Dad.'

An idea poked itself at Frankie's brain. 'Listen, back in the seventies, did they try to make women stay at home at night?' she asked distractedly, the idea slowly taking form.

'They tried,' her mum snorted.

'What does that mean?'

'Women got sick of it so they organised marches and said they were going to "Reclaim the Night". That was the slogan they used too. It was a really big deal back then.'

Frankie leapt to her feet to dash from the room. 'I need to make a call.'

CHAPTER ELEVEN

'You're still up?'

Todd yawned loudly and moved over to stand behind Frankie, placing his hands on her shoulders. She was sitting at the dining room table tapping furiously at her keyboard.

She cocked her head offering him her cheek to kiss, but her eyes didn't move from the computer screen in front of her. 'What time is it?'

'Half eleven.'

'What?' Frankie snatched up her phone and checked the time.

Her action irritated him for no apparent reason. Why ask him a question and then check for herself after he gave the answer. He had no idea why it bothered him so much, it was irrelevant, but he couldn't help it. He must be more tired than he thought.

'Don't you believe me?'

Frankie gave him an odd look. 'What? Of course I do, I just can't believe it got so late. I've been sat here researching and writing this story since I got back from Mum and Dad's about four hours ago. I completely lost track of time.'

'It's not like you to write at home. What's the article?'

'You really want to know?' It was equally unlike Todd to ask about Frankie's work.

'I asked you, didn't I?'

Frankie said nothing. Instead she pursed her lips and raised her eyebrows.

Shit.

'Sorry, babe. I'm tired – was a busy one tonight.'

'Fair enough,' said Frankie after a second and turned back to her laptop, although not sounding entirely convinced.

'I'm going to make some cheese on toast, you want some? You can tell me about your article while I do it.'

Frankie turned in her chair and gave him a hard look. He could tell she was trying to decide whether or not to forgive him now, or later, and make him suffer in the meantime.

'Okay. Just one slice for me though, I had fish and chips earlier.'

Todd's shoulders dropped and he smiled. 'Come on then,' he said patting the stool by the breakfast bar, 'tell me all about it.'

'I'm writing a piece about how things haven't really changed for women in the last forty years.'

'Right...' Todd drew the word out not quite sure what else to say.

'Specifically it's about violence against women and how they're no safer now than they were back when the police were hunting for the Yorkshire Ripper.'

'How do you mean?' Todd was cutting the cheese into thick slices just how he knew Frankie liked it.

'The advice from the police is still the same. Women shouldn't go out after dark, they should only go out in groups, not walk about with headphones in and all that stuff.'

'That sounds like some pretty good advice to me. You

wouldn't leave your phone or your handbag on show in a car for someone to nick, would you? So it makes sense for women to take precautions to keep themselves safe.'

'But why should women be the ones having to stay at home? Why shouldn't men be told *they* can't go out after dark? They're the ones *causing* the problem.'

Todd laughed. 'That's ridiculous.' He turned to see Frankie giving him a tight smile.

'You've kind of proved my point. You can't make all men stay indoors after dark because of a minority of offenders, but the police and Councillor Caldwell have no problem in asking women to do exactly that.'

'I suppose.' Todd put the toast under the grill, desperately wishing he hadn't asked what the article was about and hoping Frankie hadn't seen him roll his eyes. 'Anyway, since when were you into feminism stuff? You always said you were never going to be a "bra burner" and all that raging, man-hating feminism wasn't your thing.'

He watched as Frankie shrugged. 'It's not really about the feminism. It's more about the police being inconsistent and not doing their jobs properly because of a person's gender or job. It's the comparison of the police work from then to now I'm really talking about. And the victim blaming. And anyway, Mum reminded me earlier about all the stuff I thought was unfair between boys and girls when I was a kid, and it got me thinking.'

'Don't look now but I'm pretty sure that's what feminism is about.'

'Maybe it is, but I'd be writing the same article if it was men we were talking about.'

Todd put a plate with a slice of cheese on toast on the breakfast bar in front of Frankie. 'Not likely to happen though, is it?'

'Thanks.'

'Things have changed though, haven't they? Women basically have the same rights as everyone else now, don't they?'

'I suppose so. I mean, I know they don't get fired for being pregnant anymore like Mum was.'

'What?'

Todd stood in the kitchen leaning against the counter eating his late-night snack and listened as Frankie told him all about how her mum had lost her job and it was all because of Frankie.

'Jesus! Your mum didn't actually say that though, did she?'

'Of course not. But I'm the one who caused her to have morning sickness and be off sick and if it wasn't for that, they wouldn't have been able to "make her redundant".'

'You cannot possibly feel guilty for that,' Todd said, shaking his head. 'That's nuts.'

'I do a wee bit.' Frankie's voice was small and quiet.

'That's crazy. I think all this women's lib stuff has got to your head. You seemed so much happier before you started doing this crime reporting gig, and you always said you wouldn't touch women's stuff with a bargepole.'

Frankie shrugged again, apparently all out of words.

'Why don't you have a wee think about it? It might be this isn't for you – I don't want you being all stressed out about stuff.'

When Frankie didn't reply again, Todd rounded the breakfast bar and enveloped her into a big hug. She leaned her head against his chest, but didn't hug him back. Instead, after a few seconds, she stood up and gave him a quick kiss.

'I'm shattered. Off to bed.'

'I'll be through shortly.'

Todd tugged at the ends of his hair and then scrubbed at his face, letting out a long breath. He liked an easy life, he prided himself on being chilled most of the time, but since Frankie had started working more on crime he felt that less and less.

Ever since that article the previous year when she'd been trolled afterwards he'd worried it would get worse, thankfully it hadn't. She still received the odd comment, but it had disappeared. Todd worried now it would all start up again – there was no way that sort of article wouldn't attract nutcases.

HAS ANYTHING CHANGED FOR WOMEN IN THE LAST 40 YEARS?

A serial rapist is hunting women on the streets of Edinburgh and it appears the police are placing the responsibility for women's safety squarely on the shoulders of the female population of our city.

To date, five women have come forward and reported they were raped in one of the parks spread across the Old and New Towns. Police have yet to release a description of the suspect, apparently blaming the victims for providing inconsistent descriptions of their attacker. One thing all of the victims agree on is, the man was dressed in black and used a double-edged hunting knife to terrorise them into doing what he told them.

During a recent press conference Councillor Fenton Caldwell advised the women of Edinburgh not to go out at night, to go out in groups, not to listen to music and not to take shortcuts through parks when it's dark. When he was asked if he was going to ask men to stop going out at night so women could feel safer, he dismissed the notion as nonsense. He stated, 'I don't really think it's fair to expect all men to stay in at night, because of one bad egg', but the Edinburgh councillor was quite happy to ask women to do just that.

When you couple the clearly double-standards of the council's advice with the fact the press conference was only called after an 'innocent' victim came forward – three sex workers having already been attacked – it is clear that law enforcement place a higher value on the lives of some women over others.

But this is nothing new for the women of Great Britain. 40 years ago a serial killer terrorised women in the north of England for years before the police caught him. His name was Peter Sutcliffe and he was known by the moniker The Yorkshire Ripper.

In the late 1970s the West Yorkshire police force gave women exactly the same advice. In all the time from then until now, the police still fail to understand that women have jobs to go to. They have to work. Some work in pubs, or work shifts because of childcare, and not going out at night is not an option for them. They tell sex workers to stay off the streets, not understanding that if these women had a choice, most would not be selling their bodies by the side of the road after the sun goes down.

While the women in the 1970s never found a solution, they did fight back. The Leeds Revolutionary Feminist Movement were so disgusted by the contempt they felt the police were showing for women, they organised a Reclaim the Night march in the district of Leeds where many of the Ripper killings had taken place. Similar marches took place in many of the larger towns and cities across Great Britain.

With the police floundering and seemingly no further forward in apprehending the man responsible, is it time for the women of Edinburgh to make their voices heard? Is it time for them to demand the police and lawmakers take their safety seriously?

CHAPTER TWELVE

The alarm clock buzzed on the bedside table and Frankie reached over to shut it off. It was 7am but she'd already been awake for over an hour. In fact, she had barely slept at all. Whenever she had dropped off to sleep she'd been plagued with dreams of Fenton Caldwell looming out of the blackness and laughing at her. Calling her a silly little girl and telling her not to get involved in things she clearly knew nothing about.

This had been her routine for the past three nights ever since she'd convinced Sid to run her article. She'd sat in his office for over an hour throwing argument after argument at him, wearing him down before he acquiesced and conceded she may have a point. He told her to go and write the story and he would take a look at it. Frankie had bounced out of her seat, a triumphant smile on her face. 'It's in your inbox,' she said and breezed out of his office.

Later, he'd complimented her on her writing and the clearly detailed research she had undertaken. After a few tweaks which he insisted on, he'd passed the article for publication. At first she'd been thrilled, an excited puppy. This was her first important, proactive piece of writing for the newspaper –

everything else she had written had been an assignment, pieces anyone could have written really. *This is what proper journalism feels like*, Frankie thought.

She thought about all the people who would read the article and whose eyes would be opened by what was *still* going on. She imagined the outrage and the calls for the police to do better and it would all be because of her. She knew this was probably pushing it, but it felt good to imagine how it would feel if people really engaged with her writing.

She had imagined Fenton Caldwell's reaction – how pissed off he would be that *another* journalist had called him out in public. How this time he might feel under pressure to make real changes to the way the police were handling the investigation, and any future investigations.

Slowly though, that thought had extended to how many other people might be pissed off by what she'd written and she remembered the trolls from the previous year. How nasty they'd been over something small like the history of International Women's Day. The memory had come out of nowhere and punched her in the gut – this was going to be worse.

For the last three days she had swung between knowing in her heart this was an issue the public *needed* to be aware of, and wishing she'd never written the damned thing and wanting to retract it. Amy had talked her out of doing it at least four times since it had been accepted for publication. Promising instead to be with her the entire day to support Frankie however she needed.

'Are you making coffee?' Todd croaked from under the covers beside her.

She threw off the duvet and went into the kitchen, returning a few minutes later with two cups of cafetière coffee – she was going to need the strong stuff.

She placed Todd's on his bedside table and made her way

back round to her side of the bed while he pulled himself into a seated position, bunching up the pillows behind him.

'Thanks,' he said, before taking a sip. 'Did you get any sleep last night?'

'Not really. Sorry if I kept you awake.'

'I wasn't really awake, more aware of you tossing and turning. Is it today?'

She nodded and blew on her coffee.

'You worried?'

'Yeah, a little. I just hope it hits the right notes.'

'I'm sure it'll be fine, but I more meant are you worried about trolls again. I know it's been pretty quiet since last year, but...' He trailed off when he saw her staring at him.

'I thought you'd forgotten all about that.'

He shrugged. 'Not really something you forget. I take it it *has* been quiet? You haven't mentioned anything so I just assumed...'

'There's been the odd thing, but nothing like the last time. I don't think I'll get away with it today though.'

'Maybe don't look at the comments?'

Frankie rolled her eyes. 'Not gonna happen is it – I'm not going to stay off social media forever, am I?'

'I thought—'

'I need to get ready for work.'

Frankie stopped to pick up a takeaway coffee and a copy of the paper. She'd left early to give herself some time and planned to read her article, in print, at her desk before everyone else arrived.

She cleared away the clutter that was spread across her work surface and laid the paper out flat. She read through the copy slowly, trying to be critical. She'd strived not to come across as one of those women who thought all men were the spawn of the devil and deserved to be hung by the balls for the crimes of the few. Still, she knew there were good men in the world, she only had to look at her dad and Todd – even Sid at a stretch.

She sat back and took a sip of her coffee, feeling better for having seen her article in all its published glory.

Frankie enjoyed the peace and quiet of the office for a few minutes before people started filing in and wishing her a good morning. Frankie waved back in their general direction and decided she would sort through her emails before she got down to any serious writing.

She deleted the junk that had made it through the spam filter first and then concentrated on the rest. There was an email from Sid about the current article she was working on, which she marked as important and would read in detail later.

The next email down was from an address she didn't recognise. Frankie thought nothing of it, her email address was on the website and people would often email in with 'interesting' stories – *some people need to look up the definition of 'interesting'*, she thought and snorted at her own joke.

'What's funny?'

It was Amy.

'Nothing, don't worry about it.'

'Tea?'

'Please. Better make it a green tea though, I've had three cups of coffee already and I'm buzzing slightly.'

'Have you looked at any comments yet?'

Frankie shook her head, her lips tight.

'Good. We'll do it together in a minute.'

Frankie turned her attention back towards her emails and opened the 'interesting' story one – just in case.

You'd better watch your back you fucking
whore.

You're next in our little game.

Make sure you don't go out at night by
yourself.

BITCH!

Frankie gasped. She couldn't tear her eyes away from the screen, reading the words over and over again. With a shaking hand she manoeuvred her mouse and clicked on the address, a reflex reaction that she knew would tell her exactly nothing, but something she felt compelled to try. To do nothing would make her feel inadequate, powerless even, and neither were feelings she was used to.

What else could she do?

She would reply – that's it.

Her fingers lay on the keyboard ready to type out a pithy and assertive response to the pathetic attempt to scare her, but the words wouldn't come. She wasn't scared, but the email had given her a fright. She'd been expecting the trolls to comment online, but she hadn't been prepared for this kind of attack in her inbox. Somehow this felt more personal.

She was still trying to grasp at a reply when Amy came back with their hot drinks. She took one look at Frankie's face and said, 'I thought I told you not to look at the comments yet?'

'I didn't,' replied Frankie as Amy set the teas down. She turned her monitor to face Amy.

Amy's eyes scanned the screen for a few seconds before her reaction mirrored Frankie's own, except Amy added a, 'Shit!'

'I was trying to think of a reply.'

'No!' said Amy, her eyes wide. 'No replying – we've got to report this to IT, to the police. This is a threat, Frankie.'

Frankie turned the monitor back and read the words for the hundredth time. 'I suppose it is.'

'You suppose!'

Amy picked up her phone and punched at the numbers with a finger.

'What are you doing?'

'Calling IT and then I'm phoning the police.'

Frankie leaned forward and stilled Amy's hand. 'No, don't. It's one silly email and I doubt anyone will be all that fussed anyway.'

Amy gave Frankie a hard look.

'I'm fine, I promise. It's probably some lanky streak-of-piss fifteen-year-old trying to look hard in front of his mates. I'll save the email and then block the address – how does that sound?'

Amy replaced the receiver slowly, put one hand on her hip and leaned on the desk with the other. 'Fine, but if you get anymore, we're reporting it.'

'Are we going to report every single troll comment I'm bound to get today as well? Look, it was a shock, but I'm ready for it now. I've pulled my thick skin on and nothing can hurt me. If I've riled them enough that they're bothering to get in contact then I must be doing something right.'

Amy didn't look quite so sure, but agreed nonetheless.

———

By lunchtime Frankie could feel her thick skin slipping from around her.

When she had logged on to social media to look at the comments under her article there had been over a hundred. The number had grown exponentially throughout the morning and now there were thousands.

The vast majority were ridiculing in nature and pointed out

all the ways Frankie had got it wrong in her article. They were clearly of the belief that their opinion should be taken as fact, and Frankie's facts were wrong. As eye-rollingly frustrating as it was, Frankie could deal with it – opinions were like arseholes, everyone had one.

Amy made a point of cheering whenever she found a positive or supportive remark and then reading it out in a triumphant voice – one finger stabbing out every word as a victory. It was little defence against the onslaught of sickening, vile and deeply misogynistic comments that Frankie couldn't tear her eyes from.

She'd lost count of the number of rape threats detailing exactly what the writer would do to her if they ever found her. Did these men not have mothers, wives, daughters?

They debated whether she might be a lesbian, or if she did have a boyfriend, if he shouldn't be doing more to keep her in check – some even suggesting a slap might 'do her good'.

There were some she didn't even understand.

Another example of why we need White Sharia Law – NOW!

What the hell is White Sharia Law?

Have you seen her picture? Slut thinks she's too good for the likes of us. Frigid bitch only shags if he's rich and hot.

Which was it? Was she a slut or a frigid bitch?

Frankie gave herself a shake – she was being dragged into their weird little world and it was her they were trolling.

She read the next couple of comments.

Real men rape. It's no fun if she says yes.

If they won't give it up willingly, rape is the only way some of us can have sex.

Enough – she couldn't read any more and she closed down the internet tab. Frankie leaned forward, elbows on her desk and her head in her hands. She'd done no work that morning, the comments having utterly consumed her. It was like a car crash, she couldn't not look – except she was the victim.

The phone on her desk rang and she eyed it warily. Earlier, a caller had somehow managed to persuade the switchboard to put them through and when Frankie picked up the phone she could clearly hear the sound of heavy breathing followed by a groan. The caller, whoever he was, had been masturbating down the phone to her. After that, the switchboard had been given strict instructions to only take messages, so she was surprised when her phone made a noise.

She took a deep breath, picked up the handset and said, 'Frankie Currington.'

Silence.

'Hello?' Frankie was scared and pissed off, she'd had about all she could take that morning and a silent phone call was the last straw. 'What the fuck do you want?' she screamed down the phone.

'I want you,' said the low voice.

Frankie's hand trembled and her mouth went dry.

'*We* want you. We know your name and we know where you live,' a pause, 'remember that when you're walking home tonight. Or will you get the bus? The number 31, isn't it? We can't wait to ram our co—'

Frankie slammed the phone down and realised she was trembling all over. She eased herself back in the chair and whispered, 'What the fuck?'

CHAPTER THIRTEEN

He stood over her, knife in hand, panting hard.

It was close to midnight and he'd followed her through Roseburn Park until she'd reached the trees in the middle. That was when he'd pounced.

She was lying back, one hand behind supporting her, the other held up in front – as if that was any defence against a knife.

'Please! No! Don't!'

'Shut up, bitch, or I'll slit your throat.' Liam said the words, but even he could hear there was no real energy behind them.

'P-please, let me go. I won't say anything. I haven't even seen your face.'

He feigned forwards with the knife and she shrank back and tried to scuttle away.

'I said shut up.' This wasn't how it was supposed to be, it was supposed to be easy, that's what they'd said. How could it be easy when the bitch kept crying and wailing? How was anyone supposed to get a hard-on with all that noise.

He thought about leaving and walking away, was it really

worth it? Then he remembered Kirsty Boyd and felt his determination return.

The girl was whimpering and Liam eyed her chest; she had quite the set of tits on her. He felt something stirring and said, 'Take off your jacket and your top.'

'No... I...'

He knelt down in front of her and used the tip of the knife to lift her chin. 'Take them off, or I'll cut you.' This time his words felt powerful.

Slowly her trembling hands moved to unzip her jacket; she removed it and her top, leaving a plain white bra underneath. The girl wrapped her arms around herself.

'Fuck sake, not even a decent bra.' Still her boobs were enormous. Liam leaned forward and cut the front of the bra open, nicking the skin at the breastbone – she gave a yelp. 'Shut it,' he growled pulling the bra away so he could see her nipples.

He groaned and reached forward grabbing a tit in his left hand. God that felt good.

Leaning back on his heels he swapped the knife into his left hand and stuck his right down his trousers to help himself along.

'Why are you doing this?'

He ignored her.

'Why me? What did I do to you?'

'Shut the fuck up.' She was ruining his buzz.

She kept talking. He tried to ignore her – his hand working hard.

'What would your mother say if she knew what you were doing right now?'

Liam's eyes flew to hers. 'What did you just say?'

'I said, what would your mum say if she knew you were out here trying to rape me?'

Liam's already struggling penis flopped in his hand. 'For

fuck sake!' There was zero chance of him getting it up with the thought of his mother in his head. 'You fucking bitch!'

Liam got to his feet, stood over the woman and punched her hard in the face before running away.

———

Liam arrived home via the Water of Leith where he'd dumped the knife as he'd been instructed. The balaclava had gone in a random street bin, which he'd then set light to.

Thank God his mum was out, he didn't think he could face her after what had happened.

He sank onto his bed and dragged his hand across his forehead. What was he going to do now? He'd failed in his task and there would be no revenge on Kirsty Boyd.

He sat that way for a long time, his mind turning over and over, trying to think of a plan. He would need to go online soon and confirm. It was all part of the deal. Once he scoped out his shag, he had to tell everyone else the where and the when so they could keep an eye out in the news the next day. He was expected to verify that the plan had been executed and to pass on the details of his target.

Jesus Christ! Why did I get involved? I should've known I could never do it.

Now it wasn't only the lack of revenge that bothered him. He would, once again, be the target of abject humiliation. What kind of man couldn't get it up to shag a lassie? There was no way he could face that again. He really would have nowhere to go if they found out what happened.

Think, think, think!

He smacked at the side of his head, trying to force an idea out. He felt himself close to tears as time slipped away. He could simply not log on, but he dismissed the idea. He'd never felt like he belonged anywhere else and he wasn't about to give it up easily.

The tears slid from his eyes unchecked; at least no one could see him in this state.

No one could see him... That was it! No one could see him! No one would know if he actually did it or not – he was always reading about how *so many women* were too scared to report assaults. Since he hadn't actually touched her – a quick grope of the titties didn't really count, did it? – he could claim she was obviously too traumatised to go to the police.

He dried his eyes, took a deep breath and logged on to the forum. Quickly navigating to the right message board and with words that conveyed a confidence he didn't feel, Liam told them all about what had happened. He stuck closely to the truth, only leaving out the embarrassing bits, and embellishing the end.

They'd clearly been waiting for him and the responses filled with congratulations came flooding through. Liam sank back onto his pillows and relaxed.

He was still scrolling a few hours later, his eyes scratchy and tired, but he was enjoying himself too much. Having been offline to prepare most of the day, his mates had been filling him in on the latest – a newspaper article written by some bint who thought all men should be locked up.

That's fucking ridiculous, he typed out. *You can't keep us all inside because of a few nutters!*

@omega1998:
    That's not even the half of it. Go and read the article and then we'll show you what we've been up to.

Liam did as he was told.

He quickly realised the rapes referred to in the article were actually the revenge shags they'd been dishing out on each other's behalf. Apart from the prossies – they had started as a bit of fun and it was from there the game had developed.

He was worried for a minute, what would happen if they got caught? He quickly dismissed the thought though – this was why they were all involved and they only did one each. It was much harder to catch loads of men, especially when they actually had nothing to do with the women they were scaring.

He laughed when he realised the reason the police were so confused was because they thought there was only one guy. They didn't believe the different descriptions given to them by the eyewitnesses and assumed they were too traumatised or it was too dark for them to see properly. Apparently eyewitnesses were notoriously unreliable – brilliant!

He switched back to the forum tab and typed out a message saying as much.

@KTHHFV
Tell us about it – bloody hilarious!

@gingercel2003
Although, is she seriously trying to suggest men shouldn't be allowed out at night and we're all the same?

@mentalcelAJ
Yeah – fucking bitch, I don't know who the fuck she thinks she is telling us what we should and shouldn't be allowed to do. She needs to be taught a lesson, and clearly that man of hers isn't up to the task. This is the problem with these Stacys – they don't know their place...

As Liam read on, the things his online mates had been saying for over a year slipped into place. He felt his eyes had been opened to a whole new world. He was seeing clearly for the first time in his life.

He could see the matrix now, the raining numbers from the Keanu Reeves film.

There was nothing wrong with *him*, it was *them*. It was all those fucking women who put him down, humiliated him, told him what to do, stopped him from having sex. Girls like Kirsty Boyd and that slut from earlier. She'd taken her top off for fuck sake – no way she would've done that if she hadn't wanted it – then she goes and changes her mind? Fuck her.

Fuck them all.

Then it hit him – he'd finally swallowed the red pill.

CHAPTER FOURTEEN

'No! Not a fucking chance!' Todd marched around the living room gesticulating like a crazy person. 'What planet are you fucking on?'

'I just want your help, Todd. It makes much more sense for you to do it since you are actually a man.'

'Let me make sure I've got this right,' he said, sitting down on one of the dining room chairs, his elbows on his knees. 'You want me to go into some godawful blokes-only forum, where they all hate women, and pretend to be one of them? For research?'

He watched as Frankie opened her mouth to speak, but Todd hadn't finished.

'Research for articles about the *manosphere*, whatever the fuck that is. And how do you even know about that anyway?' He was waving his arms around theatrically, clearly on a roll. 'Where these crazy bastards, who threatened you earlier, hang out. Where these fucking nutjobs that meant you had to get a taxi home hang out? That's what you want me to do?'

'I know it seems a little bit... deranged, but this is important, someone has to report on it. I found out about it because one of those arseholes commented *White Sharia Law now* and it seemed like such an odd expression, so I googled it. There's a whole underworld of this crap out there. No one really knows this shit is going on. Literally no one is talking about it – this could be my big break. It could make my career.'

Todd let out a strangled groan. How could she not see this was a terrible idea? It was only a couple of hours earlier he'd received a call at work from Amy to say Frankie had had a funny turn. He'd rushed over there because Frankie had refused to go to hospital – God she was stubborn – and between Amy and Sid he'd got the full story.

They'd refused to show him the messages, but assured him they would be shown to the police. The website had been taken down so no one else could post their filth, but it hadn't stopped them taking to Twitter to spout their bile. Todd felt sick reading them.

Amy and Sid had told him, because they felt he deserved to know – how fucking generous of them – that some of the messages had mentioned him. Not by name of course, at this stage no one had figured out who Frankie's boyfriend was, but it sure as hell wouldn't take them long. The last thing Todd wanted was to be dragged into this mess and he certainly didn't want his girlfriend involved.

At first he had wondered if they might be messages expressing some sort of sympathy for him, because his girlfriend clearly hated men so much. He was quickly put right on that point. No, these messages were calling him a pussy, and under the thumb, and anything else they could think of decrying his masculinity because he couldn't 'keep his woman under control'. The air quotes were added by Amy for special effect.

He was angry and he was scared. Angry because he'd been dragged into Frankie's fight which he wasn't even a part of – didn't want to be a part of. Scared because of the sheer number of threats made against his girlfriend. He knew ninety-nine per cent of them were sad gits with nothing better to do than hide behind their keyboards trolling women online – faced with Frankie in real life they'd shit themselves. But that final one per cent put the fear of God into him. Those one or two who were just crazy enough to crawl out from behind their keyboards and actually do what they said they were going to do.

'Frankie,' he said her name with extreme patience, 'these people have threatened to follow you home – they even know what bus you get. Amy and Sid wouldn't tell me exactly what the worst messages said, but I've seen what they're saying on Twitter... How can you want to carry on? You'd be deliberately putting yourself in danger.'

Frankie shuffled forwards, balancing on the edge of the sofa and leaning on her knees. Todd could see she was readying herself to make her case. 'I know you're worried, and I'm worried too, but I really don't think anything will happen. These articles are going to take me months to research properly and put together. I'll be writing my usual nonsense pieces between now and then and it'll all die down.'

'Your work are worried enough to pay for taxis for you to and from work for the foreseeable future. How can you not see this is serious?'

'They're just being overprotective in case anything *does* happen to me. This way they can say they did everything they could.'

Todd stood, shaking his head and made his way over to the kitchen. 'I need a beer, you want one?'

'Yeah, thanks.'

Todd handed a bottle to Frankie and they both took a long swig.

Todd sat back down on the dining room chair and leaned back, dropping his head to look at the ceiling. When the ceiling didn't give him the answers he was looking for, he closed his eyes and begged some deity or other for divine intervention.

He knew how important Frankie's writing career was to her and he could see how this story had exploded, so if there were more like it, then yeah, this could be her big break.

What Frankie didn't seem to be considering was, she was important to *him*. He could never forgive himself if something happened to her and he *allowed* it to happen because he'd helped her. He only wanted her to be safe.

He opened his eyes and sat straight when he felt Frankie's hand on his arm.

'I'm going to bed. I'm exhausted.'

Todd said he'd be through shortly.

Frankie stopped in the doorway and turned back to him. 'Look, I know today's been... a lot and I probably didn't get the timing right.'

Todd snorted.

'Please promise me you'll at least think about it?'

Todd sighed and said nothing, simply nodded once.

Half an hour later, Todd crawled into bed beside Frankie and snuggled into her. 'Babe,' he whispered in her ear. 'Babe, are you awake?'

'Am now...' her sleepy voice drifted up from the pillows.

'You're gonna do this anyway, whether I help you or not, aren't you?'

'Yep,' she said softly.

'Thought so.' But Frankie was already back asleep.

The next morning Todd had made a decision. 'I'll help you with your research, but if anything, and I mean anything, else happens, you agree to stop. We both stop.'

'But—'

'Frankie, I would never forgive myself if something happened to you. I don't like this, I don't like it at all, but you've made it quite clear you're going ahead even if I don't help you. The way I see it is, if I'm the one in these forums I can at least keep an eye on what's going on and I won't have to rely on you telling me the truth.'

'I—'

'Because let's face it – there's no way you'd tell me if there was anything dangerous because you know I'd make you stop.'

He watched a sly smile grow on her face – he knew her too well.

'Deal?'

'Okay – deal, but I want to have your log in details so I can see for myself what's going on when you're not around. I might need to go back and double-check some stuff.'

Todd considered it. He'd much rather be around when she needed information, that way he could keep an eye on things, but he got the impression that wouldn't fly. 'Fair enough.'

'Eek! Thank you!'

Frankie jumped up and wrapped Todd in a bear hug. He hugged her back and hoped to God he'd done the right thing.

CHAPTER FIFTEEN

The bedroom door creaked slightly as it opened.

'Don't you knock?' Liam grumbled from under the duvet, pulling it tighter round him. He'd been up most of the night trolling some lassie who'd rejected one of his mates. Apparently the proper name for it was doxing. He didn't really care what it was called, it was hilarious and it wasn't even illegal, you just had to know where to look to get the information you wanted.

There was a bloke in the forum known as the Data Guy. He was clearly some kind of hacker because if you needed information on someone, he could get it for you. Didn't matter what kind of info it was – home address, bank details, tax returns – he was your man. Most of the time he'd dig up what you wanted for fun, it would take him seconds to find the basic stuff, but if you wanted anything hardcore, it would cost you. On more than one occasion he'd found nudie pictures of girls who'd upset him and posted them all over the internet for a laugh.

The Data Guy had found this particular bitch's address and phone number and posted it in the forum for them all to have some fun with. It was tame by comparison to what they had done before. Liam signed her up to a load of porno websites – she'd be getting emails by the bucketload before long. Someone else had ordered a shitload of pizza to be delivered to her address, and a few of the others had taken it in turns to phone her up and tell her all the ways they wanted to hump her.

She may or may not know yet, but she had also been signed up to a lesbian dating app – complete with pictures, her email address and her phone number. Liam called it a night when his mate came back online to share a screenshot of her Facebook page *begging* whoever it was to stop and that she'd done nothing to deserve it.

'I did knock, you just didn't hear me.'

'Whatever. What do you want?'

'I want you to stop speaking to me like that for a start.'

Liam really couldn't be arsed with her shit on so little sleep.

He poked his head out from under the covers. 'Sorry, Mother. How can I help you this morning?' His tone was dripping with fake sincerity, but he knew she wouldn't comment any further.

She glared at him for a few seconds before she said, 'I want you to get up, have a shower and get out of this room for a bit. It bloody well stinks in here.'

Liam rolled his eyes. Same shit, different day. Why couldn't she leave him alone? He went to school, didn't he? What more did she want?

'It doesn't stink. Anyway, I'm tired, I'll get up in a wee while.'

'You wouldn't be so bloody tired if you didn't stay up half the night playing on your computer, would you?'

'Leave me alone,' he snapped and disappeared back under the covers.

His mum was partly right, he did spend all his free time

online these days. He couldn't remember the last time he left the house for anything other than going to school and he hadn't spoken to any of his 'real life' friends for months.

At first he'd felt guilty about not getting in contact, but then he reminded himself it was a two-way street. They had his number, just as well as he had theirs, and they hadn't so much as sent him a text in all that time. In the beginning they'd tried to apologise, but not one of them could do it without some kind of smirk on their face. All those years of friendship clearly meant nothing to the likes of Paul and Scott.

Well, he didn't want or need them anymore. He had new mates now, people like him who understood him. They were like the family he never had. (His mum didn't count, not really.) They had his back and their loyalty wasn't in question. Liam only had to look at the way they didn't ask *why* Kirsty Boyd was on the revenge list. They just accepted she had wronged him in some way and the next man in the queue had stepped up and avenged Liam's humiliation.

Liam had been told it had happened, but because no pictures were allowed he'd had no choice but to accept it at face value. Before, he wouldn't even have questioned that it might not have been done, but since he knew he'd lied, he realised others might do the same. It didn't take long though for the clues to start appearing on social media. Sympathetic messages of support were being posted on Kirsty's Facebook profile, but she wasn't responding. Her mum had posted a message saying thank you, but that Kirsty wouldn't be replying personally and she needed some privacy.

Revenge hadn't quite given Liam the euphoric feeling he had anticipated. His anger hadn't suddenly evaporated and he'd struggled with that for a while. What would it take to rid himself of all the big feelings he'd had ever since that night in the park? He took some comfort in knowing she had also experienced abject humiliation, and not only that, but fear too. His revenge buddy had told him she was utterly terrified, to the point where she couldn't speak – didn't even fight or beg – she just lay there.

Liam dragged himself to the shower and stood underneath the jets wondering what would happen next. He'd been unable to get back to sleep after his mum woke him up, so he'd decided to have a shower in the hopes she might leave him alone for a while.

As he washed himself, he realised he felt empty somehow. He'd spent so long being furious, and planning his revenge that he hadn't looked at what came next. What was beyond ensuring Kirsty Boyd got what was coming to her?

He knew one thing for sure, he would never be put in that position again. *He* – the man – was always going to be the one in charge. Never again would he let a female call the shots, from now on they would do his bidding and he intended to have some fun with that.

Liam turned off the shower and wrapped a towel round his waist – time to ask what else he could do to help the cause.

CHAPTER SIXTEEN

An email message from the switchboard pinged into Frankie's inbox.

```
A Ruby Buchanan called to speak to you.
She says she's interested in talking to
you about your 40 years article and
could you please give her a call back.

PS — She sounded totally normal

PPS — How long do we have to keep taking
messages for you? It's manic as it is
down here.

Erin
   X
```

Frankie rubbed her forehead. There was so much to react to in such a short message she didn't know where to start.

First of all, she hated that her article was being called the 40 years article when there was so much more important content than that. Secondly, she had told Sid she no longer needed the switchboard to take messages, but he had insisted it was for her own safety. What Frankie couldn't understand was why the switchboard should have to put up with the vile low lifes who'd been calling while she was all safe and protected. Especially when the switchboard operators had done nothing wrong and Frankie was the one who'd written the article.

Apart from all of that, who the hell was Ruby Buchanan? Why did she want to talk to Frankie about the article? And what did 'normal' sound like anyway?

One thing at a time. Ignoring the 40 years article comment, Frankie replied to Erin thanking her for the email and promising to speak to Sid about the messages situation. She made it abundantly clear she was grateful for all the work the switchboard had done on her behalf and made a mental note to buy them a big tin of chocolates.

'Amy?'

'Hmm?' Amy replied without looking up.

'Have you ever heard of a woman called Ruby Buchanan?'

'Uh-uh.' Amy continued staring at her screen, her fingers a blur across the keyboard. It was clear she wasn't listening to anything Frankie said.

Frankie leaned over the desk and clicked her fingers. 'Amy! Listen to me.'

'What?' Amy didn't like being interrupted when she was in full flow, but that rarely stopped Frankie.

'I said, have you heard of a woman called Ruby Buchanan? She's left me a message to call her back. Apparently she wants to talk about my article.'

'Your 40 years article?' asked Amy – deadpan. This was her way of getting Frankie back for interrupting her, she knew how much it irritated her.

'Yes, that one.' Frankie refused to rise to the bait.

'Her name rings a bell.' Amy tapped her fingers on her lips and stared off into the distance. 'I want to say... she's something to do with one of the women's movements... I think.'

'Are you sure?'

She pointed at her screen. 'No – that's why I said, I think. Can I carry on with this now?'

'Yeah, sure, sorry,' said Frankie, distracted from the conversation anyway.

Taking a few minutes, she mulled over what to do next. Should she call the woman back and find out what she wanted? If she did that she ran the risk of wasting time talking to a crank, so maybe she should ignore her entirely. Frankie leaned back in her chair and drummed her fingers lightly on the desk.

'Google her.'

'What?'

'I said, google her. And stop bloody tapping your fingers – you're driving me mental.'

'You're a genius! Why didn't I think of that?'

'I don't know? Call yourself a bloody journalist?' Amy's eyes still hadn't moved from the screen in front of her.

How does she do that? thought Frankie as she pulled her chair in and opened up a new web page. She typed in Ruby Buchanan's name and less than a second later there was a plethora of results. She clicked on the first result and a picture of a black woman with tight blonde curls popped up. She looked to be around forty-five and her eyes held a steely determination as she made unapologetic eye contact with the camera.

Frankie read the accompanying text and was surprised to learn the picture had been taken at a protest march. There had to be chaos all around this woman, people chanting, passions running high, yet she looked entirely unflappable; comfortable in her own skin.

The article went on to say Ruby Buchanan was a founding member of The Edinburgh Coalition for Gender Equality, or TECGE for short, and her views and speeches were highly respected within the community.

Which community? mused Frankie. If they meant women, then Frankie was a total let-down to her gender having never heard of her.

Next she googled The Edinburgh Coalition for Gender Equality. Frankie still hadn't made up her mind whether or not she was going to call Ruby Buchanan, but she wanted to be as informed as possible. It seemed the group were actively involved in advocating for women's rights: they lobbied the Scottish Government and the council in Edinburgh for changes to the law. They organised marches and also gave talks in high schools across the district to try to educate both young women and young men on matters of equality.

Frankie read on for another half an hour trying to decide what to do next. Ruby Buchanan was clearly a passionate feminist, and feminism could be the only thing she wanted to talk to Frankie about. And you only asked to speak to a journalist if you wanted them to print something. Could this woman help Frankie with her articles, or was this all too close for comfort? Frankie wanted to present articles that were as balanced as possible and she couldn't see how a founding member of a women's rights group could be anything other than one-sided.

'So who is she?'

Frankie jumped as Amy spoke into her ear. 'Shit! You scared the crap out of me.'

'Just getting my own back,' said Amy casually. 'What's her deal?'

Frankie explained everything she had learned and her reticence at contacting the woman.

'You're an idiot. You hardly know anything about any of this stuff and a woman who probably knows more than anyone you've ever met gets in contact and says she wants to talk to you, and you're not sure?'

'When you put it like that...'

'Exactly. At the end of the day, you can pick and choose what information you use – if anything. At most you'll waste an hour of your time having a coffee. You never know, you might learn something.'

'I suppose you're right. I just don't want to get too radical.'

'But you're quite happy to get Todd to plunge into some extremist misogyny group for the same articles. You keep banging on about this being balanced, but so far you're researching one side of the coin. Women can be extreme too, remember?'

'Oh God, you're right.' Frankie groaned into her hands.

'Lesson learned.'

'Okay, I'll phone her now and set up a meeting.'

Frankie double-checked the number and made the call.

'Edinburgh Coalition for Gender Equality, Adele speaking.'

'Good afternoon. May I speak with Ruby Buchanan please?'

'Who shall I say is calling?'

'This is Frankie Currington from the *Edinburgh Chronicle*. I'm returning her call.'

'One moment please.'

Frankie was put through and the phone at the other end rang only once before it was picked up.

'Hello, Frankie?'

'Hello, yes, this is Frankie Currington from the *Edinburgh Chronicle*. Is this Ruby Buchanan?'

'It is. Thank you so much for calling me back, I really appreciate it.'

'No problem. How can I help you?'

'I was wondering if we could meet for a coffee, or a glass of wine, or something? It would be easier to talk it over face to face. I'm hoping we can help each other.'

Intrigued, Frankie agreed to meet Ruby after work that evening.

CHAPTER SEVENTEEN

F rankie left the *Edinburgh Chronicle* offices at the end of the day and texted Todd as she was walking to let him know she would be late home from work. She didn't bother explaining where she was going or who she was meeting, it would take too long. Besides, he probably wasn't that fussed anyway.

After speaking to Ruby, Frankie had jotted down some questions based on her research. She had groped around for a focal point, but she didn't know what Ruby was looking for from her.

Frankie had spent a frustrated hour trying to find and decide on an angle before she gave up. Ruby had come to Frankie, so it was up to Ruby to set the tone of the meeting. Frankie decided she would sit and listen to what the woman had to say, take notes and go from there. She would never normally go to a meeting so under-prepared, but then she would usually set up the meetings rather than the other way around.

Frankie tried not to let the problem unsettle her as she marched through Edinburgh city centre, rushing to beat the chilly wind blowing through the city on her way to The

Albanach. She had chosen the venue because it felt like home turf. It turned out to be perfect since it wasn't far from Ruby's offices.

Frankie was walking past Jenners Department Store when a dress in the window caught her eye. She stopped to have a look and inspect the price – it would be perfect for work. As she turned to check no one would walk into her when she stopped, she caught the eye of a man walking behind her. He looked away quickly, to look at something in the adjacent window.

Odd, thought Frankie. She watched him for a moment, but after looking in the window for a few seconds, he walked away. Frankie shrugged and turned her attention back to the dress – it *was* perfect. She checked her watch, she was cutting it fine – it would have to wait for another day.

Frankie arrived at The Albanach a few minutes early, so she ordered herself a glass of wine and found a table with a seat facing the door so she could spot Ruby when she arrived. Frankie took off her coat and settled herself at the table. Her notebook in front of her, she reviewed the questions she'd thought of and wondered if any of them would prove to be relevant.

She took a sip of her wine and checked the time, Ruby was due any minute. Instinctively she glanced up towards the door. As she did so, she saw a man watching her through the entrance. Frankie flinched, it looked like the same man she had seen outside Jenner's. It couldn't be though, surely? She'd seen him walk off in the opposite direction.

Frankie made her way towards the door, certain she had made a mistake, but needing to be sure. As she stepped outside, she bumped straight into a tall woman and started making her apologies.

'I'm so sorry, I wasn't looking—'

'Frankie?' The woman cut her off.

Slightly startled, Frankie looked at the woman properly and realised it was Ruby Buchanan. The photos online had not accurately portrayed how tall she was – easily six foot.

'Yes, sorry. Ruby, right?' Frankie offered her hand and tried to hide how flustered she was by their awkward introduction.

'Yes. Hi. Are you okay?' Ruby frowned in concern.

Frankie tried to peer past the woman and look down the Mile towards the direction the man had gone in. 'Eh, yes, I think so,' she replied, still somewhat distracted.

Ruby looked behind her and turned back to face Frankie. 'Are you sure? You look all flustered.'

'It's nothing.' Frankie gave herself a mental shake. She was supposed to be a professional and this was not a good first impression. 'I thought I saw someone I knew, but they've gone now. I've got us a table over there. Can I get you a drink?'

'Sure, what are *you* having?'

'I've got a glass of white.'

'Perfect – I'll have the same.'

Frankie went to the bar and took the few minutes while she was being served to concentrate her mind and get her head back in the game.

Returning to the table, she handed Ruby her glass of wine with a smile. 'Here you go.' Frankie sat down and took a sip of her drink. 'So, how can I help you, Ruby? I know you said it was about my article, but I must say I'm surprised you read it. You must have so many more important things to do than read an article by a lowly features writer.'

'To be honest with you, it was one of my colleagues who brought it to my attention. But the only reason I didn't see it is because it's so unlike the *Chronicle* to post anything so supportive of the equality movement. I stopped looking a long time ago, but when I read it I knew I had to speak to you and I thought there might be an opportunity for us both.'

'How so?'

'You clearly have some clout in order to get the piece published in the first place, but I noticed there were a few holes in your research. I thought perhaps I could help you with that.'

Holes in my research? Seriously? 'And in return?'

'In return, you persuade your superiors to let you write and publish more of the same. I can help you with content and provide you with all the important facts and figures.'

This was what Frankie had been worried about – on several levels. Ruby Buchanan thought she was a feminist and wanted to use Frankie to push her own agenda through the newspaper. Yes, Frankie had other plans for the subject matter, but these would be fair pieces showing both sides of the argument. She did not want to feel pushed into writing the articles in a certain way and she definitely didn't want to feel forced to do so by someone like Ruby. Using Ruby as a contact for information seemed like a good idea, but she didn't like the notion of it being a quid pro quo arrangement.

Frankie tried to articulate her thoughts as politely as possible. She didn't want to offend Ruby and hoped if she played it right, she would have a new contact at the end of the meeting. 'I appreciate your offer, I really do, but I need to tell you, the articles I write will be looking at both sides of the story. I'm not really what you would call a feminist. I mean sure, there are a few changes I'd like to see, but I don't think everything is the fault of men.'

Ruby held her hands up. 'This is probably a good time to mention what I'm not – what we're not.'

'What do you mean?'

'What we're not is extremists. When we talk about feminism and equality, we mean precisely that. We're striving for equality for men and women. Part of what we do is working with men's groups to tackle the idea of toxic masculinity; raise awareness around the subject of male suicide. For us, achieving equality is something men and women have to tackle together – present a united front. We're trying to dispel the notion that feminism equals men v women.'

Frankie was surprised, she had very clear ideas on what feminism was and here was this woman telling her she'd been wrong all along.

'And if I might add, everything you've said makes you a feminist. There are so many different approaches to feminism, but we're all under the same umbrella.'

'I'd never thought about it that way before,' she told Ruby.

'Let me guess, you thought it was all bra-burning and man-hating? Maybe all ardent feminists were lesbians?'

Frankie flushed red and Ruby laughed.

'Don't worry. It's a common misconception and one we're trying hard to reverse. It's one of the reasons I wanted to meet with you. By the tone of your article it was very clear you were trying not to come across as anti-men.'

Frankie felt a flicker of pride at Ruby's praise. 'I don't want to be pigeon-holed as a feminist writer, which is why I tried so hard to be objective. I have ideas which also incorporate looking at male suicide rates and how some of the things that affect women also affect men.'

'I can, and I'm willing to, help you with that. Another wine?'

'Thanks.' Frankie was grateful Ruby had chosen to go to the bar at that point. She wanted some time to think through everything she had heard.

In the time it had taken Ruby to buy their drinks and come

back to the table, Frankie had mulled over her options and made a decision.

'I'd like for us to work together, but I have some conditions.'

'Okay...'

'I can't guarantee anything for publication. It took some persuading for my editor to publish my Reclaim the Night article.'

Ruby nodded again thoughtfully.

'And I get final say on which subjects we cover. I need to maintain my integrity at all times.'

'Agreed. However, I have an idea for your next article already.'

Frankie eyed Ruby with suspicion. 'What is it?'

Ruby gave her a knowing smile. 'I'm organising a Reclaim the Night march, just like you suggested in your article, and I want you to cover it.'

'That could be interesting, but with something like that, there'll be loads of press there. Where's the benefit to me?'

'You get exclusive access to all the main players for comment and interview. We need to advertise the march, so I can't keep the rest of the press in the dark, but I can make sure you have content they won't. Also, I think you should take part in the march, rather than simply cover it.'

'Take *part* in the march?' Frankie had never taken part in anything like that before. Weren't these kinds of demonstrations dangerous? Sure, they started off peaceful, but inevitably a small faction always caused problems.

'We're organising it in conjunction with the police. Safety is paramount for us,' said Ruby as if reading Frankie's mind. Ruby leaned forward, suddenly earnest. 'Think about it this way, you'll be able to write your article with all the emotion and passion you feel while you're marching. You'll be right in the thick of it – experiencing the adrenaline high and walking shoulder to shoulder with everyday people who hold a common belief. The other journalists will be on the fringes, looking for picture opportunities, quotes and soundbites. None of them will truly experience the thrill and the high of the march – that will give you a unique perspective on the whole thing.'

Frankie felt herself being swept along by Ruby's enthusiasm. She had a point, Frankie couldn't recall reading anything from the perspective of a marcher; this had to be a pretty unique take.

'Okay – I'll do it.' Frankie sat back in her seat, with a mixture of excitement and trepidation swilling around in her stomach. Now she had to persuade Sid this was a good idea.

CHAPTER EIGHTEEN

Since his mother had started constantly badgering him about spending too much time in his bedroom, Liam had stayed out of the house as much as possible when she was at home. However, she wasn't happy with that either. Now she said she never got to see him or spend time with him. Liam knew he could never win with her, so he did his own thing anyway. She'd get over it, she was his mother, she had to.

In the library he'd discovered there was a suite of computers which were free for anyone to use, you only needed to have a library card. Liam was thrilled, now he could spend as much time as he wanted online and no one was going to tell him off.

After he'd made the decision he wanted to do more for the cause, Liam had got in contact with @beta2 and offered his assistance. He felt he could help spread the word and recruit new members. He wanted to bring them into the fold and make them see they were not alone and they were the real victims. @beta2 had been impressed with his enthusiasm and the fevered support he had given the other incels who had taken part in the revenge game.

Message from @beta2:

You're almost there, but we need to be sure you have a proper understanding of the cause and you fully appreciate what you're entering in to. Once you're in, there's no going back.

Message from @gingercel2003:

I am ready – I promise. I played my part in the revenge game, didn't I?

Liam had kept his fingers crossed that his deceit had still not been found out. He had no idea what might happen if it were, but he was sure it would be devastating.

Message from @beta2:

You did and you did well. Why don't you read some of our brothers' manifestos to help open your mind even more, and then we can talk again?

Liam knew there was a files section where the manifestos of members were stored for everyone to read. He hadn't bothered with them up to then. He felt he understood what was happening around him and had no reason to delve any further. But if that was what it took to be taken seriously, then that was what Liam would do. He had plenty of time after all; he had no friends and no girlfriend, so what else was he going to do?

The first manifesto Liam looked at was 140 pages long and he knew it was going to take a while. He decided to come back to the library for opening the next day to make sure he would not feel rushed.

The next morning he nicked a tenner from his mum's purse and stopped off at the shop on his way to the library. He stocked up with drinks and snacks to make sure he didn't need to leave his computer terminal, except to use the toilet. The fact libraries now allowed you to eat and drink inside was another little nugget Liam had discovered recently.

Now, he was sitting at his favourite terminal. Right in the corner near the wall, where no one needed to pass by behind him. It made him feel safer and more secure; privacy was something Liam valued these days.

He logged on to the forum and navigated his way to the files section, where he, once again, opened the manifesto written by Roger Hart. All Liam knew of Hart was that he had also been an incel, had killed eight people in a mass shooting in America and then killed himself. The manifesto was an insight into the man's life, his psyche and it provided an opportunity to understand one of the greatest advocates of men's rights who had ever lived.

Hart's manifesto went into detail about his life, from his earliest memories right up until a few hours before he set out to murder as many people as he could. Liam wasn't so sure about the ending, but he was intrigued to find out what had led him to it.

Hart's life seemed to start out just like anyone else's, Liam thought as he read. Normal childhood, apart from his parents moving to the USA when he was younger. Soon after though, his parents had divorced and Hart had found the whole process incredibly difficult.

Liam read the words and felt a connection. His mum and dad hadn't divorced, his dad had left, but the upheaval Liam felt was equally as strong. Was it all his dad's fault? Is that why he had never been able to talk to girls? Have a girlfriend? Was it because he'd never been taught? He'd had no male role model to rely on as he grew up. No one to look up to and emulate. Liam pondered on this for a few minutes and carried on reading.

Hart talked in detail about being teased and ridiculed by girls for being weird. He wanted to know why they couldn't see he was one of the good guys, he was intelligent and far superior to the boys the hottest girls were dating and having sex with. Hart began to resent them, despise them and blamed all women for his inability to have sex. How dare women pick and choose who they sleep with and leave him by the sidelines.

Liam read and read, consuming page after page of information and understanding his life was not so different. Hart detailed all the times he was made to feel inferior by girls and all the times his friends had abandoned him instead of trying to help him. Instead of trying to understand what he was going through.

When Liam arrived at the page where Hart explained he had come to the realisation the only way to fix things was for sex to be outlawed Liam took a moment to think on it. Did *he* want sex to be outlawed? If he couldn't have sex, did he not want anyone to have sex?

No, Liam still wanted to have sex if he could. He was sure it would happen one day and he wasn't ready to give up on it yet.

He felt he agreed with Hart that women needed to be punished for rejecting men like himself, but he didn't think murder was the answer. No, he was quite sure on that. There were plenty of other ways of making girls' lives a misery without taking that final step. Apart from anything else, Liam did not want to die for the cause. He wanted to live, he just wanted to have a normal life.

The final part of the manifesto described to anyone who read it how Hart had come up with the idea and how he planned for it. His aim was to kill as many happy couples as possible and he intended to do so over a party weekend. Liam felt a chill as he read how it had taken Roger Hart five months to plot his shooting spree. This was not a man who had snapped; he had planned and calculated everything, even down to changing the event date from Halloween to another weekend because there would be too many police around.

Liam now understood why @beta2 wanted Liam to take his time before immersing himself further into the cause. There was a line and he knew he did not want to cross it.

CHAPTER NINETEEN

F rankie turned to gaze at the people behind her.
When she'd first arrived in Princes Street Gardens there had only been a dozen or so people gathered, including Ruby. For a moment she wondered if she'd made a mistake. There's no way Sid would agree to run a piece about a protest march attended by only fifteen people. She was about to waste hours of her life for nothing.

It hadn't taken long for the crowd to swell though. Half an hour later and Frankie was looking at hundreds, if not a thousand people lining up behind her. She couldn't see to the end and her stomach was fizzing – with nerves or excitement she wasn't sure.

The crowd was largely women, but she could see quite a few men as well. Many were holding signs with pithy slogans on them and Frankie thought about taking some photographs. Then she remembered Sid had said he'd send a photographer to cover the march, so she didn't need to worry, she could concentrate on absorbing the whole experience and trying to remember as much of the detail as she possibly could. This wasn't going to be a report of the march, this was going to be about the entire experience.

It hadn't taken much to persuade Sid to let her cover the protest. Initially he wanted to give the job to Andrew since this was very much his area of expertise. Frankie had argued that she'd earned the right to cover the march given that it was her story that made Ruby get in contact and she was the one who'd made the deal for exclusive access to the main players. Privately, Frankie also thought since it was her who had been on the receiving end of the vile trolls, she deserved to be given the story. She felt if it went to someone else, the trolls might think they'd won and that was the last thing she wanted.

'I think we're almost ready. Frankie, you good to go?'

'Yeah, I think so.' There was a slight tremor in Frankie's voice and hands.

Apprehension and adrenaline were converging to make Frankie's body behave in a way she'd never known it to before. She watched Ruby as she spoke to her colleagues and started the process of galvanising the marchers, looking for any sign of nervousness. Frankie saw none. Instead Ruby's eyes were glittering and alive, and she was bounding around like a puppy who couldn't sit still. Ruby wasn't nervous, she was revelling in the anticipation of what was to come.

Frankie continued to take in the sights around her. As promised, there was a large police presence. They stood around in their high-vis with their hands stuffed into the arm holes of their stab vests. They were chatting to one another and at first glance, appeared completely at ease, nonchalant even. But as Frankie paid more attention and looked more closely, she could see their eyes never stopped moving. They scanned the crowd, jumping from face to face, looking for who knew what? Frankie couldn't decide if the police presence made her feel more or less safe.

Ruby came back to Frankie's side holding a loudhailer. 'The plan is to get everyone going using this,' she said, brandishing the contraption, 'and then once we're on the move, you and I will slip into the crowd so we're immersed in the whole experience. Sound like a plan?'

Frankie nodded. 'Sounds like a plan.'

'You nervous?'

'A little, but also a bit excited. There's so much energy already and it feels like I'm being filled up by it. Like there's no room for anything else but this.'

Ruby was all smiles. 'I know, it's amazing and so addictive. Right, let's get this party started!' With a nod to the nearest police officer, she turned to face the crowd and brought the loudhailer to her mouth. 'Ladies and gentlemen, it's time to march!'

An almighty cheer went up from the crowd. It was like being at a football match, the only thing that had ever come close to what Frankie was experiencing.

With the cheer, placards and signs were raised high into the air in a fluid movement. Frankie hoped the photographer had this amazing spectacle in the sights of his camera lens. Some of the placards looked extremely professional and others looked like they had been knocked up at the last minute on a piece of old cardboard. Every single one held a message important to the person holding it though.

EVERY Woman I Know Has Experienced Sexual Harassment

Help Our Boys – Toxic Masculinity is REAL

Curfew for Men After Dusk

Reclaim the Streets

Inequality Costs Us ALL Our Humanity

I Just Want to be Safe Walking Home

Big Boys DO Cry

Men Are 3 Times More Likely to Die by Suicide

Frankie was struck by the number of signs supporting men as well as women. Although Ruby had told her this march was about equal rights, she had expected the majority of the placards to be women orientated. Frankie snapped a picture of a couple of the signs with her phone and then tapped out a quick note to remind herself to make a point of this in her article.

As she put her phone back in her pocket, the crowd moved; surging forward, slowly at first, but soon picking up speed. Frankie stuck by Ruby's side and they shrank back into the crowd, allowing the others to lead the march. Frankie's nervousness disappeared entirely and she swelled with excitement.

After a few minutes, someone in front of Frankie started a chant. At first she couldn't make out the words, but slowly it was taken up by everyone around her and Frankie marvelled as she watched it take hold. As the chant passed by her, she turned around, walking backwards so she could watch how the words flowed like a wave over the crowd and one by one they joined in.

Within a few minutes over a thousand people were shouting the words into the air: 'One, two, three, four. We won't take it anymore! Five, six, seven, eight. No more violence! No more hate!'

Frankie was in awe. This column made up of individual people was moving and speaking as one organism. It weaved its way through the gardens and out onto Princes Street itself. This powerful force held up traffic, it stopped the trams and it stopped people.

The police flanked the marchers at regular intervals along the entire length of the column. Frankie watched as their heads swivelled constantly, taking in both the protesters and the crowds gathering to watch.

Frankie's apprehension disappeared. The police presence

combined with the safety she felt in the numbers around her meant she could relax and start to enjoy the whole experience. People were laughing, smiling, enjoying themselves: even the police officers seemed relaxed and unworried.

The marchers reached the end of Princes Street and turned right, passed the Balmoral Hotel and onto North Bridge. Frankie knew the plan was then to turn left onto the Royal Mile and on to the Scottish Parliament Buildings.

The front of the march was passing the Hilton Hotel when the first missile was launched from the crowd. The police officers, no longer looking relaxed and unworried, shouted into their radios.

Then the screaming started.

CHAPTER TWENTY

The internet connection was doing Todd's head in. Frankie was out for hours and he had loads of free time to play on his Xbox with Craig. It was typical today was the day the crappy internet company couldn't get their act together.

He'd been trying to play through it for about an hour, but his screen kept freezing and he was continually having to restart the game.

Todd pulled off his headset and threw it on the floor in disgust. He picked up his phone and sent Craig a text.

Internet's fucking gone again – I give up!

But I was winning!

The only reason you were winning is because I couldn't move my players, ya knob!

Still winning though. You want to go to the pub instead?

Todd mulled it over. He could go to the pub, he wasn't

working until the following afternoon and had no idea what time Frankie might be home. They had talked about spending that evening exploring this bloody men's rights activist forum, but she might be tired when she got in. Then he would've wasted a whole afternoon when he could've been out enjoying himself.

He could always text Frankie and ask her to let him know when she got home, he reasoned. There's no way she could be annoyed by that. They would both get to do their own thing, but he would still be able to help her out like she had asked him to. It sounded like a win-win to Todd.

Sounds like a plan. I can't get smashed though, got to help Frankie out with something later.

You are so under the thumb! Abbotsford?

Yeah. I'm gonna have a quick shower, so I'll see you there in an hour?

You take longer to get ready than Frankie! Fine, an hour.

Less than an hour later Todd was sitting in The Abbotsford Bar on Rose Street, nursing a pint and waiting for his friend. It was a beautiful place and he could see why it was usually packed full of tourists. The red and gold decor screamed opulence and the price of some of the whisky supported the notion.

He had almost finished his first pint when Craig arrived. He stopped at the bar and came and sat down with two pints.

'So what's this thing Frankie needs your help with later? It's not like you two to get involved in each other's work.'

Todd explained what Frankie wanted him to do.

'Hang on. She's getting even more involved in this stuff, even though she says she *isn't* a feminist and *doesn't* want to be pigeon-holed? Have I got that right?'

Todd nodded slowly.

'And after the threats she received following the last couple of things she wrote, including rape threats if I remember correctly, she basically wants to go undercover in their world and take you along with her?'

'That pretty much sums it up,' said Todd as he nodded and then took a sip of his beer. 'I really don't want her to do it. What happens if one of these arseholes does try to attack her? Why can't she be happy with the articles she was writing?'

'You're right, she's bringing it on herself. If she keeps going then she's only got herself to blame when the trolls start commenting, or worse. What are you going to do?'

'I've promised I'll help her now. It's got to be better than her trying to do it herself. At least I'll sound like a bloke – they'll be less suspicious that way.'

Craig shook his head. 'It's about time you grew a pair and stood up to her, mate.'

'Maybe, but I just don't want her to get hurt. She said she'll do it with or without my help, so this seems like the safest way.'

Craig raised his glass to Todd. 'If you say so. Right, it's your round. Let's have some chasers and turn this into an interesting afternoon. I've had enough of talking about your kamikaze girlfriend.'

Todd spent the next few hours in his own little version of bloke heaven. There was beer, whisky chasers, football talk and even a bit of flirting with a couple of tourists from America. 'What

Frankie doesn't know won't hurt her,' Craig had whispered with a wink.

The American girls had moved on, apparently wanting to drink in as many Rose Street pubs as possible and Todd was beginning to feel the effects of an afternoon spent drinking beer and whisky. On his way to the toilet he looked at his watch and made an exaggerated oops face. It was probably about time he headed for home and hopefully he would've sobered up a little by the time he got there. He would suggest to Frankie they ordered pizza, that would help absorb some alcohol.

It was only as he stumbled slightly coming back from the toilet he realised Frankie was supposed to text him when she was on her way back to the flat. That was the plan; they were supposed to arrive around the same time. So clearly, it was entirely her fault. He grinned to himself, he was off the hook.

'What are you laughing at?' asked Craig. 'Did you get your end away in the toilets?' Craig laughed uproariously, clearly finding himself rather funny.

Todd landed in his seat with a thump. 'Frankie hasn't texted, so I'm not in trouble,' he said and started giggling.

'Eh?'

'I said to her to text me when she was heading home and I would too. But she hasn't texted me, so it's not my fault I'm not there yet.' Todd waggled his phone at Craig.

'Let me see that,' said Craig grabbing Todd's phone. He held it out of the way as Todd tried to snatch it back off him. 'I don't believe she hasn't texted you all afternoon.'

Todd gave up trying to get his phone and sat back in a huff. He watched as Craig typed in his pin code – he really ought to change that – and navigated his way to Frankie's texts.

Craig started laughing.

'What is it? Have I missed a text? Shit! She'll kill me.'

'No, Toddy-boy, you haven't missed a text. You never texted

her.' Craig handed Todd back his phone and creased up all over again.

Todd grabbed at the phone and looked at the screen. Craig was right, he'd never texted Frankie to let her know where he was going or ask her to text him. Shit. He could imagine her at home silently fuming and waiting for him to come through the door to give him both barrels. Should he go home and face her? Try to explain what happened? Or should he carry on drinking, seeing as he was in enough trouble anyway.

Craig was still laughing and taking the piss, and Todd had just about had enough of his 'jokes' for one day. 'Right, I'm off. I'm hungry anyway and I better get home and face the music.'

'Off you trot like a good little boy.'

'Don't be a twat all your life, Craig.' Todd rolled his eyes and left his friend to his own wee joke. He knew in about ten minutes Craig would finish his pint, look up and realise he was on his own. He wouldn't be laughing then.

The night air was nippy as Todd stepped out the pub door, and he pulled up the zip on his jacket and buried his chin into the collar. He stuffed his hands in his pockets and tried not to stagger as he made his way up Rose Street.

Even at this time of night, it wasn't as crowded as Princes Street, which ran parallel, so he intended to walk as far along it as he could before turning off.

As he walked, Todd noticed there were a few more people around than usual. He didn't pay too much attention, Edinburgh was a tourist city after all and it went with the territory. He tried not to stare when he saw a young woman in floods of tears being supported by, he supposed, her friends who all looked equally as upset.

He really paid attention when he saw a second, third and fourth group of people doing the same thing. That was when he noticed some of the people around him were injured. One man was holding a piece of bloodied cloth to his head. A teenage girl had her arm around another and was hopping along, the pain evident on her face.

Todd stopped in the middle of the street and looked around him. No one was smiling, no one was laughing. The faces he saw were filled with anguish, many were crying or looked like they had been. More still were pale with what he assumed was shock. Had there been a terrorist incident and he and Craig had missed it? Surely something like that would have penetrated the little world they had been in that afternoon.

All of a sudden, Todd felt completely sober. The repercussions of too much booze had vanished from his system. He needed to help these people. But how? And who to start with?

First he needed to find out what had happened. He made his way over to a group of four women and two guys. 'Excuse me, sorry. I was wondering what's happened?'

One of the men turned to him. 'They attacked the march, right on North Bridge. Some of us managed to get away, but they tried to pin us in at both ends. We've all come off Princes Street to get away.'

Todd looked at the man incredulously. 'Surely the police wouldn't have allowed there to be two marches...' He trailed off and as he did so he made eye contact with the man.

'Are you all right?' he asked and reached out to grab hold of him.

'Frankie. I've got to find Frankie.'

'Was she at the march?'

Todd could only nod, his brain whirring with awful thoughts and possibilities.

'Todd! Todd!'

The sound of someone calling his name brought him back to earth. It was Craig.

'Craig!' he said as his friend ran up to him. 'Frankie—'

'I know. That's why I came to find you. Someone came in the pub and I heard what happened.'

'We need to find her.'

'Have you phoned her?'

'Not yet,' Todd said fumbling for his phone. Why hadn't he thought to do that straight away? 'It's going to voicemail.' He looked at his friend, he needed guidance, Todd had no idea what to do next. He felt a hand on his arm.

'I don't want to upset you, but there were quite a few bad injuries. She might be at the hospital.'

Todd stared at the man, his brain unable to process what he was hearing. He turned to Craig. 'What if she's...'

'She's not. Come on, we're going to the hospital – now.'

Craig tugged at Todd's arm and they set off at a jog.

CHAPTER TWENTY-ONE

Frankie sat in the uncomfortable moulded plastic seat and leaned forward, her hands covering her eyes. Her head throbbed from where the projectile had struck her right on the top of her head. The bottle hadn't smashed, but it had been hard and it hurt.

She felt a hand on her shoulder. 'Here.' It was Ruby holding out a cup of water.

'Thank you,' she said as she took it, but only held it, using it as a focal point.

'Are you okay?' asked Ruby, sitting in the seat next to her.

'I think so. My head hurts and I've some scrapes, but I'll live. I'm nowhere near as bad as some of the people I've seen being taken in. Is there any news?'

Ruby shook her head and continued to hold the cold compress to her jaw. Somehow she had been punched in the ensuing panic and a purple bruise covered most of the lower left-hand side of her face.

'What even happened?' Frankie had been trying to figure it out ever since she arrived at the hospital and had had time to think.

'The police are still gathering information. They're going to give me an update later.'

Frankie cast her mind back to the march, only a few short hours earlier, but it seemed like days.

It had all been going so well. She'd relaxed into the carnival-like atmosphere and joined in with the chanting. The people not involved had been paying attention, trying to understand what the march was about, but she hadn't noticed any angry or aggressive faces. Certainly not in the numbers needed for the attack they'd sustained anyway. She'd been keeping an eye on the police, she knew they would be the first to react to any trouble, but they looked happy, so she wasn't worried.

As they walked over North Bridge, a glass bottle had been lobbed by someone in the crowd. Frankie had watched, not fully understanding as it sailed over her head. It landed somewhere behind her and seconds later she heard a woman scream. She had looked to Ruby. 'Was that a—' Frankie started to say, as she saw a hail of bottles soaring through the air.

'Get down!' The nearest police officer was shouting and gesturing with his hands for the protestors to drop to the ground. Frankie had no idea what use that would be, the bottles could still hit them. But even so, all around her, people were covering their heads and cowering in an effort to make themselves smaller targets.

She looked the other way and saw several more police officers speaking urgently into their radios as they drew their batons and flicked them open.

'Move! Get away, as safely as possible!'

Frankie could hear what the police were saying but it made no sense, go where?

The sound of screaming rent the air and suddenly there was pandemonium. People were trying to escape the attack, but there was nowhere to run. The attackers were in front of them and behind them – the protestors were stuck on the bridge with nowhere to go.

The police were trying to fend them off, but as soon as they removed one, another filled their place. Some of the protestors saw no option other than to fight the attackers in order to make spaces for everyone else to escape.

Frankie was not a fighter, she would be no help on that front. Instead she tried to assist the wounded, some of whom were collapsed on the ground, writhing in agony or not moving at all. 'Ruby! We've got to help them!' But there was nowhere for them to go. They could pull the casualties to the side of the road, but there wasn't much more shelter there.

'We've got to get them out of the firing line!' Ruby shouted.

Frankie could see she was right, a little more shelter was all they could do.

One by one, they supported those who were injured to the side of the road, and asked those who were uninjured to look after them, talk to them, apply pressure to their cuts and assure them the emergency services were on the way. The screaming and shouting raged on around them as they tried to help, their endeavours being hindered by more flying objects.

Frankie spotted a man prone on his side, apparently not moving. She dashed over to him screaming for Ruby to come with her. As she turned him over, she saw a cut to the side of his head and he wasn't breathing. She pressed her fingers into his neck to feel for a pulse, but there was nothing, not a flicker. Panic welled up from Frankie's stomach and she tried to focus her mind and *think*. What was she supposed to do?

She closed her eyes to try to concentrate. A pinprick of a memory stabbed at her brain.

Compressions.

Compressions to the tune of 'Staying Alive'.

She placed her palm on his breastbone in line with

where she imagined his nipples might be and then placed her other hand on top. She pressed sharply downwards and hummed the tune in her head. She felt the panic well up in her again as she realised she had no idea if she was pressing hard enough, nor how long she would have to keep it up until an ambulance arrived. She looked around for Ruby, and saw she was helping someone else over the other side of the street.

Suddenly, the deep guttural noises around Frankie changed to cheers and sounds of hope. Continuing with the compressions, she looked up, distracted by the noise and saw a sight which caused her to cry with relief. A troop of mounted police officers and police dressed in riot gear had arrived and were breaking up the fights and chasing off the attackers. It was over.

'Frankie!'

She turned at Ruby's cry, as the glass bottle landed on her head.

Although she hadn't been knocked unconscious, she had been dazed and confused when a police officer came over to help her and he'd insisted she go to the hospital. Frankie had asked him about the man she'd been giving CPR to and the policeman promised her the paramedics would take care of him from here.

Now she was here, she wished she'd just gone home. There were far more critically injured people than her, and the wait was likely to be a long one. Frankie had considered slipping away quietly, but then Ruby had turned up and insisted she wait with her until the doctor came to see her.

All Frankie wanted to do was go to sleep, but a nurse had told Ruby to make sure she stayed awake at all times and every time Frankie started to drop off, Ruby would shake her and chastise her.

'It's my fault you're in this mess, so you will absolutely *not* go unconscious on me, okay?'

Frankie didn't understand the logic, but couldn't form a coherent thought to argue the point either, so she did as she was told. 'Have you heard anything about the man I was...' Frankie struggled for the right words, '... the man I was helping?'

'The nurses aren't giving out any details, other than to say he's alive. They're saying you saved his life.'

Frankie made no more comment. Her only thought was at least being here meant she had first-hand access to any emerging information. No other journalists had been allowed in the hospital and this could only be good for the story she would need to write when she got home.

Story.

Home.

She had to tell Sid and Todd what was going on. They must have heard and they'd both be worried, but she also needed to tell Sid she was fine to write something for the morning paper.

She turned on her phone and became frustrated by the pinging of all the messages and missed calls coming through. She ignored them and tapped out a text to Todd.

I'm okay, but I'm at the hospital. You probably saw there was a problem at the march today. Don't come down, it's mental here. I'll let you know when I'm on my way home.

She averted her eyes from the sign on the wall forbidding the use of mobiles and called Sid. She explained she was fine and she would write a report on the riot once she was back from the hospital. She would start typing it out on her phone and email it over later. He tried to argue, but Frankie hung up before he could say any more. She texted him instead.

I'm writing the report, so there best be some space for me. I'll get it over ASAP. You know I'm right on this one.

Switching over to the notes app on her phone, Frankie tried to ignore the headache that had taken up residence, and typed out the details of how the riot had started and what happened. She just needed Ruby's police contact to come up trumps and tell her who the attackers were for her exclusive.

CHAPTER TWENTY-TWO

Todd and Craig jogged down Hanover Street hoping to jump in a taxi at the rank, but as soon as they turned the corner Todd realised how naive they'd been. Everyone was looking to get out of the city centre as quickly as possible after the violence and there was a queue all the way up the street.

'Fuck sake!'

'Two options,' said Craig, breathing heavily, 'we either go up to George Street and try the rank there or we head down to Princes Street and try our luck?'

'George Street's in the opposite direction, we'll go down to Princes Street, but I reckon that'll be worse.'

Todd was right. Princes Street was full of police, and the taxi rank was even busier. For a moment he considered getting a bus, not ideal, but better than nothing. He watched as one drove past them and realised it was full – standing room only.

'Fuck!' he shouted, scaring a couple of teenage girls who were hurrying past them.

Craig clutched his friend's arm. 'Todd, take a breath, mate. You're scaring people.'

'How the fuck am I meant to get to the hospital? There's no

fucking transport and in case you hadn't noticed, they've shut the bridge.' Todd pointed towards the police preventing traffic and pedestrians from crossing North Bridge.

Craig turned, looking for a solution that would stop his friend from losing the plot completely. There really was only one option. 'Right, here's what we'll do. Todd! Are you listening?'

Todd was staring hard at the police cordon wondering if he might be able to get past them somehow. 'Yes! Yes, I'm fucking listening.'

'Right. We go through the gardens, it's not busy, and we go up the stairs to the castle and then over to the road and down to the Grassmarket. We'll be able to get a cab from there, no problem.'

Todd looked to where Craig was pointing and imagined the route they would take. With the bridge shut it was about the only way to get south without going the long way around. The stairs would be a bitch to climb, no one in their right mind would usually do it, but needs must. And Craig was likely right about the taxis.

'Todd! Are we going?'

'Yeah, let's go.'

And for the second time that day, the two friends set off at a jog.

Once they reached the top of the stairs Craig bent over and was pulling in great lungfuls of air. Todd tugged at his arm, eager to keep moving. If he kept moving, he worried less.

'You can recover on the jog down. Come on!'

Craig rallied and allowed Todd to pull him along.

As they descended West Bow and into the Grassmarket

they dodged groups of tourists seemingly intent on getting in their way. They soon jumped back once Todd started growling at them.

Down on the Grassmarket they were easily able to hail a cab and as they piled in Todd said, 'Edinburgh hospital A and E.'

The driver flicked a glance in his rear-view mirror at Todd's abruptness. He was likely used to rudeness from tourists but Edinburgh people knew better.

'Sorry, mate,' said Craig. 'His missus was caught up in that trouble on the bridge and he hasn't heard from her.'

'Nae bother. Shoulda said.' With that he pulled out into the road and roared off in the direction of the hospital.

Todd fidgeted the whole way there. Rotating between staring out the window and staring at his watch. He was grateful to Craig for not speaking, there were no words that would help anyway. Todd willed each of the traffic lights to be green as they approached.

As the car drew to a stop at the hospital, Todd threw open the door and sped off towards the entrance, leaving Craig to pay the taxi driver.

Todd was arguing with a policeman by the time Craig caught up to him.

'I'm telling you, I think my girlfriend is in there and I need to get in and see her.'

'And I've told you, nobody gets in. We've had reporters try all sorts to sneak inside, so we had to lock it down. Look, you said you don't even know if she's in there. Have you tried to call her, or text her?'

Todd felt like screaming. Of course he'd bloody tried to call and text her.

'Try again,' said Craig. 'You haven't tried since Rose Street. Her phone might be on by now.'

Todd pulled his phone from his pocket and stared at it.

'What? What is it?'

'A text from Frankie.'

'What does it say? Is she okay?'

'Hang on! I'm reading it.' Todd read the short message several times as he absorbed what was written. Finally, he let out whoop of relief. 'She's fine. She's here.' Todd beamed at Craig and the policeman.

Craig leaned back against the wall and lifting his face to the sky breathed a sigh of relief. 'Thank fuck for that.'

'Does this mean I can go in there now? Now I've got proof she's here?'

'Let me see what I can do.' The policeman walked a few feet away, spoke into his radio and waited for a reply. After a few sentences toing and froing he returned to where Todd and Craig were waiting somewhat impatiently. 'You can go in,' he said pointing to Todd, 'but you have to wait outside. Sorry, too many people in there already.'

'No problem, officer.' Craig turned to Todd. 'Tell Frankie I said hi and give me a shout if you need anything.'

'How are you going to get back?'

'Don't worry about that, I'll figure it out. Let me know how she is later, right?'

'Right. Thanks, mate.'

'Nae bother.'

Todd turned and walked through the sliding doors in search of his girlfriend.

He didn't have to look far. He found her seated in the waiting area, tapping furiously on her phone and oblivious to anyone else around her. Todd walked up to where she was sitting and waited for her to see him.

He smiled when she noticed his feet and her eyes slowly travelled up his body until she realised who was standing in front of her.

'Todd!' Frankie jumped up and wrapped her arms around him in a tight embrace.

Todd didn't think he'd ever been so pleased to see her. He buried his face in her hair and squeezed his eyes shut against the onslaught of emotion. 'I was so worried about you,' he whispered into her hair.

Frankie pulled back and looked at him quizzically. 'But I texted you?'

'I know, but I only got that when I got here. When I first found out what had happened I was on Rose Street and I tried to call you. It went straight to answerphone, so I sent you some texts. By then Craig and I were on our way here – and let me tell you what a mission that was – and I didn't think to check my phone until I was outside.'

'Craig's here?' Frankie asked looking behind him.

'They wouldn't let him in, had to persuade the policeman to let *me* in. Tell me what happened.'

Frankie sat down and gestured for Todd to do the same. She took a deep breath and then launched into the story of what had happened that afternoon.

When she got to the part about texting Todd and calling Sid to talk about the story, Todd interrupted.

'Wait a minute.' He closed his eyes and shook his head. 'You... texted me and rang... Sid? About a story?'

Todd watched as Frankie fiddled with the hem of her jumper.

'You knew I would be worried sick when I found out what had happened, but instead of phoning me, your boyfriend, you decided the story was more important. Have I got that right?' Todd's voice was getting louder and more indignant as he realised he had not been a priority for Frankie.

'Todd, shh!' Frankie glanced around. 'Keep your voice down. It wasn't like that.'

'What was it like then?' Todd's voice lowered to a dangerous growl.

'I didn't want you to worry, I thought a text would downplay it.'

'Fine, but you don't need to write this story so why call Sid?'

'Are you joking? I am literally involved in this story and you imagine I wouldn't write it? Look around you – I'm the *only* journalist in here. I'll have an exclusive. Maybe even the front page.'

'You have a head injury, Frankie! Listen to yourself. You should be resting not writing stories about violence you were involved in.'

They were both silent for a few minutes. Both fuming that the other could not see their point.

Todd calmed down first. 'Do they know who it was?'

'Who what was?'

But Todd knew Frankie was deliberately misunderstanding. 'Who started the violence.'

Frankie could not, would not meet his eye. He lifted her chin so he could see into her eyes. 'Who was it, Frankie?'

She pulled away. 'Men's rights activists.' Frankie practically whispered her answer, knowing how he would react – and she was right.

Todd was on his feet. 'Are you fucking kidding me?'

He didn't wait for an answer. Instead he walked off up the waiting area, growling under his breath, ignoring the stares from the other patients. He couldn't believe what he was hearing. Everything he had worried about since Frankie started on this... on this crusade, was coming to life. He had to make her see... She had to stop. This was dangerous!

He stormed back over to where she was still sitting and bent over, his finger raised. 'Listen to me,' he said through clenched teeth, 'this is it. You stop this now. You're going to get hurt. How do you know these twats weren't targeting you?'

'They—'

'I'm not finished. Even if they weren't targeting you, they were targeting a Women's Rights march, which is everything you're planning to write about. You're planning to try to infiltrate these... these wankers, who have no problem attacking a group of protesters who are surrounded by the *police* for fuck sake! What's wrong with you?' Todd paused, his breath coming in short, sharp bursts as if he'd run a marathon. This was exhausting, why could she not see the danger? Why was she not running from it? This was *not normal*.

'Listen, I know you're worried and trust me, it was scary. But I can't walk away from this, I can't back down.'

'Why *not* though?'

'Because I can't let them win. Women have been backing down for years and it's got us nowhere. I'm not doing it anymore.'

Todd stared at Frankie, unable to believe what she was saying. He searched her eyes for some clue, some chink in her determination and saw none. She had made her mind up and Todd could think of no other argument that might convince her to back down.

'I won't help you. I'm not going into that forum. That deal's off.'

'It's okay, I don't need you to anymore anyway. Ruby already has someone in there.'

Todd's laugh was mirthless. 'Okay then. Have you got money for a taxi home?'

'What?'

'I said, have you got money for a taxi home? Because I'm not going to sit here and worry about you with a head injury while you're quite happy tapping away on your phone to write a story with no concern for your own safety. And clearly you don't need me anymore anyway.'

Frankie stared at him. 'I've got money,' she whispered.

'Good. I'll see you at home.' Todd turned his back on the woman he loved and walked away.

CHAPTER TWENTY-THREE

Liam ran.

As soon as he saw the mounted police, most of the horses well over six feet tall, he knew the game was up. There was no sense in him getting caught and he knew his mum would make his life unbearable if she found out what he'd been up to that afternoon. He also wasn't quite sure he could bear to look at the disappointment in her eyes if he was arrested.

He ran down Princes Street, dodging in and out of the crowds of people until he had put enough distance between himself and North Bridge. He slowed to a walk, slowed his breathing and tried to look as casual as possible. He couldn't, however, stop glancing at the faces around him, wondering if any of them were plain clothes police officers and he was about to be caught anyway.

After a few minutes, he relaxed. It seemed like all the activity was still concentrated on the bridge and no one was looking for anyone who'd disappeared – yet.

He ducked into Burger King and ordered himself a large Coke. Upstairs he found a seat by the window that showed him a view all the way up to the Balmoral Hotel and at least some of the activity going on.

Despite the urge to flee when he realised he would no longer be on the winning side, Liam could still feel the adrenaline coursing through his body. The high he'd experienced while he was in the midst of the fight was like nothing he'd ever felt before.

He'd felt alive. He'd felt important, like he really was somebody. Nobody here was underestimating him, taking the piss out of him, humiliating him. No, they were taking him very fucking seriously indeed and he *loved* it.

There'd been a message in the forum a few days earlier telling them all there was a Women's Rights March being organised to take place in the city centre that weekend. The message was a call to arms. A call for those who truly cared, to show up and be counted. To show up and *do* something to protect their way of life; the *right* way of life.

Liam had not hesitated. He instantly volunteered for the job without even fully understanding the details of what would be expected of him. When he found out they were to cause as much disruption, panic and chaos as possible, and by any means available, he'd thought about it for a second.

But then he was all in.

He collected glass bottles as directed and put them in a carrier bag. No one was going to look twice at a bloke in Edinburgh carrying a shopping bag full of bottles at the weekend. That stuff was par for the course.

First thing on Saturday morning they were told to make their way into town and take their allotted positions at either end of the bridge, or on the bridge itself. There would be no meet up in advance. They would not be attracting attention to themselves in any way. They were looking for one hundred per cent shock and awe with no chance for anyone to anticipate what might be coming.

Liam arrived on Princes Street as the march made its way from the gardens onto the main road. He had to wait for them all to pass before he could make his way up to the corner. At the corner he would wait until the last of the marchers was on the bridge and then follow them onto it.

A few minutes later he was in position and looking at the faces of the men round him, trying to figure out if they were with him or not. He spotted a few guys with shopping bags, but that didn't necessarily mean anything.

Liam was twitchy and the adrenaline was building in his stomach. He checked his watch, once, twice, three times. He had no idea why, because the signal to start was the first bottle being thrown from the front of the mass of people.

Liam missed the first bottle, but he saw the second and third and he saw some of the men around him pull bottles from their own bags and start lobbing them into the crowd. Liam did the same, not caring how far they went or who they hit.

There was screaming, so much screaming, Liam wondered if someone was dying. He hadn't considered the harm the bottles might actually do before then. He'd been so excited to take part in something that mattered, he hadn't thought about *why* they'd all been asked to bring, and throw, glass bottles.

So when he saw blood pouring from a gash on a woman's arm he'd stopped short and stared at it for a few moments. Then he started looking at the rest of the crowd, really looking. Almost everyone had cuts and grazes and there was so much blood.

Liam was jolted from his thoughts when a man grabbed him by the arm. 'Come on!' he yelled and dragged Liam towards a group of men fighting.

He had no choice but to join in, throwing punches at everyone and anyone who got near him. He had no idea who was on his side and who wasn't, there was no way to know for sure, so he just kept swinging and trying to deflect any punches that came his way.

Thankfully, none of the men were really fighters and any blows that came near him were glancing. There was one guy who kicked at everyone near to him, but Liam hadn't the time or the wherewithal to even consider that his legs were going to be covered in bruises later.

Then the mounted police had turned up and Liam had realised it was time to get lost. He wasn't the only one, a group of the fighters peeled off and disappeared into the crowd.

Liam looked back at the carnage he was leaving behind. There were injured people littered all over the street and Liam knew their group's name would be in the news that night. @beta2 had told them all he would phone anonymously and take credit for the attack – there would be no choice but for the news outlets to cover it.

Princes Street looked to be calming back down to its normal Saturday afternoon chaos from Liam's view out of the first storey window. He was eager to get back online and celebrate with his incel mates about what a fabulous success that afternoon's project had been.

He left Burger King and set off for home, still feeling on top of the world.

⸻

When he arrived home an hour later, he went straight to his bedroom, ignoring his mum's calls from the lounge. Once there he turned on his laptop and waited for it to load up. He also knew his mum would be up any second and he waited for her to appear.

As he'd expected, a few minutes later, there was a knock at his door.

'Come in.'

'Did you not hear me calling you?'

'Sorry, no,' he said, his eyes firmly on the screen in front of him.

He felt his mother's stare on him, but he refused to look at her.

'Where have you been all afternoon?'

'Out.'

'Out where?'

'Does it matter?'

'It matters to me! There was some trouble in town, I was worried.'

'As you can see, I'm fine, so no need.' Liam braced himself. His dismissive tone could go one of two ways. Either his mum would decide she wasn't in the mood for a fight, or she would take him to task on it.

He heard her sigh – excellent, there would be no arguing tonight. 'What do you want for your tea?'

Liam considered her question for a moment. His afternoon activities meant he was starving. 'Can I have a pizza supper from the chippy?'

Again, his mum considered him for a moment before her shoulders slumped. 'Sure. I'll go and get it for you. Salt and sauce?'

'Always.'

His mum left his room, shutting the door behind her. She was a good mum really. Liam just wished she wouldn't nag him all the time. It was so much easier when she was doing what she did best: cooking and cleaning, and leaving him alone.

He rubbed his hands together as the forum page loaded and he navigated to the noticeboard dedicated to that afternoon's ransacking of the march. He was about to type a comment when a DM notification popped up. *Odd.*

He hadn't had one of those since they played the revenge game. He clicked to open the message from @beta2 and froze as he read it.

Message from @beta2:
  We need to talk. We know you didn't do your part fully in the revenge game.
  This is unacceptable and there will be repercussions.

Pressure mounted in Liam's head and his brain shut down. How did they find out? How could they *possibly* know? That lassie was so ashamed, he'd seen it in her eyes, no way she'd told anybody.

And yet, that's the only way it could've happened. Had she reported the attack to the police and it had got back to @beta2?

What was he going to do now?

And what did they mean, *there will be repercussions?* His revenge on Kirsty had already happened, so it wasn't like they could take it back.

His mind was in overdrive, trying to figure out what to do – what to reply. The DMs came with read receipts so @beta2 would know he'd read the message. Leaving it too long would be like an admission of guilt.

Think.

Another message popped up on his screen.

Message from @beta2:

We received word from our man at the police station, your target reported the attack but was very insistent her attacker did not have sex with her.

Liam stared at his screen and felt a tear slip down his cheek. He typed: *I'm sorry, I couldn't do it. She wouldn't stop talking.*

There was no point in denying it, they had it first-hand.

He typed another message: *What happens now? Are you going to kick me out?*

Message from @beta2:
   We'll be in touch.

EDINBURGH CHRONICLE REPORTER HAILED AS A HERO!

Frankie Currington, a reporter here at *The Edinburgh Chronicle* has been hailed a hero by local police.

Frankie was taking part in the equality march in the centre of town yesterday when it was set upon by an unknown group of attackers. A group of men surrounded and trapped the marchers on North Bridge before launching glass bottles indiscriminately into the middle of the crowd. As the marchers tried to flee, they were attacked and forced to engage in fights in order to escape.

With nowhere to go, Currington took the only option available to her – she helped. After assisting many of the injured to the side of the street out of the way of flying objects, Frankie came across an unconscious and bleeding James Dixon. Upon realising Mr Dixon was not breathing, Frankie immediately started administering CPR with no regard for her own safety.

As help was arriving in the form of mounted police and paramedics, our brave reporter was struck on the head by a glass projectile. Thankfully, only dazed and confused, Frankie was transported to the local hospital where she was checked over by doctors.

Mr Dixon had this to say: 'I cannot tell you how grateful I am for Frankie's quick thinking and prompt actions. She saved my life and I will forever be in her debt. I hope to meet her properly as soon as possible, so I can thank her personally.'

At the same time as praising Frankie's actions, the police have condemned the attackers, but there has been no announcement as to who the group were as yet.

CHAPTER TWENTY-FOUR

The headline on the front page of the newspaper had caught Todd's eye as he passed the display on his way into the shop to buy some rolls. He'd stopped short to read it properly and someone knocked into the back of him.

'Fuck sake, pal,' muttered the teenager.

Todd grabbed a copy of the paper. 'Sorry.'

Now he was sitting at the dining room table with a roll and sausage, a strong cup of tea and the paper spread out in front of him.

He read the report for the third time. Alongside it there was a picture of a woman hunched over a prone figure. Todd knew his girlfriend well enough to know it was her, but to someone else it could've been anybody. Frankie hadn't mentioned she'd saved somebody's life! Mind you, he hadn't really given her time to talk about anything. There was a part of him that regretted his words to her the previous night, but he knew in his gut he was right about this.

Frankie had arrived home a few hours after he'd left her. Todd was in bed, but not asleep, although he'd pretended to be.

He was still angry with her, but too tired to talk about it any more that night. He couldn't imagine Frankie would want to talk either, so he left it.

In the morning his anger had boiled down to a simmer. He'd even bought enough rolls so Frankie could have one when she eventually woke – he might even make it for her.

Todd wondered if there was a chance some of his words had sunk in, but he doubted it. How could he make her see what was so clear to him and everyone else? He thought about the trolls who had started all of this and realised there would likely be more comments on the online version of the article.

He grabbed his laptop from the sofa and pulled up the *Edinburgh Chronicle* website. As he'd expected, the hero article was front and centre. He clicked on it so he could see the comments underneath. He'd known there would be some, Frankie's profile had raised slightly in recent months, but even he was shocked to see over a thousand comments.

Todd scrolled down the page, scanning the posts which were, as anyone might expect, mostly complimentary and calling Frankie a true hero. He stopped when he came to anything that was even remotely troll-like and took a screen grab. He was going to show them all to Frankie when she woke up to try to reinforce his argument.

His phone pinged with an incoming message – it was his mum.

Hi son, I hope everything's okay. I've just seen the news about Frankie. Is she okay?! She's so brave, saving that man's life like that. Xoxox

For fuck sake. His mum and dad had moved south a few years earlier for his dad's work, how on earth had they heard about it? He texted his mum back.

She's fine mum, thanks for checking. How did you hear about it anyway?!

Todd tugged at his hair with one hand while he waited for a reply. He didn't have to wait long.

It was on the news on the telly, son. Have you not seen it?

On the news? What the fuck?

Todd scrambled for the remote control and turned the telly on. He'd never bothered much with the news channels, but that morning it was the most appropriate place to go.

His eyes scoured over the screen, taking in the rolling news reel at the bottom and the headlines scrolling down one side. There was nothing there – perhaps his mum had been mistaken.

The news anchor moved on to the next story and suddenly the screen was filled with shaky footage, clearly filmed on a mobile phone. After a few seconds, the image stabilised and Todd could see his girlfriend kneeling over a man in the middle of the road. He watched as she started compressions, oblivious to the chaos and smashing bottles around her.

As the mounted police arrived, there was a cheer from the crowd and Frankie looked up – her face clear for all to see. Todd watched as Frankie was distracted by a shout and a bottle hit her squarely on the head, the force of it causing her to fall backwards. The owner of the mobile phone zoomed in and Todd could see Frankie's eyes had become unfocused. The footage ended as suddenly as it had started.

Todd sat on the sofa, stunned and unmoving. Although he'd read the report about Frankie performing CPR, seeing it in full technicolour was a completely different experience.

And now, he realised, everyone would know who Frankie

was. She was no longer an anonymous face, she could no longer hide behind the newspaper.

He rewound the live television and watched the footage again – there was no mistaking who the woman was and she would be easily recognisable.

'What's that?'

Todd whipped round, he hadn't heard Frankie get up. 'Hey, how are you feeling?'

Her eyes were trained on the TV and he had no idea how long she'd been standing there. 'A bit of a headache, but I'll live. What's this?' She gestured to the television.

There was no point in trying to hide anything, she'd find out soon enough regardless. 'There's footage of you saving that man's life. And you're in the newspaper too.'

Frankie sat down on the sofa beside him and pulled the remote from his grasp. She rewound the footage, just as Todd had done a few minutes before, and was silent as she watched.

'Where's the newspaper?' she asked when it was finished.

Todd stood up and brought it over to her. For a moment, he watched as she read the copy, her face blank. 'I'll make us a cuppa,' he said, wanting to give her space. Todd busied himself filling the kettle and getting the cups ready.

When he turned round, Frankie was engrossed in her phone, a smile on her face. 'Are you okay?' he asked.

'Okay? Of course I am, this is brilliant! I mean, forget the hero stuff, I did what anyone else would've done, but we're on the *national* news. So many more people are going to hear about us now.'

'*Us?*' asked Todd, not quite believing what he was hearing.

Frankie looked up at him. 'Yeah, us. The Edinburgh Coalition for Gender Equality – this will raise our profile monumentally.'

'Is that all you care about? People were hurt, a man almost *died* and all you can talk about is the profile of some tin-pot "equality" group.' Todd threw the teaspoon into the sink in anger.

'Of course I bloody care. It wasn't us who caused a fight though, was it? It wasn't us who started lobbing glass bottles into the middle of a crowd. We were demonstrating *peacefully*, it was them who started the violence. You should be condemning them, not me.'

'I get that, Frankie, and I'm not blaming you for the violence. I just don't understand why you needed to be there.'

Frankie groaned. 'We've been through this, it's my job. I don't know how else to spell it out for you.' She stood up and stormed out of the room, saying, 'I'm going for a shower.'

Todd stared after her and shook his head. Not only did he feel like he was banging his head off a brick wall, he was so sick and tired of having the same fight over and over again.

From the sofa where he'd left it, Todd's phone beeped to alert him to another message. 'For fuck sake,' he whispered as he marched over and picked it up. It was Craig.

I see the missus is a hero! How is she this morning?

She's fine, but oblivious to the fact her face is now all over the news and everyone knows who she is.

Your girlfriend's famous, sunshine, you'd better get used to seeing her face around. And being her bag carrier, otherwise she'll soon have no use for the likes of you! LOL!

Helpful, thought Todd. Just what he needed, someone to point out how much more successful his girlfriend was than him. He didn't bother to reply, he was in no mood for Craig's piss-taking.

Instead, Todd continued looking for comments from trolls, and selecting the very worst, he screen-grabbed them to show Frankie when she was in a better mood.

CHAPTER TWENTY-FIVE

F rankie was sitting on one side of a table, there were two chairs on the other side, but apart from that, the police interview room was bare. She'd given the blank walls a once over when she'd first arrived, but since then she'd gone over her notes and organised her thoughts.

She picked up her phone to check the time. It felt like she'd been there for hours, but in reality it had only been about thirty minutes.

After she'd stormed out of the lounge earlier, she'd taken a long shower. She allowed her thoughts and feelings to tumble and flow, not looking at any particular one too closely. She allowed them to wash over her in the hopes they would eventually make some sense.

She knew Todd had a point, but equally, so did she. She couldn't figure out though where the middle ground was, or even if there was any.

Afterwards, she pulled the towel tight around herself and padded back into the bedroom. She took two of the painkillers the doctor had prescribed for her, and sat on their double bed. She allowed her skin to air dry and checked her phone for messages. There were several, but what caught her eye was a voicemail from an unknown number. She dialled in to listen to it and when a slightly gruff Edinburgh accent started speaking, a spike of fear shot through her as she assumed one of her online trolls had found her phone number.

After a moment, she realised there was no malice in the voice and she tuned in to the words. The message was from a DC Callum Menzies and he wanted to take a statement about what happened at the march.

Now, here she was a few hours later being kept waiting after the officer who showed her into the interview room promised it would only be a few minutes.

When she'd told Todd where she was going, he'd shown her a file full of screen grabs and practically begged her to tell the police about them while she was there. He said if she wasn't going to quit, she at least needed to make the police aware of what had been going on in case something terrible happened to her.

She'd conceded the point and agreed to show DC Menzies everything Todd had gathered. Privately she also resolved to show the detective the slew of vile emails and private messages she'd received, which her boyfriend knew nothing about. She knew if she told him he would become even more unbearable and life at home was already difficult enough.

Just as she was losing the will to live and almost an hour after Frankie arrived at the police station, the door to the interview room opened. Frankie looked up from her phone at the noise and was momentarily stunned.

'Hi, sorry to keep you waiting. I'm DC Menzies. Frankie Currington, right?'

The man in front of her smiled and held out his hand. For a second Frankie could only stare. He was absolutely gorgeous.

Frankie mentally gave herself a shake and leaping to her

feet, shook his outstretched hand, hoping he didn't notice the slight blush she could feel creeping over her cheeks. 'Yes, that's me,' she said brightly.

Too brightly she realised when the policeman gave her an odd look.

He indicated they should sit down and took out his notebook and a pen.

While he was reading through his notes, Frankie took a moment to gather herself. She wasn't normally so easily struck by a good-looking man, but she'd felt completely thrown when he walked through the door. Since when did policemen get so hot?

He was tall and broad, like a fit rugby player. His sandy blond hair was cropped short on the sides and brushed forward on top – it was in no way fashionable, but on him it worked. When he'd smiled at her his deep-set navy eyes seemed to twinkle and this was what had rendered her mute for a moment.

He looked up suddenly and she quickly averted her eyes, not wanting to get caught staring. He already thought she was some kind of weirdo after taking an age to shake hands with him.

'How's the head?'

'A bit sore, but I'll be okay,' she said, brushing her fingers across the bruise hidden by her hair. The truth was, it hurt a lot, but complaining wasn't her style.

DC Menzies nodded as though he understood. 'Let's get you out of here as quickly as we can then, hey? I think it would be useful if you talked me through, in your own words, what happened at the march yesterday and then I can ask questions as and when they occur to me. That sound okay?'

'Sure, where would you like me to start?'

'Let's go from meeting in Princes Street Gardens, make sure we cover everything.'

HEATHER J. FITT

'Okay.' Frankie proceeded to tell him the details of what had occurred the day before. He interrupted on occasion when he needed to clarify a point, but otherwise he listened intently and made copious notes.

Once she had finished he said, 'And you've no idea who these people were?'

'No, no clue.'

'Did you see any of them? I mean, could you describe them or would you recognise them again?'

'No, everything was such a blur.' Frankie shook her head as she thought. 'Was it really all men?'

'It seems so. So far no one we've spoken to has reported seeing a woman involved.'

'So it's got to have been some kind of men's group then? Like incels, or men's rights activists?'

DC Menzies was looking at her curiously. 'What do you know about incels and men's rights activists? And why would you assume it had anything to do with them?'

'It makes sense, doesn't it? A equal rights march attacked by a group of men. What else could it be? And I know about it, because they've been targeting me.' She said the last part quietly. She had never actually said it out loud before, never given it a name or a label because that made it real. To her, brushing it under the carpet made it less important.

'Targeting you?'

'Yeah. Here, look.' She opened her laptop and turned it round so he could see.

He took his time looking through the screen grabs and Frankie showed him the file full of emails and DMs she'd collected over the recent months. She told him how she felt like she'd been followed a couple of times, but couldn't say for certain.

They'd both been silent for a while when DC Menzies

finally closed the laptop lid and pushed it back over towards Frankie, letting out a breath as he did so. 'That's... a lot.'

'Yeah. My boss at the paper has been trying to filter my calls and emails, and they pay for a taxi to and from work for me.'

DC Menzies nodded to indicate he was listening as he made even more notes. 'Can you forward all that to me?' He pointed at the laptop with his pen.

'Sure, I'll do it now.'

He gave her an email address and for the next few minutes the only sound in the room was Frankie tapping on the keyboard. Once she'd finished she waited patiently for DC Menzies to finish scribbling.

When he closed his notebook, placed the pen on top, covered both with his hands, he looked at Frankie. 'I'm going to be honest. With what you've told me, there's not a lot I can do. Yes, they're vile, but they're from so many different people, tracking them all would take too long and cost too much. My best advice to you is lock everything down. Change passwords, use maximum privacy settings and ask your paper to remove the vilest comments and block the trolls.'

Frankie blinked and shook her head as if clearing her mind. 'That's it? Some of these people have threatened to find me and rape me. And you're telling me to block and ignore?'

'I'm really sorry. If you get anymore then obviously send them to me, I'll be registering your complaint and these will all be kept as evidence. It just doesn't warrant an investigation at this stage.'

'What, precisely, would warrant an investigation?' Frankie could feel her temper rising, she had a funny feeling she knew the answer.

'If someone were to follow you, or approach you...' He had the good grace to look a little embarrassed.

'So, what you're saying is, once I've been attacked, you'll look into it?' Frankie almost spat the words at him.

'I'm sorry, my hands are tied.'

Frankie started packing her laptop away. 'Are we done? Can I go now?'

'Yes, of course. I'll be in touch if I have any more questions.'

Frankie stood up, firing her chair backwards and it made an awful screech as it moved across the floor. She waited for him to escort her back to the entrance, aware that as much as she wanted to storm out, she had no idea where the exit was.

He led her from the interview room and down the corridor, before opening the door that led into the public area. As she passed by him, he said, 'You know, you could always keep a lower profile. Let someone else take some of the spotlight.'

She stared at him, amazed, as a battery of retorts stormed through her mind. Instead of being rude, she turned and stomped the last few paces out of the police station.

CHAPTER TWENTY-SIX

This was it, this was Liam's way back into the forum.

He'd avoided logging on since he'd received the private messages from @beta2, unable to face the shame of what he'd done. Not everyone knew of course, but that didn't matter, *he* knew. He'd missed out on celebrating with his friends after the march and it had really upset him. He now fully understood how much this group meant to him and he was prepared to do whatever it took to make amends.

He'd been following the online reports of the violence at the march: scouring social media and reading every newspaper report he could find. He was reading an account of the march in the local newspaper when he spotted a link to a story with the headline, Edinburgh Chronicle Reporter Hailed As A Hero!

He read through the article and realised the woman mentioned was the same woman who had written the article reporting on the march itself. He wondered if she'd written anything else, and when he searched through the *Edinburgh Chronicle* website he discovered how prolific she was.

He scrolled through the headlines and noted that for the last few months, all she seemed to have written about was how hard done by women were and how awful men were. She was a Stacy, exactly the kind of woman they all hated. Maybe he could use that to his advantage. He could certainly use it to get a conversation going.

He copied the link to the main article, logged on to the forum and started a new thread.

Check out this bitch's newspaper articles. Apparently women are oppressed and it's all our fault!

Liam pressed the 'post' button and sat back against the pillows on his bed. He was nervous, would anyone reply? Or would they ignore him and move on? He was desperate to be a part of the gang again, he had to get back in – he had nowhere else to go.

After a few minutes someone replied.

Message from @truecel43
  Who the hell does this foid think she is? Do you know her?

Liam typed quickly.

No. I know where she works though, so she must live in Edinburgh somewhere

After that, the replies came thick and fast. Liam tried to keep up with them all, but soon found there were off-shoot conversations popping up all over the place. The conversations varied little, there was a lot of talk about what they would like to do to her if they ever found her. Liam read these comments his eyes shining; he was both appalled and entranced by what he was reading.

Some of the comments went too far for Liam's taste, but he

found himself getting excited at the thought of tying a woman up and making her do whatever he wanted.

Message from @omega1998
Anybody know what she looks like?
Are we taking bets? Hottie or minger?

Message from @KTHHFV
Writing shit like that I bet she's fugly! Can't get shagged so this is what she does instead, makes it out to be all our fault.

Liam berated himself. Of course they wanted to see what she looked like, that's all they were ever interested in. Why hadn't he thought of that? Although, he *had* called her a Stacy, so that should've given them some clue.

He quickly opened up a new tab, typed the reporter's name into the search engine. First of all he went to the *Edinburgh Chronicle* website and navigated to the staff pages; they were bound to have pictures of their reporters.

Liam was right, they did have pictures, but for some reason Frankie Currington's was missing. He went back to the search results, but each listing was another article for the newspaper. He smacked his hands on the mattress and tried to think of something else.

Facebook! He logged on and searched again, only to find the only Frankie Currington in Edinburgh had a picture of Gullane beach as her profile picture. *Bloody hell!* As a last-ditch attempt he went back to the search engine and re-entered the name, this time clicking on 'images' on the off-chance.

And that's where he found it. A grainy picture of a woman kneeling in the middle of the street. He opened the thumbnail and realised he was looking at an image from the march itself. Perfect.

He copied the link and switched back to the forum. Underneath @KTHHFV's comment he hit 'reply' and pasted the link into the box along with the comment:

Here you go. This is from the march itself. She's a bit of a looker actually.

Message from @KTHHFV
She is a bit. Slag would never look at the likes of us twice though.
I reckon we should have a little fun with her – what do you reckon?

Liam smiled to himself, this was going well.

Message from @gingercel2003
That sounds like a plan to me! What did you have in mind?

Message from @KTHHFV
Whatever it takes to scare her.

Liam spent the next few hours discussing and planning with his friends as to how they were going to terrify Frankie Currington into submission and force her to become the diminutive, submissive little girl she ought to be.

CHAPTER TWENTY-SEVEN

R uby was sitting at the table with a glass of wine in front of her. It was already half drunk. Frankie looked at her watch, she didn't think she was late. She wasn't, Ruby was obviously early.

Frankie made her way to the bar and attracted Ruby's attention, using a drinking motion to ask her if she'd like another across the noisy bar. Ruby gave her the thumbs up, so Frankie ordered a bottle – it had been that kind of day and she was definitely going to need more than one glass. For some reason there had been a huge uptick in the trolling comments online, and she'd lost count of the number of vile DMs she'd received and profiles she'd had to block.

A few minutes later, sitting at the table and the wine poured, Ruby asked Frankie how she had been doing since the march.

Frankie puffed her cheeks and let her shoulders slump for a moment before quickly straightening up again. 'It's been tough,' she replied, then took a gulp of wine.

'How's your head?'

'It's okay. The headaches have stopped and I've learned to brush my hair without scraping my brush across the bruise – it's still a little tender.'

'You spoke to the police.'

Frankie couldn't quite tell if Ruby was asking a question or making a statement, but she told her that she had. She then went on to explain what happened when she told DC Menzies about the trolls and the threats.

'He wasn't interested. I mean, he said he'd log it and he said I was to send him anything else, but otherwise he basically told me to ignore it and it would go away. Like I was ten and trying to get rid of some school bullies.' Frankie could feel her frustration bubbling back towards the surface as she retold the story.

'This is the sort of thing we see all the time at the centre. It's not the police's fault, not really, it comes from higher up. There's lots of them would love to be able to help, but their hands are tied with budgets and bureaucracy.'

'He basically said, unless something physical happens, there's nothing they can do. They can only protect me *after* I've been injured. It's so frustrating!' Frankie finished her wine and poured herself another glass.

Ruby smiled dryly. 'This is what it's like. This is why we set up the centre and lobby the council and the government for change, for extra funding.'

Frankie played with the stem of her wine glass and said nothing for a few moments. She had been debating with herself all day and she knew she had to make a decision. 'How many people were injured at the march?'

'Twenty-seven taken to hospital, five seriously injured. They'll all be okay and thank God nobody died.'

Frankie nodded slowly as she digested the information. 'Did the police manage to arrest any of the attackers?'

Ruby picked up her glass, ran her tongue along the inside of her mouth and shook her head. She took a sip of wine then said, 'As soon as the police turned up, they ran. Who wants to get caught being a violent misogynist?'

Frankie stared off into the distance and processed what Ruby was telling her.

'The police have been making enquiries at the hospitals, they can't believe no one on their side wasn't injured badly enough to need treatment. But so far, it's been a no-go.'

'I want to help.' Frankie leaned forward to emphasise her point.

'Cool, we can use all the help we can get at the centre. You could write some copy for us, that's always useful.'

'No, I mean... yes, of course I'll help with that, but I want to help *practically*. I want to do something *useful*. I mean, virtually everyone knows who I am now, surely we can use that somehow?'

'We could but, Frankie, you need to know, if you go public, the trolling only gets worse. These people are not going to go away overnight and they are vile little creatures who will try anything to get you to shut up and go home.'

'After today, I'm not sure it could get much worse.'

Ruby gave Frankie a considered look. 'Okay, let's talk strategy.'

For the next couple of hours they discussed Ruby's idea for going into schools and chatting to students during their Physical and Social Development lessons. They talked about the structure those presentations would take and how they could make sure they engaged both the boys and the girls. They considered publicity and which medium would be the best fit for getting their message out there.

'We need people to understand this is about *equality*. It's about everyone being treated the same, and it's not about women taking over. The world can be just as dangerous a place for our young men as it is for our young women.'

One bottle of wine turned into two and when Frankie's stomach growled, they ordered themselves some spicy cheesy nachos for fuel, and to soak up some alcohol.

It was late by the time they felt they'd talked themselves out.

'I'll write up what we've discussed tomorrow and then maybe we can decide how to implement it from there?' said Ruby.

'Sounds good to me. Right, I better be getting off, Todd'll be wondering where I've got to.'

'No worries. Text me when you get home.'

Frankie walked out of the bar into the cool Edinburgh night where the breeze blew up the Mile and woke her up a little. She started walking home, wanting to use the time to think about the plans she and Ruby had discussed that evening.

With her bag over her shoulder and her phone clutched inside her coat pocket, her thoughts switched to Todd. How was she going to tell him she'd done the exact opposite of what he'd asked her to do? He'd been annoyed the police hadn't taken her complaint more seriously, but conceded there was little more Frankie could do. He'd asked her again to reconsider her involvement with the centre, pointing out that now she was 'famous', things could only get worse.

Frankie had, once again, said no; once again asked him to see things from her side and asked for his support. She asked him to understand how important this was to her personally and for her career, but he didn't, and Frankie wondered if he ever would.

She was almost home and had left the hustle and bustle of

the city centre behind her when she noticed the footsteps. She'd been lost in a world of her own and had no idea how long they'd been there. A wave of coldness swept over her and her stomach lurched. She checked over her shoulder, trying to see who was there, trying not to make it too obvious she was concerned.

It was too dark to be able to see anything, or anyone, clearly, but there was definitely someone behind her. Trying not to panic, she pulled her phone from her coat pocket and rang Todd. He didn't answer, but that didn't stop her having a 'conversation' with him.

'Hiya, babe.' A pause. 'Yeah, I'm almost home I'll not be long now.' A longer pause. 'Pizza sounds good. Have we got any wine?' Frankie had no idea if this was working or not, but she kept it up anyway. 'Good, I could do with a glass. I'll see you really soon.' Frankie 'ended' the call, but kept the phone in her hand, prepared to use the emergency alarm if she needed to.

She picked up her pace a little and hoped whoever was behind her would get the message and back off. She considered crossing the road, but she'd only have to cross back again further up and then they would know she thought they were following her. What if it was someone walking home? She didn't want to appear rude.

Frankie panicked when the footsteps behind her also moved more quickly. The terror surged through her as she fought the urge to run, trying to tell herself she was being paranoid. She looked around for a shop or a pub she could divert into until she felt safe enough to continue walking.

As Frankie crossed in front of an alleyway, the footsteps turned into running steps and she felt something slam into her back, forcing her down into the opening of the alley. She went to scream but was slammed against the wall and a hand clamped over her mouth.

All thoughts of raising the alarm with her phone were

forgotten; she hadn't even noticed she'd dropped it as she crashed into the brickwork behind her.

In front of her was a large man, a Hearts Football Club beanie hat pulled down low over his eyebrows, his chin and mouth buried into a Hearts scarf.

'Think of this as a warning, Frankie Currington. You need to stop writing your horrible pathetic misandry-filled made-up stories. You're nothing but a little prick-tease and if you're not careful, we'll take whatever we want from you.'

Frankie's eyes grew wide when he said her name and she squirmed, trying to free herself, but he pinned her to the wall using the length of his body and she could feel his erection, hard against her thigh. She whimpered and turned her head to one side. Half of her already accepting he was going to rape her, at this point she would settle for getting out alive, and the other half praying someone would walk past and see them.

He reached down between them with one hand, Frankie assumed to pull his fly down. Instead, he slipped his fingers between Frankie's legs and gently caressed her. 'You know you want it really,' he whispered into her ear.

Frankie remained as still as possible, pulling in as much air as she could through her nostrils and desperately trying not to panic. Whatever was going to happen, she wanted it to be over. She did not want to give him any excuse to hurt her more than he already planned to.

Suddenly, he released her. He squeezed her breasts and then ran off down the road, laughing.

Frankie sunk to the ground, sobbing.

It had all happened so quickly, Frankie could scarcely believe it had happened at all.

Her phone lit up with an incoming message and Frankie picked it up off the pavement, only then realising she must have dropped it.

She could feel the panic welling up in her chest and tried to fight it off. If she could get home, she would be safe there and she could fall apart all she wanted.

CHAPTER TWENTY-EIGHT

L iam sunk back onto his bed, ecstatic. He wiped his dick, cleaned his hand and threw the wad of tissues at the bin. That might have been the best wank he'd ever had, and it was all thanks to Frankie Currington.

He never would have said she was his type, but once he was there, leaning up against her and he could see the fear in her eyes, his hard-on had been unstoppable, almost painful as it strained in his jeans. When he slipped his fingers between her legs, he'd actually thought he was going to shoot his load then and there.

The year before he would never have been able to do something like that, he was still a little boy then. But it was true what they said about teenage boys growing almost overnight; he was the same height as her, but he easily outweighed her.

Liam was pleased he'd been able to do something practical. Although he'd done his bit at the march, he knew he still had a lot of making up to do after the revenge game problem.

When they'd been discussing ways of terrorising the reporter, he'd been only too happy to put his hand up to help out. There was a whole list of things they planned to do to her, but this one needed to be done in person. Since he lived in the same city, it made sense for him to be the one to deliver the first in-person message.

It had been easy. All he'd had to do was wait for her to leave work and then follow her. Once she was in a more secluded area, he could then put the fear of God into her and make sure she understood where they were coming from. Make sure she understood, they were not messing around.

He'd expected to have to follow her for a while before he had the opportunity to speak to her. He knew women were always banging on about how dangerous it was in the city at night, so he'd thought she would take a taxi, or walk with someone else most of the time. Clearly, she wasn't as fearful of the dark streets as she'd made out in one of her newspaper reports. More lies.

He'd deviated from the plan slightly, but only because the opportunity was too good to pass up. He was supposed to get up close, deliver the warning in a menacing way and then leave. When he saw the alleyway, however, he'd decided to do things a little differently. He'd also hoped doing things this way would mean he'd gain back some of the respect he'd lost from @beta2.

She'd made it easier on him by not talking and not fighting. Seeing how scared she was, he felt the power flow through him; he could do whatever he wanted.

When he released her, feeling like he'd got his message across, he'd grabbed and squeezed her boobs, just for a laugh. He was definitely a boob man and he couldn't walk away knowing hers were there for the taking. It was *only* a quick squeeze, it wasn't as if he'd tweaked her bare nipples or anything.

When he arrived home, he'd planned to get straight on the forum and tell them all how it had gone. Explain to them exactly how he'd done it and accept their praise and adulation.

However, even by the time he'd arrived, he was still excited. His mum was out and he couldn't wait any longer.

Now, feeling satisfied but certain it wouldn't take much for him to become excited again, he logged on to the forum. Liam couldn't be bothered to read the new posts yet, he wanted to get his story out and onto the message board.

He started by pointing out how easy it had been to find and follow Frankie, sharing his theory that maybe women weren't as scared at night as some of them made out. He then went into detail about how he'd forced her into the alleyway, how he'd delivered the threat and then how he'd copped a feel. He told them about the fear in her eyes, the way she trembled and how he had been sure he could've had her if he'd wanted to. He could feel himself getting horny all over again as he typed out the words.

He didn't have to wait for very long before praise was being heaped upon him. Some wanted to know why he hadn't had sex with her then and there, some thought he'd gone too far by deviating from the plan. After all, there was supposed to be an escalation and Liam had set the bar pretty high already. Mostly, these people were told to shut up by other members who went on to congratulate Liam for his quick thinking in changing the plan to suit the situation.

Some of the other members started sharing their day of trolling and compared notes on how many profiles they'd had blocked on Twitter. By the sounds of it, the bitch reporter had had a shite day all round.

Liam was thrilled by the responses, but he was waiting for a particular one. He read through all the replies twice to make sure he hadn't missed it and was disappointed to see the name he was looking for wasn't there. He tried to shake it off and concentrate on the applause and admiration he was receiving from all over the world.

He was trying to think of what else he could do to earn the respect of the man, when another new reply pinged up. It was him! Liam took a breath and clicked on the message icon.

Message from @beta2:
You did well.

Three little words, but they meant everything to Liam. He didn't think for one second he'd made up for the mistakes he'd made previously, but at least he knew he was heading in the right direction.

CHAPTER TWENTY-NINE

There was a missed call from Frankie on Todd's phone when he removed it from his locker at work. He looked at the time, she'd rung ages ago and hadn't tried again, so it clearly wasn't important. He tapped out a quick text to let her know he was on his way and he'd see her soon. Todd could see she read the text almost immediately, but there was no response. *Maybe she's still with Ruby*, he thought with a sigh.

For the millionth time he wondered what it would take for Frankie to see she couldn't go on like this. One day she was going to get hurt and for what? He couldn't see this was a cause worth ending up in the hospital for, and he was getting to breaking point. How could he look after Frankie when she wouldn't even look after herself?

Todd let himself into the flat, and as he was taking his shoes off he could hear voices in the living room. He stopped and listened for a moment, it didn't sound like the TV. Whoever Frankie was with, neither of them appeared to have heard him come in the door. He hoped to God it wasn't Ruby, he was too tired for any of their nonsense.

He walked into the lounge and was relieved to see it wasn't

Ruby sitting on the sofa with Frankie. However, the relief was immediately replaced with confused anger. There was a man sitting on the sofa with his arm around his girlfriend, her head on his shoulder.

'What the bloody hell's going on here?'

Their heads snapped up and he could see Frankie had been crying. The man stood and walked towards Todd, his hand outstretched. Todd glared at it while trying to figure out how the scene before him and the man's actions slotted together.

'Hi. I'm Detective Constable Menzies. I guess you're... Todd?' He turned to look at Frankie as he said it and she nodded.

'Police?' He looked around the large man stood in front of him and addressed Frankie directly. 'Why are the police here?'

Frankie was still crying and hadn't yet said a word.

'Why don't you sit down, Todd, and we'll tell you what happened.'

We'll tell you...? Todd did not like the sound of the 'we'll' in that sentence one little bit. Who the hell did this guy think he was? And policeman or not, what was he doing with his arm around Frankie?

'Todd, sit down, will you?' Frankie snapped at him.

He did as he was told and it was only then he realised how upset she was. Her whole face was red and puffy and she looked like she'd been crying for hours. He softened and realised he'd been a bit of a dick. He put his arm around her and pulled her to him. 'What happened?' he asked softly into her hair.

He heard the policeman clear his throat and when he looked up he realised Menzies had pulled a dining room chair over and was sitting opposite them with his notebook opened.

'Frankie, would you like me to explain?'

'Please. I don't think I can...'

Todd stroked Frankie's arm and listened as DC Menzies

187

explained what had happened to Frankie on the way home that evening. The more he heard the more disgusted and angry he became. How dare some little prick put his hands anywhere near Frankie.

'Why didn't you call me?' he asked when Menzies had finished the story.

Frankie sat up and blew her nose. 'I tried to call you while I was walking, but you didn't answer and it was just after that he jumped me.'

'My phone was in my locker, you should've called work.'

'I was panicking, Todd. I wasn't exactly thinking straight. Anyway, I'd forgotten you were working. When I got home and you weren't here, I called DC Menzies and he offered to come straight round. I knew you'd be home before long anyway.'

'That was very good of you, DC Menzies.' He wasn't gay, but even he could see the policeman was good looking and he couldn't help but feel a stab of jealousy at the thought of this man comforting his girlfriend instead of him.

'Please, both of you, call me Callum. DC Menzies is far too formal for these situations.'

Todd nodded once and Frankie said, 'Thank you, Callum.' She gave him a watery smile that Todd did not miss.

Todd wanted to take back control of the situation. 'Do we need to do anything else... Callum?' The familiarity felt wrong to him, but he thought calling him by his title would be too confrontational after being asked not to.

Callum got the message and standing up, he flipped closed his notebook and put it in his pocket. 'Not right now. Frankie, when you're feeling up to it, we'll need a proper statement from you. As horrible as it is, now this has happened we can do some investigating. I can see myself out, no need to get up.'

Todd watched as Frankie got to her feet and hugged the policeman. 'Thank you.'

Callum looked a little uncomfortable, but hugged her back lightly. 'Just doing my job.' He gave Todd a stiff nod and let himself out.

The following morning, Todd was wide awake hours before he needed to be. He'd had very little sleep and spent most of the night tossing and turning, his thoughts and fears tumbling over each other as he tried to decide what to do.

He was sitting on the sofa nursing his third cup of coffee and wishing he'd been bothered to go out for rolls. He needed to speak to Frankie, but he was loath to wake her. He could only imagine how exhausted she was after her ordeal and all the crying.

After DC Menzies, *Callum*, had left the night before, Frankie had stood and said she was going to bed. She'd stopped in the doorway and turned to look at him. 'I know we need to talk, but I can't tonight.' She hadn't even waited for a reply.

Todd was sick of talking. They always said the same things and it was draining. Something had to change and Todd had realised during the night when he was somewhere between sleep and consciousness that he was going to have to be the difference. There was no way Frankie was going to change.

He went to the kitchen and made himself some more coffee. He didn't really need a fourth, but he needed something to do.

Frankie walked in, rubbing her eyes as he was pouring the hot water into a cup.

'Do you want coffee?'

She yawned loudly. 'Yes, please.'

Once he'd made both cups, he turned and saw Frankie standing in the middle of the floor, staring at a holdall by the side of the sofa.

'What's this?'

"Here.' He handed her a cup. 'Come and sit down, we need to talk.'

'I know we do, but I was expecting to be awake before we did,' she said, taking the cup from him and sitting on the sofa with her legs tucked underneath her.

'I'm sorry, but I can't wait.' He closed his eyes and took a deep breath, this was do or die time. 'Frankie, what happened last night was just about my worst nightmare come true. I know you weren't physically hurt, but you could have been. I have been saying for months that something like this could happen and now it has. These trolls aren't keeping it online anymore. This is serious and they will end up hurting you, badly, if you keep going. I'm asking you, begging you, to please choose another avenue for your reporting.' He implored her with his eyes to make her see he was serious.

'And what if I don't?' she asked, her eyes catching the bag once more.

'If you won't look after yourself, well, I can't watch you get hurt. If you won't take these threats seriously, then...' he trailed off. 'If you say no, then I'm leaving, for a while at least. I'm going to stay with Craig. I can't keep having the same argument with you and the thought of you being seriously hurt terrifies me.'

Todd watched the tears in Frankie's eyes, her gaze had not wavered from the bag. Todd could feel himself start to well up and he prayed Frankie would make the right decision.

He took her hand, he thought maybe he could get the strength of his emotions to flow from his heart and into Frankie. 'Please.'

His heart nearly broke in two when she pulled her hand away and looked at him. 'No,' she whispered. 'I can't and I won't quit. If you can't or won't support me, then you do what you have to do.'

He watched her walk away and for a few minutes he was utterly distraught.

Then he dried his eyes, blew his nose and grabbed his bag. On his way out the door he dialled Craig's number. 'It's me. Yeah, I'm coming to yours now.'

CHAPTER THIRTY

Frankie was sitting in the reception area of Radio Edinburgh and checked the time on her phone. Realising it had only been a minute since she'd last looked, she told herself to get a grip and forced the phone down the inside of her bag. She thought perhaps if it were not sat right at the top, she wouldn't be so tempted to keep checking it.

Not wanting to be late, she had made sure she arrived thirty minutes early, but that had only made her even more nervous. Giving herself time to sit and think and consider, not for the first time, if she was doing the right thing had been about the worst idea Frankie could have had.

She knew it had been her idea for her to get more involved in the centre's cause and she and Ruby had discussed the likes of radio interviews. However, it had all happened rather too quickly for Frankie's liking. She had thought there would be more time for her to learn about the facts and figures that backed up the centre's messages, she thought she'd have time to practise, to do some reading and fully immerse herself in the cause.

So when Ruby had called her three days later about the

possibility of appearing on the daily lunchtime show on Radio Edinburgh, alongside Fenton Caldwell no less, Frankie had panicked. 'I'm not ready, Ruby. Especially not after what happened the other night. I wouldn't even know what to say. I thought I'd have more time.'

'What happened was awful, but you can use it to your advantage. You have first-hand knowledge of what it's like to be a lone woman on the streets of our city, and that is exactly what the interview is about, Are Our Streets Safe for Women? And anyway, it's not for another week – we can get you prepped in that time.'

They'd chatted for a while longer and Ruby had managed to wear her down. Now, here Frankie was, waiting to be taken to the studio. The whole segment was to last no longer than fifteen minutes and then there would be comments and questions from the listeners afterwards. This was the part that worried Frankie the most.

They'd discussed the questions she was likely to be asked and the kinds of answers Caldwell would give and then prepared and practised various answers. The audience questions were a complete unknown, and although the station had promised to vet anyone who phoned in, the idea her trolls may call sat at the back of her mind.

She heard the automatic entrance doors swish open and allow a din to enter through the open space. Frankie peered behind her and saw Fenton Caldwell entering with his entourage who all appeared to be speaking into mobile phones. *Are they all talking to each other?* Frankie thought with a giggle.

The councillor stopped in the middle of the reception area and waved a hand at one of his minions, who scuttled over to the desk, removing his phone from his ear for a moment. 'Councillor Fenton Caldwell for the Neil Stuart Show.' He didn't wait for a reply, he simply put his phone back to his ear.

Frankie watched as her opponent, as she'd started to think of him, checked his watch and took in his surroundings. He was quite a short man, maybe five foot six – Frankie was definitely taller than him – with a skinny stature that made him look like he might break in two with a decent gust of wind. In fact, with his balding head and smattering of grey, he was reminiscent of Monty Burns, Homer's antagonistic boss from *The Simpsons*.

Frankie giggled again, except this one was louder. She tried to turn it into a cough, and looked away when she realised the noise she made had attracted Caldwell's attention.

She turned back towards him and saw he was giving her an appraising look. After a moment, he strode towards her. Frankie thought he was going to be curt with her, so was surprised when he said, 'Councillor Fenton Caldwell, pleased to meet you,' gave her an extremely cheesy smile and stuck out his hand.

Frankie tried not to laugh and hoped he would take her smile as friendly, rather than disparaging. 'Frankie Currington from the *Edinburgh Chronicle*,' she said standing up to shake his hand.

'Oh! I see. I was so sorry to hear about what had happened to you the other week. Especially after your heroics at the march. Are you sure you're feeling well enough?'

'I'm fine now, thank you.' Frankie wanted to say so much more, but decided she would save it for the interview. Caldwell's concern for her well-being didn't fool her, but she didn't want him to realise that quite yet.

'If it all gets too much up there, no one would think badly of you, so you just say if you need to step away.' He emphasised his point by touching Frankie on the arm and she forced herself not to flinch.

'That's very kind of you, but as I say, I'm absolutely fine.' And she gave the brightest smile she could muster. Yes, she had been through a lot recently, but now she could do something about it. The thought of the nasty comments she'd received, the threats, the violence at the march, her attack and now Fenton Caldwell's underestimation of her, all clustered together in her belly and gave her a steely determination that she allowed to flow through her and swallow her up.

She could do this and the reason was because she had lived it. It had happened to her, she'd experienced it. Fenton Caldwell had none of that and that was how she was going to best him live on the radio.

Their cosy little 'chat' was interrupted by a runner who had arrived to escort them to the studio. Once inside they were made comfortable, given a set of headphones each and shown where their 'cough' button was.

Neil Stuart introduced himself and explained once more how things would proceed, and then, before she knew it, the time had arrived.

The host introduced both Frankie and Caldwell, explaining who they were and why they had been invited on the show.

'Frankie, you have first-hand experience of this if I'm not mistaken? You were actually attacked on a main road walking home one night, weren't you?'

'Yes, that's right, Neil.'

'Why don't you tell us what happened?'

Frankie took a deep breath and told her story, leaving nothing out. She explained how she'd been on a well-lit road, she'd tried to call someone to put off any would-be attacker – all the things she and her friends had been taught to do.

'Why didn't you take a taxi home?' asked Caldwell.

'I needed to do some thinking and the walk home would give me the time to do that.'

'You walked home on your own, late at night, knowing there is still a rapist at large so you could do some thinking? Don't you think that was a bit irresponsible?'

Frankie smiled – this was the opportunity she had been waiting for. 'Councillor, are you saying I am responsible for being attacked? Are you blaming me because a man pushed me into an alleyway and groped me?'

Fenton Caldwell's face turned puce. 'Of course not, but I do think women should take some responsibility for their own safety. Some of them clearly do, because this isn't the sort of thing you hear about often.'

'Apart from in recent months in Edinburgh, Councillor,' Neil Stuart cut in.

'You don't hear about it because we don't usually report it,' said Frankie, not giving Caldwell time to reply. 'The stats show around sixty-four per cent of all women have experienced sexual harassment in public. That figure goes up dramatically when you look specifically at young women. I think what we all want to know, Councillor, is what are you going to do about it?'

After that, Frankie relaxed and started to enjoy herself. Councillor Caldwell was on the back foot and, realising his initial mistake, tried desperately to retreat and make himself look like a good guy – the kind of politician who wanted to help.

By the time Neil thanked them both for coming and asked the listeners to call in with questions, Fenton Caldwell looked like a defeated man. As the music started playing, his shoulders sagged and he raked both hands through what was left of his hair.

No one said anything during the musical interlude, everyone seemed to be taking the time to reflect on what had already been said.

The first couple of callers were extremely supportive of Frankie and expressed how awful they felt at the things that had happened to her. It was the third caller who changed the tone.

'Next on the line we have Dale Anderson from Wester Hailes. What's your question, Dale?'

'Not so much a question, more of an observation. Females who go out on their own at night only have themselves to blame. They know the chances of them being attacked is high, so if they do go out, surely they're only asking for it?'

'Thanks for that profound insight there, Dale,' said Neil rolling his eyes and cutting the caller off. 'Okay, next up is Stephen Baxter from Morningside. What's your take on the situation, Stephen?'

'My take is that Frankie Currington needs to wind her neck in and stick to reporting actual news, otherwise she might find she gets more of the same – or worse. Watch your back, Frankie.'

Neil and Caldwell turned to stare at her, mouths agape. Frankie was momentarily stunned, but the words came to her from nowhere. 'I have no intention of stopping, you nasty little man. You and your mates can go and crawl back under the stone you came out from. Do your worst.'

Frankie sat back, smug she'd managed to reply for once. After a moment or two though, the dawning realisation of what she'd said swept over her and she thought she might be sick.

She'd publicly called out her attackers, the aggressors who knew exactly who she was. What had she done?

CHAPTER THIRTY-ONE

'Do you want to listen to the interview?'

'No chance.'

'Do you not think it might help?'

'How on earth could it possibly help, Craig?' Todd couldn't for the life of him see where his mate was coming from.

'I just thought, if you listened to what she has to say, it might help you to understand.'

'I thought you were on my side.'

'I am on your side, but you've been moping around my flat for over a week – it's clear you still love her. As I see it, understanding her point of view is the only way you're going to be able to square it away in your head and go back to her.'

Todd stood. 'You want rid of me, is that it?'

'Course not. You know you can stay as long as you want, but you're miserable and definitely no fun. Look, what harm can it do?'

'Fine.'

Todd knew Craig was right, as much as he was loath to admit it. He did still love Frankie and he regretted leaving like he had. The problem was, he was stubborn and backing down was not going to happen easily. If he did go to her, rather than the other way around, he was going to have to find a way of doing it that didn't dent his pride.

Craig fiddled about with his phone and after a minute or two, Todd could hear the Edinburgh Radio jingle.

Craig placed the phone on the table and then went into the kitchen where Todd could hear him rattling around and switching on the kettle.

Trying to look casual, Todd relaxed into the sofa and stared off out of the window. He desperately missed Frankie and wanted nothing more than to go back to being the happy couple they'd been not so long ago, but he couldn't see a way back to that. Whatever happened, it was going to be different.

There was another thing bugging him, one he'd barely admitted to himself, let alone anyone else. He'd been wondering, with Frankie's star rising, where did that leave him? She was practically famous, certainly in Edinburgh, and what was he? The boyfriend? The plus-one? He felt inconsequential and dare he say it, a tiny bit jealous. His mates took the piss badly enough as it was, and things were only going to get worse now Frankie was appearing on radio shows. What next? TV?

He knew none of these thoughts showed him in a particularly complimentary light, but he couldn't help having them. He felt so undermined when Frankie was around, she took charge of everything, why couldn't she let him be the man?

Craig handed him a coffee. 'She's on next.'

When the host introduced Frankie, Todd leaned forward, the cup in both hands, and stared at the floor as if in concentration. The truth was he couldn't look at Craig, didn't want him to read what was in his eyes and he didn't know what else to do.

Todd gripped his cup as he heard Frankie recounting the story of the night she was attacked. He was proud of her. She'd kept her voice even and although there was passion behind her words, there was no sign of the tears he had seen the night it had happened.

He bristled listening to Fenton Caldwell effectively blame his girlfriend for being attacked and his pride in her only intensified when she stood her ground and called him on it. For the first time he looked up and smiled at Craig, only to see his friend doing the same thing.

When the music came on, Craig stood and walked towards him, right hand raised. 'Man! She nailed it!' he said and high-fived Todd.

He smiled. 'Yeah, she did.'

They lapsed into silence as the music ended and Neil Stuart chatted to some of the listeners. There were more grins as they heard the support Frankie was receiving; everyone really seemed to get it.

'Not so much a question, more of an observation. Females who go out on their own at night only have themselves to blame. They know the chances of them being attacked is high, so if they do go out, surely they're only asking for it?'

Todd tensed and looked over at Craig who was rolling his eyes. 'Dickhead,' he said and they both laughed.

Their amusement stopped suddenly as they listened to the next caller.

'My take is that Frankie Currington needs to wind her neck in and stick to reporting actual news, otherwise she might find she gets more of the same – or worse. Watch your back, Frankie.'

Before Todd realised what was happening, he was on his feet, fists clenched. 'I'll kill him, I'll fucking kill him!'

Craig held up a hand. 'Shh.'

'I have no intention of stopping, you nasty little man. You and your mates can go and crawl back under the stone you came out from. Do your worst.'

Todd stared at the phone. Had he really heard what he thought he heard? Did Frankie really just call out a group of men intent on stopping her.

Craig looked at Todd. 'Oh fuck.'

Todd was fumbling for his phone. He needed to speak to Frankie and he needed to do it now. What the hell was she thinking?

'This isn't a good idea,' Craig warned.

Todd ignored him and swore when his call was sent to answerphone. He dialled again, this time pacing the floor, his entire body tight with tension. 'For fuck sake!' he screamed when, once again, his call was sent to answerphone.

Craig put a hand on his friend's shoulder. 'Mate, chill.'

Todd shrugged him off and instead of calling, typed out a text message.

I listened to you on the radio. What the fuck is wrong with you?!
You're going to get yourself killed.

Todd paced the floor some more, and watched as the three dots appeared on his phone.

I don't have time for this right now. Leave me alone.

Todd threw his phone at the sofa and growled with exasperation.

Craig appeared in front of him and grabbed him by both arms. 'Stop. This is not going to work. Do you want her back?'

'Yes.'

'Then tell her that. Explain your frustrations are out of love and you're ready to get behind her and support her.'

Todd tipped his head and took a deep breath letting it out slowly. 'I need to go for a walk.' He picked up his phone, put on his hoodie and left the flat.

He didn't know how long he'd been walking when he felt calm and rational enough to send a text to Frankie explaining how he felt. He sat down on a park bench and took out his phone.

I'm so sorry, baby. It's just that I love you so much and I don't want anything bad to happen to you. Look, I heard you on the radio today and I was so proud of you. The way you handled Caldwell and how you really knew what you were talking about. I think I get it now – I want to come home and I'm ready to get behind you and have your back. Xxx

He replaced his phone in his pocket and headed back to Craig's flat. For one, he didn't want to be hanging around waiting for Frankie's reply, that would drive him crazy. And for two, he needed to pack so he could go home.

He took the quick route and twenty minutes later he let himself into Craig's place. He showed his friend the message he'd sent and explained he was going to pack up his stuff. He didn't want to waste any time once he heard from Frankie.

Todd was doing a final circuit, double-checking to make sure he hadn't forgotten anything, when his phone pinged announcing a text.

It was Frankie.

'What did she say?' asked Craig from behind him.

Todd turned to face him and there were tears in his eyes. He couldn't say anything so he showed Craig his phone screen.

I'm sorry Todd, but I don't want you to come home. I don't see how you can go from one message to the other in the space of an hour and expect me to believe you. We can talk some more when I've got some head space. Frankie

CHAPTER THIRTY-TWO

Frankie had escaped from the studio as soon as she was able to, managing to thank the host and no more.

At first she'd stormed out of the front door, but as she set off up the pavement, she realised how foolish she was being. She had a taxi pre-booked, the newspaper was still footing the bill, and anyone listening to the radio would know exactly where she was if they wanted to come looking for her.

While she was waiting to leave the studio, her phone had lit up with a call from Todd, which she'd declined. She did the same with the next one, but by the time she'd got down to Reception there was a text waiting for her. *Not now, Todd!* she thought. She sent a terse reply, she had more important things to worry about than whether or not Todd thought she was an idiot.

Now, she was pacing up and down the reception area, arms folded tightly against her stomach, waiting for her taxi.

'Excuse me, Frankie? I just wanted to see if you were okay?'

Frankie turned to see Fenton Caldwell standing a few paces away. 'I'm fine, thank you,' she replied tightly. The last thing she wanted was to have any more conversation with this man. She already felt slightly grubby having been in close quarters with him and the elation she'd felt earlier after he'd shown himself up was long gone.

'What you said up there was idiotic and you'll only have yourself to blame if something happens to you. I would strongly advise against going anywhere by yourself for a while, even in the daylight.'

The way he said it, made it sound like a threat, and Frankie could only stand and watch, mouth open, willing herself to say something, as he turned and walked away.

She stared after him and watched as he climbed into a black BMW with his minions. As the car drove away, another one pulled up behind it and a short, balding, fat man got out. He waited for the automatic doors to open and poked his head through. 'Taxi for Frankie?' he said, looking at her.

'Eh, yeah, thanks,' she replied, giving herself a shake.

She climbed into the back of the taxi and hoped he wouldn't be chatty, she was in no mood to make small talk. All she wanted to do was get back to her flat and lock herself inside.

'So, where am I taking you?'

'Home,' she said and gave him the address.

Frankie lost herself in her thoughts. She needed to figure out what to do about Todd and although she knew it was a pressing issue, all she kept thinking about was what an idiot she'd been – inviting trouble to her door she didn't need. Maybe she could speak to Callum and ask him to suggest some safety ideas. She pointedly ignored the fact that the thought of him brought a small smile to her face.

It dawned on Frankie she'd been in the car for quite a while. She looked out of the windows in all directions, but she didn't recognise any of her surroundings.

She checked her watch, the show had finished forty-five minutes earlier. She was certain she should be nearly home by now. Frankie leaned forward and addressed the driver. 'Excuse me? I think you might've gone the wrong way.'

There was no reply; not even a hint he'd heard her.

She tried again. 'I'm not sure where we are, but I'm pretty sure this isn't the way to my house.' She leaned to one side, looking to see if the driver registered her comment on his face.

Nothing.

A prickling sensation crept up Frankie's spine and she shivered.

'Can you hear me? I said, we're going the wrong way.'

Maybe he was deaf? No, Frankie had given him her address earlier and he'd repeated it back to her.

'You're freaking me out here. Can you at least say something?'

'Black Knights and Black Pills.'

Frankie felt the blood drain from her face. Her thoughts stuttered along, trying to piece together what had happened. What *was* happening.

'W-what?' she said, buying time, hoping he hadn't heard the slight stutter.

'You heard me.'

'Where are we going?'

'You'll see.'

Frankie was paralysed. All she could think about was the words her attacker had spoken in the alleyway. The words the caller had used on the radio show earlier. They tumbled through her mind on a loop. She imagined looking down on herself after the taxi driver had finished with her. Her body broken and bruised – a message delivered loud and clear to anyone else who had thought about taking them on.

A silent tear tumbled down Frankie's cheek. Her poor parents – they'd done nothing to deserve this. Then she was angry. *How* could she have been stupid enough to get into a taxi without checking first? Now she thought about it, was it even a taxi? There hadn't even been any signwriting on the doors and a glance at the centre console told her there was no meter.

Frankie was furious with herself. She was ready to fight this man if she needed to, but first she needed to make sure help was coming.

Not taking her eyes off the driver, she slid her phone from her bag. Frankie was desperate not to make any obvious movements to draw the man's attention. She lifted the phone up and tipped her head down just enough to activate the facial recognition and then held the phone down by the door.

Frankie caught him looking at her in the rear-view mirror and realised she wasn't behaving like she had been kidnapped. 'Please, let me go. Drop me off here. I'll stop I promise.' She even allowed a few tears to well in her eyes; he didn't need to know they were tears of frustration.

Frankie could see him smirking in the mirror, his eyes back on the road. Only flicking her eyes to her phone for a second at a time, Frankie navigated to her text messages, selected the Google Maps icon and tapped the send button. She followed this up quickly with two words, 'help' and 'kidnapped'.

'What the fuck are you doing?' The driver was leaning back and trying to grab at Frankie's phone. 'You fucking bitch.'

They were in the middle of a deserted industrial estate and he pulled off into a car park. Slamming on the brakes, he tore off his seat belt and threw the door open. Frankie tried to do the same, but quickly realised the child locks had been activated. She tried to climb between the front seats to escape through the driver's door that had been left open, but he grabbed her by the ankle and pulled her backwards.

Frankie screamed and kicked out at his fingers with her other foot.

'Bitch,' he swore as he instinctively loosened his grip.

Frankie didn't hang around. She carried on climbing through the car and, once out, she started running. Running and screaming for help.

It was useless, the whole area was deserted. She opted to save her breath for running. He was a short fat man, surely she could outrun him?

Frankie looked behind her and let out a sob. Short and fat he may be, but slow he was not.

Too late she realised she'd been running herself into a blind alley. The only place she could go was up. Up the metal stairs leading who knew where?

Reaching the bottom she started running up them, taking them two at a time. Near the first landing, she felt nails dig into her calf and another hand grabbed her ankle, tripping her face first onto the next flight. Frankie put her hands out to save herself, but she wasn't quick enough and her forehead connected with the edge of one of the treads.

Pinpricks of light appeared behind her eyelids and she had to force her eyes open, determined not to pass out in such a vulnerable position.

'You fucking bitch. Think you could get away from me, did you? Saw a fat man and thought you could outrun me?' Breathing heavily he turned her over, pinning her arms painfully to the stairs. 'You little fucking slut,' he said bringing his hot, wet, panting breath inches from her face. 'I'm going to take great pleasure in showing you what little guys like me can really do.'

Spittle rained down on Frankie's face as she tried to clear her head.

Suddenly she was aware of him pulling up her skirt and yanking at her underwear. He'd let go of one of her arms. She punched him as hard as she could in the side of the head, and then kept punching him over and over again until he let go of her other wrist as well.

Heaving, she pushed him off her and somehow he tripped over his own feet and tumbled back onto the landing.

Frankie didn't wait. She pulled herself to her feet and launched herself down the stairs, determined to put as much distance between herself and her attacker as she could before he could catch her.

Frankie ran back towards the car, hoping to find the keys still in the ignition so she could escape that way.

Behind her she could hear the driver clanging down the metal steps and calling her a cunt. Knowing how quickly he could move, she didn't waste time looking behind her. She rounded the car, desperately trying to see if the keys were still there.

The ignition was empty. 'Fuck!'

Frankie had no idea what she was going to do next. All she knew was that she had to keep going and hope to God her attacker ran out of steam before she did. Or failing that, someone came to her rescue.

Terrified that neither would happen and he would catch up with her again, Frankie began casting her eyes around to try to find a weapon. Anything she could possibly use to stop his unrelenting assault.

Frankie felt tears prick at her eyes as she realised there was nothing. Not even a stone she could throw at him.

A noise penetrated her ears and sharpened her focus. Was that a car she could hear?

She tried to gauge which direction it was coming from and ran towards it, knowing if she got it wrong, she would likely be dead soon.

She could still hear the taxi driver behind her, panting and spewing obscenities between breaths.

Up ahead, she saw a car turn onto the road at speed and come hurtling towards them. At that moment, it occurred to Frankie, whoever was in that car may not be there to help her. What if the driver had arranged for someone else to meet them?

She was left with only one option – she carried on running past the car as it came to an abrupt halt beside her.

'Frankie! Where are you going? Get in!'

She turned at the sound of his voice and saw Callum racing after the driver of the faux taxi. But the driver had turned around, leapt into his car and driven off before Callum could get anywhere near him.

Frankie was leaning against the bonnet of Callum's car trying to catch her breath against the exertion and sobs that were racking her body. Her tears flowed freely as she realised she was safe and as Callum rushed back towards her, Frankie's knees gave way.

Callum caught her before she hit the ground and eased her down gently, until he was sitting against the wheel with her held tight in his arms.

'Shh, I've got you now,' he whispered.

CHAPTER THIRTY-THREE

'Excuse me? I'm sorry to disturb you, but do you think you could help me with something?'

Liam jumped and looked up at the sound of the girl's voice. He looked around a little confused, he wasn't sure anyone had spoken to him while he was in the library before.

Actually, that was the whole point of him being there instead of using his own computer at home – no one was likely to nag him for being online too long. He *had* been at home, but his mum had started nagging him again and he'd heard enough. While she was out the back hanging up some washing, he'd got his stuff together and snuck out the front.

He'd been in the library long enough to set up the screen just as he liked it and log in to his favourite websites. Since he was on a public computer, he planned to spend some time trolling a few bitches. They deserved it and watching their outrage was hilarious.

'Hi, over here.'

Peering round the side of the computer opposite, Liam could see a cute blonde with elfin features smiling and waving at him. He smiled back reflexively and found he couldn't stop.

'Hi. Everything okay?'

'Yeah, I think so. Well, I can't seem to figure out how to get this to print. I don't suppose you know how it works, do you?' She beamed at him and all thoughts of trolling anyone, or doing anything else for that matter, fled from his mind.

'Let me have a look.' Liam stood up so quickly his chair crashed into the wall behind him. His face reddened as he hurried round the group of tables, he hoped she hadn't noticed. He'd never printed anything at the library before, so he didn't actually *know* how to print, but how hard could it really be? It wasn't rocket science, was it?

She was watching him, a smile on her face, as he rounded the table and walked towards her. *How do you walk again?* The floor felt like it was moving underneath his feet, as if he were trying to walk on a boat. He smiled back and tried not to lose himself in her silver-grey eyes. *Play it cool, Liam. Don't forget to breathe.*

She scooted her seat slightly to one side to allow him access to the keyboard. He bent over and looked at the screen. 'Is it the whole document you want to print?' he asked, trying to sound like he knew what he was doing.

'Mmm.'

Liam's eyes twitched to the side. She was close; so close they were almost touching, but her eyes were firmly planted on the screen. *She's only trying to see what I'm doing.*

He clicked on a few menus and made a few selections, feeling quite sure it was the same as printing something at school. The library system couldn't be that different, could it?

As he clicked the final 'print' button, he noticed a warning flash up briefly in the bottom corner of the screen. 'Have you got any money in your printing account?' Liam looked towards the girl who was already turning red.

'Oh! No, I assumed you paid afterwards. I didn't realise we

had to have a printing account,' she replied casting her eyes around the desk as if looking for something. 'Is there a slot where I put my money?'

Liam stifled a laugh, not wanting to offend her. 'No, if you take your library card over to the counter, they'll add the money to your account there.'

'Oh! Of course. Well, thank you for your help...' She tilted her head.

'Liam,' he replied, almost shouting.

'Thank you for your help, Liam. I'm Trish by the way,' she said with a self-conscious wave and beaming that smile at him again.

Liam grinned back. 'You're welcome. I'll be over there if you need help with anything else.' He cringed as he realised he was pointing, as if she hadn't found him first.

'Thanks. I'll just go and sort this out.'

'No problem.'

Liam stumbled his way back round to his computer, following this gorgeous girl with his eyes. He landed back in his seat with a thump and found he could not stop himself from smiling. She glanced over at him and he quickly busied himself with studying what was on the screen in front of him, which was precisely nothing.

For the next couple of hours, Liam tried to focus on what he was doing. Not that it was terribly important, but it was the only way he could stop himself from staring at Trish, and he was certain she had caught him a few times.

As the afternoon turned towards early evening, Liam realised the library would be closing soon and there was a better than good chance Trish would leave and he would never see her again. The thought made him panicky. Did he have the balls to ask her out? Ask her for her phone number? Even just ask if she would likely be there the next day? He'd never seen her before, so he figured it was unlikely she would be a regular visitor.

In his head, Liam practised different ways of asking her out. He was sure she must like him – she'd asked him for help over everyone else sat around the table. Should he try asking casually if she fancied a coffee? Or maybe he could go the whole hog and ask her out for a pizza? He didn't have any money, but he was pretty sure when his mum found out what it was for she'd give him twenty quid.

Right, he would do it.

He leaned forward over the desk and opened his mouth to attract Trish's attention. At that precise moment, his mouth dried up and his palms started sweating. Horrified he leaned back in his chair and rubbed his hands on his trousers. He couldn't do it.

He smacked a hand on his leg and silently berated himself for being such a pussy. He imagined what @beta2 and the other boys would say if they found out what a wimp he was being. Liam allowed the thought of their ridicule to give him the motivation and courage to speak a few simple words.

As he was about to lean forward again, Trish stood up and looped her bag over her head.

'Thanks again, Liam.'

'No problem.'

She started to walk away.

'Trish, wait.'

She turned, slightly startled, and Liam realised he'd shouted.

'Sorry,' he said, hurrying over to where she was standing. 'Listen, I um, I don't suppose you might fancy going out for a pizza with me?' Liam eventually met Trish's eyes and realised she looked rather shocked. 'I... I don't mean tonight. I thought maybe you could give me your number and we could chat, and sort something out...' He was waffling and he knew it. He clamped his mouth shut in an effort to allow her to speak.

'Oh, Liam... um... that's really lovely of you, but I don't think so.'

'But I thought... when you asked me to...'

At least she has the good grace to look embarrassed.

'Oh! No, I really did just need some help.'

'But you could've asked at the desk.' Liam was confused.

'Yeah, but you were right there and you looked like you were such a sweet person. I honestly didn't think you'd mind, or I wouldn't have asked.'

'Do you often go up to strange men and trick them into helping you?'

'Trick you? How do you figure that?'

'You're trying to tell me you didn't smile at me and flirt with me?'

'No! I was being nice and if I thought for a second you'd be expecting something in return for helping me I would never have asked you.' Her words were coming fast and the volume rising.

Liam was furious. How dare this slag lead him on? He stepped forward, bringing his face close to hers and hissed at her. 'You're nothing but a nasty little prick tease, you little slut.'

She looked scared. *Good*, thought Liam, *that'll teach her.*

'Fuck off, you fucking weirdo. I don't owe you anything!' she screamed at him and ran off.

Liam considered going after her, but there were still a few people around and their discussion hadn't exactly been quiet.

He slammed his fist into the table making the computer's mouse jump and causing the screen to come to life. As he glanced at it, he saw a familiar photo. It was the picture of Frankie Currington performing CPR at the Women's Rights Demonstration.

Liam grabbed hold of the mouse and clicked on a few buttons. What he read caused his temper to rise even further. The bitch had been researching Currington's articles and clearly what she'd read had given her ideas.

That fucking cunt Frankie Currington had a lot to answer for and Liam was going to make sure he was the one to ask the questions.

CHAPTER THIRTY-FOUR

After receiving Frankie's text telling him she didn't want to see him, Todd spent the following week moping around even more than he had been. He called in sick to work and never left the flat, only moving when absolutely necessary.

Craig came home from work one day and Todd was sprawled on the sofa, exactly where he'd been when Craig left for work. Todd dragged his eyes from the TV screen when he realised his friend hadn't said anything and hadn't moved from the doorway.

Craig stood, framed by the door, his laptop bag by his feet, one hand on his hip and the other rubbing at his jaw. He was looking around the room and Todd did the same. The lounge was a mess. There were beer bottles left where they'd been dumped, a half-eaten pizza in its box lay on the floor in front of where Todd sat, the bins were overflowing and Todd could see at least four empty cups.

Todd started to speak. 'Mate... I—'

Craig held up a hand to interrupt him. 'Don't. Look, I get you're in bits about Frankie, I honestly do, but this,' he gestured around him, 'has to stop. This is my home. I don't even mind you making the mess or drinking all my beer, but you don't even tidy it up. You just sit in it all day. When did you last have a shower?'

Todd straightened on the sofa and looked at his T-shirt. There were pizza stains down the front and he realised he'd probably been wearing it for a couple of days now. He stood and started clearing some of the beer bottles. 'I'm sorry, you're right, I'll get this tidied.'

Craig sighed. 'Leave it. I'll tidy up in here. You go and have a shower. I'm not getting close enough to find out, but I'm pretty sure you stink. We'll figure out what you're going to do afterwards.'

'Thanks – you're a good friend. Oh,' said Todd, looking a little embarrassed, 'we're out of beer. Might be an idea to put in an Amazon order. I'll pay – obviously.'

'Obviously,' replied Craig with little humour, as he surveyed the mess.

Todd stood underneath the hot cascading water, allowing it to flow over his head and down his body without moving for ten minutes. He did his best to blank his mind; he was trying to reset his brain so he could figure out a way forward. He wasn't a man with many problems, but he often found this the best way to resolve any he was faced with.

He knew he needed to prove to Frankie he was serious. Serious about them staying together – he didn't think they were broken up yet, were they? – serious about supporting her in her work and in her new-found belief in feminism. Todd could appreciate it wasn't a subject he knew a lot about, but did any man? Maybe that was the route he needed to take? Maybe he needed to do his research and try to understand the world from a woman's point of view?

The other problem bugging Todd was how he could protect Frankie. She wasn't going to back down and he couldn't see this gang of wankers backing down either, so he needed to know what he was up against. He needed to know what made them tick and he needed to be one step ahead of them at all times.

An idea bloomed. There was no reason why he couldn't continue with Frankie's original plan. She had wanted him to infiltrate the forum for research, why not do exactly that? The research purpose was slightly different, but it would be easier for him to get involved without Frankie peering over his shoulder all the time.

Buoyed by his idea and pleased to have a way forward, Todd finished showering, dried himself and got dressed, eager to explain his idea to Craig. He was hoping his friend would agree to help him out.

He barrelled into the lounge, almost colliding with Craig holding a bulging black bag.

'Whoa!'

'Sorry, sorry. I've got a plan.' Todd was bouncing on the balls of his feet like a puppy waiting for a reward.

Craig chuckled at his friend's new-found enthusiasm. 'Let me take this out,' he said holding up the bag. 'You can order pizza and beer and then you can tell me all about your amazing plan.'

'No worries.' Todd jumped out of Craig's way and pulled out his phone to place the order. Then he went in search of his laptop, which he found under the bed.

Back in the lounge and sitting at the table, he opened up his laptop and then swore loudly when he realised the battery was flat. Had he remembered to pack the charger?

After a few minutes of rummaging around in the spare

bedroom he located the charger in one of the small side pockets of his bag. Triumphant he returned to his laptop and plugged it in. While he was waiting for the computer to come to life he imagined showing Frankie everything he'd done and proving to her he'd learned as much as he could. He was desperate to show her exactly how prepared he was to support her and her career – wherever it took her.

Craig returned and opened the fridge door. 'We must have *some* beer left. Or some ciders or something? Did you order yet?'

'Yeah, shouldn't be too long.'

'Aha!' Craig held up two dodgy-looking cans of supermarket lager.

Todd screwed his face up. 'Where the hell did they come from?'

'Dunno.' Craig shrugged. 'Probably left over from a party. Anyway, they'll have to do until the delivery arrives, since someone drank all the good stuff.'

Todd reached for a can. 'Good point, well made.'

Craig sat down on the chair opposite him and cracked his tinny. 'So, what's this big idea of yours then?'

Todd explained the plan of attack he'd come up with in the shower. How he was going to pose as an incel and get inside information on the plans they had for their vendetta against Frankie. He also told Craig how he wanted to at least try to understand feminism. 'The way I see it is, there must be *something* in it for it to be such a hot topic. If it's going to be important to Frankie and it's going to form part of her job, then I need to be supportive. How would it look if I undermined her position?'

Craig looked doubtful. 'Are you sure this is what you want? If you go down this road, you might make yourself a target too. These arseholes aren't going to take too kindly to "one of their

own" siding with the opposition. I mean, I want to call you hen-
pecked, and I'm your mate.'

Todd looked up sharply to see Craig stifling a laugh.

'I'm joking, mate. Don't look so serious,' he said, laughing.
'But I can guarantee you *they* won't be.' His tone serious.

'I love her. And if this is what it takes to keep her, then this
is what I'm going to do. Plus, I need to be able to protect her.
You were right, I've moped around for too long, I need to do
something practical.'

'Okay then.' Craig rubbed his hands together. 'Let's do this.
Where do we start?'

Todd spun the laptop and showed him the screen. 'I've
already set up a fake profile. Now I need to take some time and
have a look around. Get to know the etiquette and maybe
comment on a few threads. See what's what.'

As he spoke, Todd's eyes were flitting across the screen and
his fingers tapped and dragged across the trackpad.
Occasionally he chewed on his thumbnail while he read longer
posts. He soon realised he was going to need to keep track of
what he was reading and learning if he wanted to avoid making
mistakes.

'Mate, you got a notebook or something?'

When Craig didn't reply, Todd looked up from the screen to
see his friend smirking at him.

'What are you smirking at?'

'You.'

'What about me?'

'You've been staring at that screen for the last twenty
minutes. I don't think I've seen you so engrossed in anything
apart from FIFA.'

'True. Notebook?'

Todd sat back in his seat and tapped his pen against his mouth. He quickly read over the notes he'd made, realising there were pages and pages filled with his handwriting. He grabbed his beer to take a swig and found it empty.

He stood up to grab a new one from the fridge. 'Beer, mate?'

When he received no answer, he turned only to see his friend asleep on the sofa. Todd looked at his watch. It was two in the morning and he'd been trawling the forum for over six hours.

He desperately wanted to tell Craig what he'd learned so far. He was sure there was something big coming, but he couldn't figure out what it was yet and no one was saying anything explicit.

He considered waking Craig up to talk it through and get his take on it, but he could imagine his reaction.

Todd scrubbed at his face and decided things might make more sense in the morning. Leaving Craig where he lay, Todd went to bed.

CHAPTER THIRTY-FIVE

'Why don't you sit down and I'll make us a cuppa?'
Frankie nodded vaguely and stared off into space as she lowered herself onto the sofa. She must've zoned out on the journey home because she couldn't remember any of it.

Callum had held on to her while she cried on the ground in the car park. When her tears ran dry, he helped her up and guided her gently into the passenger seat of the car. The next thing she knew, he was opening the car door again and when she looked up they were outside her block of flats.

A mug of steaming tea appeared in her eyeline. When she didn't immediately take it, Callum put it down in front of her.

'Maybe I should have taken you straight to the hospital. You look like you're in shock and that bruise looks quite nasty.' He nodded at her forehead.

The last thing Frankie wanted was to go anywhere else. She was safe, in her own home, and Callum was with her.

'I'm fine, I promise. Just tired.' In an effort to prove she was okay, Frankie lifted her cup of tea from the carpet and took a sip.

Callum gave her an appraising look before saying, 'Okay but I'm going to hang around for a while, just to make sure.'

'That seems like a fair compromise.'

Frankie closed her eyes and sunk back into the sofa.

'Don't go to sleep.'

'I won't.'

They lapsed into a comfortable silence.

Frankie was glad Callum had said he would stay. Yes, she felt safe with him around, but it was more than that. She didn't feel like he expected her to be anything other than her. He'd asked her once about backing off for her own safety and when she'd said no, he'd accepted that.

He was the complete opposite of Todd, who'd seemed to spend all his time nagging her recently. She'd tried to explain to him so many times why this was important and he couldn't wrap his head around what had changed. He was exhausting and she could no longer find the energy to fight him about it.

'You know we need to report what happened, don't you?'

'Yeah, I know.' Frankie would've said the same thing to anyone else, but that didn't make it easy.

'Do you think you ought to let Todd know as well?'

Frankie glanced up at Callum, unsure if there was a change in his tone when he mentioned Todd, but his expression gave nothing away.

'No, I can't deal with him at the moment. He's... he's staying with a friend for a while.'

'Oh.'

This time there was definitely a change in tone, which Callum quickly covered by saying, 'I'm sorry to hear that.'

'It's fine,' she said, waving him away. The last thing she wanted to talk about, or think about, was Todd. 'Do we need to go to the police station?'

'No, I can call it in and take your statement here if you'd prefer?'

Frankie's shoulders relaxed a little. 'Thanks, that would be easier.'

'Do you want to do it now? Or do you want to wait for a bit?'

Frankie was grateful to Callum for his calm and practical approach. It was possible for a man to be kind and supportive without coming across as patronising or condescending. Someone should tell Todd, she thought a little unkindly.

'Let's do it now, get it over and done with. Then I can try to forget about it.'

Callum borrowed Frankie's laptop and typed as she spoke, occasionally clarifying a point, or asking gently probing questions to tease out as much detail as possible.

Callum visibly tensed when Frankie described how the man had tried to yank down her pants.

'Did he hurt you when he did that?' he asked with barely concealed anger.

'A few little scratches, nothing terrible.'

'We're going to need to take photographs,' said Callum gently.

Frankie understood. 'Can I take them myself on my phone?'

'I'm sorry, but it would need to be an official police photographer, otherwise they would be inadmissible.'

Frankie closed her eyes and took a deep breath. 'Fine.'

They finished the statement and read it through together to make sure it was accurate and then Callum emailed it to his work email and said he would print it off later for her to sign.

'You know, thinking about sending me that Google Maps pin was amazing. Most people would clam up in that situation.'

'I was ready to fight him, but I needed to be sure someone could find me... whatever ended up happening.'

All at once an overwhelming wave of emotion crashed over

Frankie as the reality of what had happened and what might have happened slammed into her chest. She started crying again and gulped in great big lungfuls of air.

Very quickly she was panting – she couldn't breathe properly and a darkness closed in at the edges of her vision.

'Frankie. Frankie, look at me.'

She did as she was told, her eyes wide, still gasping for breath.

Callum took her hands and held them firmly. 'You're having a panic attack. Sit up straight and breathe with me. Okay?'

She nodded quickly.

'Breathe in and hold it.'

Frankie watched him do as he'd instructed her and copied him.

'Now, breathe out slowly,' he said blowing out and emptying his lungs.

They repeated the sequence and after a few minutes Frankie's breathing had more or less returned to normal.

'Okay?'

'I think so.'

'Come and sit down on the sofa, you look wiped out.' Callum stood and held out his hands for Frankie to lean on. He guided her over to the sofa and they sat.

Frankie leaned back and closed her eyes. A tear sneaked out from under her eyelids and slid down her face.

'Come here,' said Callum as he enveloped her in a hug, her head on his chest.

They sat like that long enough for Frankie to relax, her breathing slowed and she eventually fell asleep.

When Frankie woke up some time later, she blinked away the sleep and tried to make sense of where she was. She felt the warmth of another body underneath her and all at once she remembered Callum had been holding her while she cried and realised she must have fallen asleep on him.

Frankie sat up quickly. 'Oh, I'm so sorry!'

'It's okay. You needed it. I was going to wake you up soon anyway.' Callum's smile was kind and reassuring.

'Thank you. Do you need to get going? Please don't feel you have to stay.'

'I don't mind. Besides, you probably shouldn't be on your own.'

'Probably not,' Frankie conceded, 'but I'm pretty sure this is over and above your duties as a police officer?'

'I'm not doing it because I'm a police officer, I'm doing it because I care.' Callum's expression grew serious. 'To be honest, I've been a little unprofessional, but I couldn't leave you on your own.'

The atmosphere in the room turned super-charged. Frankie could feel the energy crackling and her breathing shallowed again; only this time it was in anticipation.

'I... thank you.'

'I mean it, Frankie, I really care about you and when you sent me that message, I... Well, knowing what might have been happening to you terrified me.'

Somehow, they had edged back closer to one another on the sofa and Frankie could feel the warmth of Callum's leg pressed against hers.

'I wanted someone to know where I was – whatever happened. I had no idea how long it might take you.' Frankie picked at her thumbnail.

Callum tilted up her chin. 'I would always come for you.'

The intensity of his words combined with the gentleness in his eyes caused Frankie's skin to prickle. She watched as his gaze dropped to her lips and he leaned in slowly. His pace almost asking for permission, giving her time to pull away if she wanted to. Did she want to?

Frankie already knew the answer and as their lips met and eyes floated closed, Frankie's heart and mind soared with happiness.

CHAPTER THIRTY-SIX

L iam left the library soon after Trish. He made sure to leave it long enough so it didn't look like he was going after her, but he also didn't want to hang around after she'd screamed at him. He was ignoring everyone around him, but he could feel their eyes on him all the same.

The walk home did nothing to quell his temper, if anything he arrived even more wound up. He was fucking livid. The more he thought about Frankie fucking Currington, the more he decided she was the cause of all his problems. The epitome of his regrets.

There she was telling girls they deserved more and that they should raise their standards and stand up for themselves, meaning nothing would ever be good enough for them. Men like Liam could try their hardest and do their best, but it would never be good enough for the likes of Frankie Currington. The more she was allowed to encourage women to be brash and bold, the less chance there was for normal guys like him to find a girlfriend. Surely he deserved some slack? Surely he deserved to be loved? Surely he deserved to have sex?

At home, he was relieved to find his mum wasn't in. He

went straight up to his bedroom and logged on to the forum. It was time to come up with a plan to put the bitch back in her box.

He sent @beta2 a private message. Although it wasn't the done thing, he felt sure, on this occasion, it was the right thing to do.

Liam took his time composing the message. He needed to get it right and be sure @beta2 had all the facts as Liam understood them. He explained what had happened in the library and how he had felt completely humiliated and then palpably livid when he'd realised who was behind Trish's rejection. He ended his message by saying:

> *I know there are plans in the pipeline to deal with her, but I want to be involved. I want to be the one to do it and I want to be there when she pays the ultimate price. Once she is brought crashing back to earth the Stacys and Beckys will realise they can't fuck with us anymore.*

Liam leaned back in his chair and ran a hand back and forth across his head while he read his message. Satisfied he had explained himself clearly, he hit the send button and waited.

At first, he just sat and stared at the screen waiting for the read message to appear and then the three little dots to tell him @beta2 was replying.

After ten minutes of impatiently refreshing the screen, Liam realised a quick reply would not be forthcoming. Instead, he decided to have a browse through the posts and see what been happening.

His attention was drawn to a long post that had attracted over 2,000 likes and 400 comments. *This looks juicy.* Liam clicked on the header and began reading.

He was quickly engrossed as he realised it was a post

discussing their latest strike against Frankie Currington. He'd forgotten about the plan to kidnap her after she appeared on the Neil Stuart show. He got more and more excited as he read the driver's account of what had happened. Liam could hardly believe she'd been stupid enough to get into a random car without actually checking it was a taxi first. Mind you, from what he'd heard about the radio interview, it was no wonder she'd been distracted.

He had not anticipated the failure of the plan at the final hurdle and couldn't help but swear at his computer screen when he read how Frankie had been rescued by some police guy. The driver had gone on to apologise for forgetting to take Frankie's phone from her, but he'd been so surprised when she got in the car no questions asked, all thought of it had gone from his mind.

I'm going to need to take a step back now. Although I used fake number plates, they both got a really good look at me and I can't risk being involved in anything high-profile for a while. Obviously happy to help out in the background if you need me to though.

Although Liam was a little gutted Frankie had managed to escape, in a way he was glad too. It meant the glory was still there for the taking. He still had the opportunity to be the one to destroy her once and for all.

After posting a congratulatory comment, Liam checked again to see if he'd had a reply from @beta2. Noticing the little red dot that indicated there was an unread message, a thrilling spark shot through his core.

His eyes raced over the message, but it took a couple of passes for him to fully understand what was being said.

@beta2 had a plan and it *did* involve Liam.

If Liam successfully executed the plan, then his debt for the revenge game would be settled.

The question Liam had to ask himself was, was he prepared to pay the extortionate price being asked of him?

For the next few minutes he considered his options. As he did so, his thoughts drifted back to Kirsty and how she'd humiliated him, and then to Trish, and finally to Frankie Currington and he knew what he had to do.

His reply to @beta2 simply said:

I'm in. What do I need to do?

CHAPTER THIRTY-SEVEN

The following morning over breakfast, Todd filled Craig in on what he had learned from the forum the night before.

'They talk in code, so it's kinda hard to figure out what they're on about half the time. Although, I was able to google some of it. It definitely looks like there is some sort of vendetta against Frankie, but I can't see what, if anything, is coming next.'

'Jesus, it's all a bit scary. Do you not think maybe you should take this to the police?'

'I thought about that, but Frankie said her mate, Ruby, had a man on the inside, so I think I can assume he's taking care of that. My main concern is being able to alert Frankie to any danger.'

'So what are you going to do now?'

Todd glanced at his watch. 'I need to go into work. They're not going to put up with my shit for much longer. And anyway, I'm feeling better now I'm doing something proactive.'

After his day shift at the gym, Todd went straight back to Craig's. Retrieving his laptop and notepad from the bedroom, he carried them to the dining table and logged on to the Black Knights and Black Pills forum.

He could see straight away there had been a flurry of activity while he'd been at work. Turning to a clean page in his notebook he clicked on the top post, which seemed to be attracting a lot of attention, and began reading.

Horror filled Todd as he read what these monsters had done to Frankie that afternoon. When he read about the moment the bastard had climbed on top of her, Todd felt sick. It was quickly followed by pride when he read about how she fought back and then anger when he realised she'd asked for help from the policeman.

When Frankie needed someone the most, when she thought she might not be able to help herself, instead of turning to her boyfriend, the man she supposedly loved, she had turned to a stranger. That's what Todd told himself anyway, Menzies was a stranger. He tried not to think of the time he'd come home and found him with his arm around Frankie after she'd been attacked in the street; the way they'd looked so comfortable sitting together on the couch.

No, he was definitely not jealous, just annoyed that Frankie would think to go to him before she turned to Todd.

As Todd read through the replies, the sick feeling returned to his stomach. Each comment was congratulatory in tone, with a few also commiserating that 'the bitch' had managed to get away. He picked up his phone, checking to see if he'd missed a call or a message from Frankie. Surely she would have thought to tell him what had happened? Just because they were taking a break didn't mean he didn't care anymore. He knew if something ever happened to him, she would be the first person he called. But there was nothing. He even checked to see if a message had somehow been marked as read, but the last message from her was the one telling him to stay away.

Todd's instinct was to call her immediately and demand to know what happened, but he knew that wouldn't work. Frankie would clam up and he'd make things worse. Should he send a text? Or should he go round there?

He checked his watch. Craig would be home from work soon, so Todd decided he would wait and ask him what he thought he should do.

———

Craig was running late though, and when he finally did arrive home almost two hours later, Todd was prowling around the living room like a caged tiger.

'Where've you been?'

'Err, did we get married and somebody forgot to tell me?'

'I needed to speak to you. I thought you'd be home ages ago.'

'Seriously, mate, one of the benefits of being single is no nagging. Pack it in. Grab me a beer while I get changed and then you can tell me why your knickers are in a twist.'

When Craig came back into the living room, Todd handed him a bottle of Coors and took a long swig of his own. Craig settled himself on the sofa in an overly dramatic fashion and sighed contentedly.

'You finished?' asked Todd.

'I'm ready, you may begin.'

'Thank you.' Ignoring his friend's eye-roll he, once more, explained what he'd found out and then asked what Craig thought he should do.

'You mean you haven't been round there to see her?' Craig leaned forward in his seat, eyes wide.

'No. I didn't know what to do. I was about ready to explode and the one thing I did know was that wasn't going to help.'

'No, I suppose you're right. But I tell you what, if it had been me, I wouldn't have been able to stop myself.'

'Right, but what do you think I should do *now*?'

'It's too late to turn up there now, really. Maybe text her and ask how she is? Ask if she minds if you go round?'

'Okay, okay, that's good. I'll do that. Text message.' Todd pulled out his phone and tapped away on the screen. 'There, sent.'

'What did you say?'

'Exactly what you told me to!'

'Yeah, but—'

'Sh, she's replied... ah shit!'

'What?'

'She wants to know how I found out.'

'Oh fuck. She doesn't know you're in the forum, does she?'

'No, she doesn't. I told her I wasn't doing it and she said I didn't need to anyway.'

'You're going to have to tell her.'

'Fuck.'

Todd decided a phone call might be better than text messages.

'Hi, it's me. I found out from the forum. I've been having a poke around to see if I can find out what they're up to. I thought if I could, then I could warn you and help keep you safe.'

'Todd, please tell me you are fucking joking? I asked you to stay out of it, I asked you to give me some space and now you tell me you've found out I was attacked from the people who attacked me? Can you not see how fucked-up that is?'

'I was only trying to help! I don't want to lose you, Frankie, and I thought if I could learn about this stuff you're interested in all of a sudden, I could understand more. But I also wanted to look after you – it's too much. They're coming after you, you know that, don't you?'

'No, they came after me. They wanted to put the fear of God into me and they have.'

'So you're going to stop then?'

'No! I've spoken to Callum and he doesn't think it'll escalate any further.'

'Oh, Callum is it now?'

'What the hell is that supposed to mean?'

'Nothing. Look, can I come and see you? I need to see for myself you're okay.'

'You'll have to take my word for it. I'm fine. I don't want to see you.'

With that, Frankie ended the call.

'For fuck sake!' He launched his phone onto the sofa then dropped down beside it and held his head in his hands. He knew what Frankie wanted, but he wasn't sure he was capable of walking away.

CHAPTER THIRTY-EIGHT

Amy was gawping at Frankie across the table in their favourite pub. Frankie took a sip of her wine and feigned nonchalance, even though she knew she'd dropped two bombshells on her friend.

'So, let me get this right? You were kidnapped by a taxi driver—'

'He wasn't a taxi driver, he was pretending to be one.'

'Whatever.' Amy batted the air. 'This guy kidnaps you, takes you to some abandoned industrial estate and attacks you. Except you've managed to get a message to Top Totty Callum, so he comes to your rescue. Have I got that right?'

Frankie cringed at Amy's new nickname for Callum. 'That's pretty much it.'

'And then, when you get home and TT Callum is supposed to be behaving like an upstanding member of the police force and looking after you, he shoves his tongue down your throat.'

'It wasn't quite like that. It was actually a really nice kiss and I definitely wasn't upset about it.' She grinned at her friend. In fact, she had barely stopped smiling since Callum had left her flat and said he'd be in touch about the photographs they needed to take of her injuries. Then she remembered Todd had been in contact and her face dropped.

'What? What's the matter?'

'Todd.' Frankie sighed. 'He just doesn't get the message. He's been looking into the Black Knight forum to try to "protect me" and he found out about the attack. Why can't he understand the more he tries to "look after" me, the more smothered I feel?'

'He cares about you.'

'I know he does, but he's been trying to wrap me in cotton wool recently and all it does is make me feel claustrophobic and want to push him away. He doesn't seem to realise I'm an adult and I don't need a protector. At least not like he's trying to be anyway.'

'What *do* you want?'

Frankie had been asking herself that for a while now and the truth was, she really wasn't sure. She did know that what she was doing, her writing and raising awareness, felt important. It felt like she was making a difference in the world.

Up until recently, if asked, she would have said her and Todd were in it for the long haul. The volcanic eruptions part of their relationship had passed and now they lived in comfort together; flowing nicely through life. Todd had always been supportive of her job and although she knew she could have been more supportive of his, she only pushed because she knew he was capable of so much more.

Maybe that was it. Maybe when it came to it, Todd was giving her a taste of her own medicine?

Or maybe they had become too much like friends. Sure, the volcano had died down, but shouldn't there be fireworks sometimes? Frankie couldn't remember the last time she'd felt a flutter in her stomach when Todd was around.

'I think maybe it's over between me and Todd,' she

whispered. 'I think it has been for a while, but we've been too comfortable to see it. It's taken us to fundamentally disagree on something for us, or me at least, to see what's been there for months now.'

Frankie's throat started to close and a single tear slipped down each cheek.

Amy reached across and squeezed her hand. 'It's okay. We'll get you through this, I promise.'

Frankie gave her friend a watery smile and squeezed her hand back.

After a moment, she cleared her throat and pulled a tissue out of her bag. She wiped her eyes, careful not to smudge her mascara, and blew her nose. With a shake of her head she looked up and tried to put a sparkle in her eye.

'Anyway, enough of that. Ruby will be here soon and I don't want to talk about this with her. It's all a bit raw.'

'Understood. More wine?'

An hour later, Frankie and Amy had been joined by Ruby and their second bottle of wine was almost finished.

Frankie had caught Ruby up with everything that had happened since they'd last seen each other, but left out all the Todd/Callum stuff. It was hard enough admitting her feelings to Amy, let alone someone she didn't know very well.

Ruby stood up and picked up the empty bottle. 'I'm going to get us another one of these, and then I want to talk to you about something.'

Frankie raised her eyebrows. 'Intriguing.'

Ruby pressed her lips tightly shut and wandered off to the bar.

'What do you think she wants?' asked Amy, her face animated.

'God, knowing Ruby it could be anything.'

Ruby returned to the table a few minutes later, complete with a fresh bottle of wine. She spoke as she poured them each a glass. 'Do you remember ages ago we talked about doing school events? Talking to boys and girls, aiming to make them aware that feminism isn't only about women?'

'Yeah, I remember. I've always thought it would be a good idea for you to do that. So many people assume it's about women getting their own way. And yes, I'm fully aware I was one of those people,' said Frankie, catching the look on Ruby's face.

Ruby smirked and raised one eyebrow. 'Well, the opportunity has come up for us to do exactly that at Corstmount High.'

'Corstmount?' said Frankie. 'I went to Corstmount.'

'I know, which is why I think you should do the talk.'

Frankie stopped and stared, glass of wine halfway to her lips. Slowly, she lowered her glass and her gaze to the table. Only when she had positioned the base of the glass exactly in the centre of the beer mat did she look up.

'I'm sorry, but I could've sworn you said you wanted me to do a feminism talk at Corstmount?'

To the side, Frankie could see Amy glancing back and forth between her and Ruby.

Ruby held Frankie's gaze. 'That's exactly what I said.'

'Did you forget about the part where I told you I was kidnapped and he attacked and attempted to rape me? Do you really think it's a good idea for me to be putting myself in the public eye so soon?'

'Of course I didn't forget. Anyway, isn't that the point? That you show them you're not scared of them and you're not going to stop because they say so?'

'Of course, but...' Frankie was floundering. She had said all of those things, but the physicality of the attack had left her reeling. Although she'd put on a brave face, she hadn't gone anywhere on her own since the assault. If she was being really honest with herself, the whole experience had left her shaken.

In her own mind, Frankie had planned to let things die down, although she refused to accept this meant Todd was right. It wasn't the same thing at all. She would still be assisting in the background; writing copy and helping out at the centre, that sort of thing.

'I completely understand how scared you must have been, who wouldn't be, but we're talking about a bunch of teenagers. Fifteen and sixteen-year-olds who still giggle when you say the words vagina or penis. And if it makes you feel better, we can arrange security for you.'

An image passed through Frankie's mind. One of her entering the theatre flanked by two large men in black suits and shades, complete with earpieces, firmly moving people out the way to create a gap for her to walk through.

Frankie looked to Amy for help or inspiration, she wasn't sure. Whichever it was, Amy wasn't helping in the slightest, she just shrugged and took another sip of her wine.

'The kids will listen to you, Frankie. Everyone knows who you are now, and the fact you went to Corstmount will be a big bonus for them. They'll see you as one of them, not as some adult coming in to tell them what to do and how to think. And if I'm honest, the fact you were attacked recently will give you extra kudos.'

Amy choked and looked like she was going to spit her wine out; her eyes wide as she stared at Ruby. Frankie herself couldn't quite believe Ruby had gone there. Someone needed to remind her there were some things better left unsaid.

'*If* I agree to do this, we will *not* be mentioning the attack.' Frankie held up her hand as Ruby tried to interrupt. 'It's not up for discussion.'

'So you'll do it?'

Frankie pressed her fingers to her eyes and then massaged her temples. Looking to the ceiling she grasped her hands together as if praying. For the next few moments, nobody said anything for which Frankie was grateful – she needed the thinking time.

Bringing her gaze back to eye-level she realised neither Ruby nor Amy had taken their eyes off of her.

'I'll do it.'

Ruby cheered.

'But I have conditions. I want a car and a driver to pick me up and take me home, you have to be with them. And I want Callum to be with me. I won't have security there, as you put it, that's weird, but I'll feel safe with Callum there. Plus, you have to agree to prep me fully.'

'Done, done, done and done.' Ruby looked triumphant.

Frankie still wasn't convinced she was doing the right thing, but backing down wasn't really something that sat well with her.

CHAPTER THIRTY-NINE

It had been a few days since Frankie had told Todd she didn't want to see him. He was confused and hurt, and had no idea what to do. Doing nothing had been killing him, but all he could do was wait until she got in contact. That was exactly what she'd done.

He was now on his way over to their flat 'for a chat' as she'd put it in her text that morning. Frankie was back at work, so Todd had had to wait all day for the visit and he'd driven himself round the bend with his inability to sit still.

When he arrived outside the block of flats, he had no idea whether he should let himself in, or knock. Technically it was still his flat too, but somehow he didn't feel like he could just walk in as if the last few weeks hadn't happened.

He let himself in the main entrance and reasoned he would knock on the flat door, that seemed respectful enough. As he jogged up the stairs his phone pinged in his pocket. It was Frankie, his heart sank, was she going to tell him now wasn't a good time after all?

Let yourself in. I'm just out the shower and getting dressed. Won't be long.

Todd did as he was told. 'Only me,' he called down the corridor.

Frankie's voice came back. 'Be through in a minute.'

He ventured into the living room and had a look around. Nothing had really changed, he wasn't sure why he had expected it would have. He gave his head a wobble and got a beer from the fridge.

He sat down at the table and took a long pull from the bottle. There was paperwork everywhere. Todd looked at the sheet nearest to him and realised it was information from The Edinburgh Coalition for Gender Equality.

Interested, he read through some of the scattered pages, nodding a few times and screwing up his face when he read about pockets being a feminist issue. The next page he found was part of an email, apparently from Ruby. He read it quickly and then scrambled around trying to find the rest of it. *Is she fucking serious?*

'Hey.'

Todd looked up. Frankie stood in front of him dressed in her favourite comfy gear, her hair still damp from the shower. For a moment, Todd forgot about the email. God she was a sight for sore eyes.

'What's that?' she asked gesturing towards the papers in his hand.

'I was reading some of your information. I've been trying to do better, learn more, but then I found this.' He thrust the pages of the email towards her.

Frankie took them from him and read a few words. 'These are private.'

'Maybe you shouldn't have left them on the table then?'

'I'm in my own fucking house!'

'It's my house too, Frankie.'

'That's not what I meant,' she replied more quietly and closed her eyes.

'Is that right? What that says. Are you going to give a talk at a school?'

Frankie slumped on the sofa, her head in her hands, still clutching the papers.

She took a breath as if strengthening her resolve. 'Yes, I'm going to give a talk at my old high school.'

Todd stood up. 'I don't fucking believe this. You're not serious? You were *attacked*, Frankie. A man tried, and almost succeeded, in *raping* you! You said yourself you weren't sure if he was going to kill you. How have you not learned anything? I can still see the bruise on your head for fuck sake! How can I protect you when you won't even look after yourself?'

Frankie leapt to her feet. 'I never asked you to protect me.'

'I'm your boyfriend, it's what I do. It's my job!' Todd paced up and down the carpet, his temper at boiling point. He heard Frankie mutter something behind him. 'What?'

'It's not your job anymore,' she whispered, not meeting his eye.

The fight drained from Todd and he stumbled over to the sofa where he sat down next to her.

'What do you mean it's not my job anymore. Of course it's my job.' He took Frankie's hand in his and rubbed the back of it with his other hand.

Frankie was staring at her toes and Todd leaned forward trying to see her face. 'Talk to me, Frankie.'

She looked up, her face drowned in tears. 'I don't want this anymore. I don't want us to be together anymore.'

'No,' Todd moaned. 'You don't mean that, please.'

Fat tears dripped from Todd's chin and landed on his hand,

still clutching Frankie's. If he didn't let her go, then she could never leave him.

'I'm sorry,' she breathed through her own tears. 'We want different things. You have to let me go. I can't be the woman you want me to be, I've changed.'

'I can change too, I'm trying to change. I've been reading and learning and I'm ready. I'm ready to support you and be the man you need me to be.'

'And I love you for trying, but you shouldn't have to change because of me. You're a kind and lovely man and you deserve a woman who wants to be looked after. I'm not that woman. I'm so sorry.'

Todd's heart felt like it might burst. He couldn't think of anything else to say to persuade her to change her mind.

A ringing phone distracted him from his thoughts. Frankie stood up and went to answer it.

'Hi, Callum, now's not a good time, can I call you back?... Sure, I'll give you a buzz later.'

Rage flared in Todd's stomach. 'It's him, isn't it? He's the reason you're dumping me.'

Frankie looked up from her phone. 'What?'

'That fucking policeman, Callum. Are you shagging him?'

Frankie stared at Todd, shocked, for a second before her features hardened. 'No, I'm not, not that it's any of your fucking business.'

'Then why was he calling you?'

'Because I have to go and have my thighs photographed as evidence of my attack!' she screamed at him.

'Frankie, I'm sorry...'

'Get the fuck out of my house!'

Without saying another word, Todd did as he had been asked.

On the walk back to Craig's house Todd's emotions vied for

attention. Sad because Frankie had tried to end their relationship. Angry because he was convinced she wasn't telling the truth about the policeman. Terrified because somewhere in his gut he was convinced the talk at the school was a terrible idea.

CHAPTER FORTY

I n the few days since Liam had told @beta2 he was ready to repay his revenge game debt and stop Frankie Currington once and for all, they had spoken via messenger almost constantly; first through the forum and then via mobile phone.

Almost immediately @beta2 had told him to be on the lookout for a package addressed to him. It was a brand-new iPhone and Liam was to use it to aid him in the planning of, and throughout, his mission. Most importantly, Liam was now only to contact @beta2 using the device. He'd explained to Liam how it was untraceable and it would add a layer of security to stop anyone finding out what they were planning ahead of time.

Make sure you turn the GPS tracker off. We don't want any hiccups and if someone does happen to find out about the phone, at least they won't be able to track you.

Unfortunately Liam's mum had got to the package first and demanded to know where it had come from.

'A friend sent it to me.'

'What friend? You never talk to anyone these days, you're on your computer all the time and none of your old friends could even dream of owning a brand-new phone like this.'

'You don't know them. Just leave it, will you.'

'Liam, is there something I need to know? Have you got yourself involved in something and can't get out of it?' she asked softly.

Liam hesitated for a second and then remembered what they'd said in the forum. *No one else understands you. Your family love you, but they can't understand. We get it, we know how you feel and what you're going through. We know you love your mum, but she's had sex, she had you, remember? So she can't comprehend how you're feeling.*

'For fuck sake, I've told you, no!'

Back in his room Liam told @beta2 his mum had seen the phone and was asking questions.

What did you tell her?

Nothing, I told her to mind her own business. This is going to destroy her though.

She'll be fine, Liam, there are lots of people around who will look after her. But there's only us who can look after you. We're your family now; the dads and the brothers you never had. You're one of us and we always look after our own.

Liam asked if anyone else had done what he was planning to do. He wanted to get a sense of how these things happened and what might go wrong. He wanted to know if @beta2 had been involved directly before; Liam knew he was the mastermind behind most of the planning, but had no idea if he'd ever personally been involved.

Liam needn't have worried; @beta2 sent through pictures and videos showing Liam the before, during and after of a plan like theirs. At first the pictures were hard to look at, the violence contained within them was like nothing Liam had ever seen. After a while though, they didn't bother him, especially once he started watching the videos.

He watched the videos until he was numb to them. Once that happened, he paid attention to the structure of the plot; the tactics of what had gone on and how it had been executed. Once Liam had the location he could then piece together his movements and plan out exactly how it was going to go down. Until then, all Liam could do was learn as much as he could from his predecessors and write down his story, as instructed by @beta2.

A new message buzzed through from @beta2. They seemed to come through constantly, but this was the message he'd been waiting for; they had a location for the execution of the plan. Liam was thrilled, clearly the gods were looking down on him. This was an area Liam knew intimately. There wasn't a nook or cranny, not an alleyway or shortcut Liam didn't know.

Liam replied:

This is ideal, I know this place like the back of my hand.

Perfect. I have someone standing by to plan the finer details, but if you're sure you know it so well, I'll leave it to you.

I'll handle it. We can always run it by them to do a double-check.

Liam started by opening Google Maps on the iPhone and tapped in the location he'd been given. He did know it almost as well as he knew his own home, but he didn't want to make any mistakes.

He spent hours poring over his phone and more than once being tempted to load the information onto his laptop to save his eyes. Each time he thought about it though, he remembered what @beta2 had warned him about leaving a trail of evidence, and ploughed on. Liam came up with several scenarios and plotted ideas for each one. Eventually he came up with a plan which allowed for small deviations depending on what the whore actually did on the day.

Liam rolled the word around in his mouth, *whore*. It was what @beta2 called her and he'd started doing it himself. He found the more he did it, the more he despised her and the more adamant he was that his plan succeed. @beta2 had backed up the notion by showing Liam pictures of her snogging a man they knew wasn't her boyfriend. Her poor cuckolded boyfriend who she'd thrown out. Liam had needed to look up 'cuckolded' but once he knew what it meant, he'd had to agree with the summation.

How dare that whore, that slut, tell women to withhold themselves from men like Liam, only to go around shagging two different men at the same time. It wasn't right and it made Liam even more determined to teach her a lesson.

Liam emailed @beta2 the details of the plan and asked a few technical questions, which were answered in a timely fashion.

```
You've done well, Liam. We're all very
proud of you and you should know you
have    the    backing    of    the    entire
```

```
community.  Go  onto  the  forum  now,  via
the  phone,  and  you'll  see  what  I  mean.
```

Liam logged on as instructed. Pinned to top of the page was a post telling everyone, in their unique code, what Liam was going to do for them all. Underneath there were already thousands of comments cheering Liam on and commending him for taking a stand.

They all loved him and Liam filled with pride that the group respected him enough to show this outpouring of emotion.

He was ready and prepared to carry out the bidding of the members. They would whisper his name reverentially, the same as they did the others who had gone before him.

Not long to wait now.

CHAPTER FORTY-ONE

F rankie's phone buzzed across on the bedside table. She picked it up and groaned quietly when she saw the caller ID.

She took a deep breath, clicked the green icon and said, 'Todd, what do you want?'

'Listen, Frankie, I know you don't want to talk to me—'

'You're right, I don't.'

'Please, just listen. I... I think you might be in danger.'

'For fuck sake, Todd, not this shit again!'

'Frankie, I'm being serious. I've been on the forum—'

'Honestly, you don't fucking listen, do you?'

'Frankie, I think they're going to do something at your talk – at the school.'

'Why on earth would you think that?'

'I saw it, on the forum, they're planning something. Please, you have to cancel.'

'Oh, well if you saw something on the forum I should do exactly what you say, shouldn't I?' Frankie's words dripped with sarcasm. 'So, what's the plan then? What exactly are they going to do?'

'I... I don't know, I just have this feeling it's going to be at the school.'

'You have a feeling? You don't actually know anything, you have a *feeling something might* happen during my talk?'

'Well, yeah, but—'

'Stop! Stop talking. This is the last straw, Todd. I've fucking had enough of you telling me what I can and can't do. In case you have forgotten about the last conversation we had, you are no longer my boyfriend. You do *not* get to tell me what to do anymore. Do not contact me. I will get in contact with you about the flat and coming to get your stuff. Do you understand?'

'Frankie, I just—'

'Do. You. Understand?' Frankie needed to get Todd off the phone, otherwise she was going to say things she knew she would regret.

'Yes,' came the feeble reply.

Frankie ended the call and tossed the phone onto the bedcovers. Her head in her hands, she growled out her frustration.

'Are you okay?' Callum asked.

'He just can't leave it alone.'

Callum had been asleep beside her, breathing softly, when she answered the call. To his credit, he hadn't said a word, or even moved, while she spoke to Todd. He'd popped round to see how she was the previous night, and after a couple of glasses of wine, one thing had led to another.

'What's he saying now?'

'He reckons this bunch of twats online are planning something during my talk at the school.'

'Did he say what?'

'No, only that he "had a feeling",' she replied using air quotes.

'Even if they are planning something, you've already got security in place, haven't you?'

'Yeah, Ruby's going to have some people on the door and some people inside.'

'There you go then.'

Frankie looked at Callum appraisingly for a moment. 'Aren't you going to try to talk me out of it?'

'Would it make a difference?'

'It would make a difference to how quickly I kick you out of my bed.' She was only half joking.

'Would I rather you didn't do it? Yes, of course I would, the idea of you being in any sort of danger scares me. But, I'm also of the opinion, being scared of these kinds of people only makes them bigger and scarier than they are. We have to carry on with our lives and as long as you're taking sensible precautions then I think you should do it. That, and trying to talk you out of it would be the quickest way to make sure I never saw you again, and I want to see you again.' He smiled sheepishly at her.

Frankie smiled back at him. 'Will you be there?'

'Do you want me to be?'

'I think you're the only person I trust completely enough to be right next to me. Ruby says her security guys are sound, but *I* don't know them.'

'I get it. I'll be there, right by your side the whole time.'

'Thank you.' Frankie leaned back into Callum and he wrapped his arms around her.

CHAPTER FORTY-TWO

My name is Liam Wallace and these are my reasons why.

I feel I should start by saying I never wanted this to happen, it was never part of the plan. It didn't even occur to me until very recently – until she got involved and became the head of the snake that needed to be cut off. But I'm getting ahead of myself.

I was a good son, a good student and, I like to think, a good friend. This despite there being no father or father figure in my life. My mother told me that my father walked out when I was very small; I have no memory of him. I cannot help but think had he been around to teach me things, masculine things, explain to me how being a man works, then things might have turned out differently. For that, I blame my mother. Not only could she not keep my father happy, but after he left, she could not satisfy another man enough to fulfil a role I needed in my life.

In the last eighteen months I have lost all of my friends, after the abject humiliation I encountered at the hands of the girls in my year. It wasn't enough that they considered themselves worthy enough to reject me sexually, but they also shamed and degraded me in public. Compounding their vile behaviour by sharing the evidence on social media. Know this, Kirsty Boyd – I have had my revenge and it was sweet.

To this day, I am celibate, involuntarily celibate, and this is through no fault of my own. The whores I have encountered are so selective in who they have sex with, I and other men like me, cannot hope to ever experience sex without taking it for ourselves. How is it fair that they hold all of the power and get to make all of the choices, leaving good men with nothing?

I have found a group of like-minded people who understand me, who are going through what I am going through and it is for them I carry out this redress in the balance of power; the family I have chosen for myself.

We have all felt hounded for our beliefs recently after she began spreading the lies of the females for the world to read. My most recent, and final, foray into romance was halted before it even began because she had given the slappers permission to lead us on and flirt and prick-tease without ever having to follow through. This was my epiphany moment.

Until they learn to bend to our ways, live by our laws, they leave us no choice but to wipe them from the face of the earth, one by one until they see the light.

This is my day of retribution for you, my family.

Liam sat back in his desk chair and took a sip from his can of Irn Bru. He desperately wanted a beer, but he needed to keep a clear head until he was satisfied this was one hundred per cent right. This was going to be his legacy.

He read it through again and then sent it to @beta2 for a final proofread. Once they were both happy, he might treat himself to a bottle of beer to help him sleep. One wouldn't do any harm, he reasoned, and a good night's sleep could only be a benefit.

He knew it wouldn't take @beta2 long to come back to him, he'd been in constant contact ever since the plan had been given the go-ahead, but while he waited, he decided to read through the details one more time. He knew it as well as he knew the layout of his own home, but he wanted to be sure he had the movements of the target memorised specifically. This was the absolute key to a successful mission.

> *Message from @beta2:*
>
> *This is perfect. We are all very proud of you, as you have seen from the support on your post. Remember: help will be there at the other end, and everything is in place for a successful operation. Your manifesto will be published tomorrow morning and we will talk for the final time then. In the meantime, I suggest you get some sleep – tomorrow is a big day.*

Liam replied thanking @beta2 for his support and advice, and then powered down his laptop. He did not want the excitement of the forum to cause his adrenaline to kick in, he needed all of that for tomorrow. Instead, he went and found a beer from the fridge in the kitchen, and then settled onto his bed to read more of the literature he had downloaded from the internet earlier in the week.

He was ready and tomorrow was game day.

CHAPTER FORTY-THREE

Todd woke but his eyes remained closed. His tongue was stuck to the roof of his mouth, and there was a pounding in his head, which he knew instinctively would get worse if he opened his eyes. He groaned and rolled over wondering if Drunk Todd had thought to put some water by the bed for Sober Todd.

With effort he managed to open his eyes enough to see there was a pint of water on the bedside table alongside a packet of paracetamol. Maybe Drunk Todd wasn't such a twat after all.

Very carefully, he swallowed down two of the pills along with the full pint of water.

'Stupid,' he whispered to himself afterwards. Todd knew the water wouldn't stay there for long, he'd drunk it too quickly.

He leaned over the side of the bed looking for a bin so he didn't have to leg it to the bathroom in his hung-over/maybe-still-pissed state. Turns out Drunk Todd was an absolute godsend – by the side of the bed was an empty washing-up bowl, which Sober Todd promptly filled when he threw up.

After spitting out the last of the bile, he lay back on his pillow and tried to remember the events of the night before.

This level of hangover suggested a marathon session, but Todd couldn't quite figure out why. The previous night was a dark blank space in his mind.

He picked up his phone, which Drunk Todd had remembered to charge, and looked at his messages to see if they could give him a clue. There was nothing, sent or received, and he hadn't put anything on social media for ages. He checked his call log, just in case, and was momentarily surprised to see a call to Frankie.

A second later, the previous evening came back to him like a steam train crashing into his mind. Frankie hated him. He *knew* she was in danger and she didn't believe him. She had yelled at him to leave her alone and forbidden him from getting in contact. After that, Craig had taken him to the pub and got him so drunk he couldn't remember coming home.

Todd checked his watch, 9.45am. He had a little over an hour to figure out what was going on and warn Frankie. Swinging his legs over the side of the mattress he sat on the edge of the bed and groaned. Swaying every time he moved was not going to help.

Gingerly, Todd dressed himself and grabbing the paracetamol, he headed towards the kitchen. He needed *all* the hangover cures today.

He found Craig making coffee and while he poured himself another glass of water, they grunted at one another with sufficient clarity that meant Craig knew he wanted strong coffee and food.

Back at the dining room table, which had become a home from home for him, he fired up his laptop. The last dose of paracetamol having ended up in the washing up bowl, Todd swallowed some more pills, only sipping at his water this time.

Craig placed a cup of coffee and a bacon sandwich on the

table next to the laptop and sat down on one of the vacant chairs.

'What are you doing?'

'I need to find out what their plan is. I know I'm right about this, so I need to prove it to her, and I only have an hour.'

Todd slouched back in his seat, pursed his lips and stared at the wall as Craig closed the laptop lid.

'Stop! You've warned her, she has the information, it's now up to her what she does with it.'

'But she doesn't believe me, so I need to prove it to her,' said Todd opening the laptop once more.

This time Craig shut the lid, picked up the computer and held on to it. Todd tried to snatch it out of his grasp, but Craig moved out of the way and held up one hand.

'Wait a minute, listen to me for a second, will you? Do you really think you're going to find a detailed plan posted in this fuckin' weirdo forum? Because that's what it's going to take to make her believe you – concrete evidence.'

Todd said nothing, simply glared at his friend.

'Fine.' Craig sighed and handed him back the laptop. 'Here, do whatever you want. I'm done trying to help you with this. You know if you keep going you'll lose her forever?'

'Yeah, but if it saves her, then I can live with that.'

Todd ignored Craig's stomping around the flat and concentrated on his laptop. He heard the front door slam and felt bad for a moment before refocusing on the task ahead of him.

Inside the forum, the furore around the 'announcement post' – as he'd taken to thinking of it – had mostly died down. There were a couple of new comments, but there were no replies to them and it seemed everyone had moved on.

He carried on scrolling through, reading the odd post and a few comments, but there was nothing else big being talked about. Todd slammed his fist down on the table causing everything to jump and his coffee to spill.

He ate his sandwich and drank some of his coffee while he tried to decide what to do next. By the time he was finished, he had no new plan. Frustrated, he decided he ought to go for a shower. Not only would that help with the thinking thing, it might also help with the hangover thing.

Once out of the shower, Todd checked the time, 10.45am. With no bolt of lightning having hit while he was showering and Frankie's talk due to start in about fifteen minutes, Todd decided to check the forum one last time.

And then, he promised himself, *I'll leave it.*

There was a new announcement pinned to the top of the forum, timed fifteen minutes previously when Todd had still been in the shower.

Fuck.

He clicked on the title and quickly read through the post. As Todd read the last few sentences everything became very clear and precise, both around him and inside his head. The clarity was simultaneously startling and terrifying in equal measure.

He darted from the table, knocking over the chair, and raced to his bedroom. Scrabbling for his phone, he pulled it free from the charger and phoned Frankie.

'Answer the fucking phone!' he screamed into the empty flat.

She sent the call to voicemail.

'For fuck sake!'

He slapped at the phone again to redial her number, this time she answered.

'I don't have time for your shit, Todd, I am just about to—'

'Frankie, listen, you have to listen to—'

'No, I don't. I'm hanging up now and then I'm blocking your

number. Oh, and I'm blocking Craig's as well, so don't even bother trying that.'

Before Todd could utter another word, he had been cut off.

'No, no, no!'

He tried once more, but, true to her word, Frankie had blocked his number.

CHAPTER FORTY-FOUR

Frankie took a deep breath and put her phone back into her bag. Taking out a tissue she angrily wiped the tears of frustration from her cheeks.

'I take it that was Todd?' Callum asked.

'He doesn't know when to give up. I've blocked him now, and Craig too, so...'

Callum gave her arm a rub. 'You've done the right thing.'

'I'll unblock him and deal with it once I've got through this,' she said focusing her gaze on the microphone on the stage.

'You've a couple of minutes yet. Are you ready?'

Frankie licked her lips and nodded determinedly. 'I think so. I just don't know how they're going to react.' She gestured to the auditorium before her which was filling up with teenagers.

'No doubt there will be some little pricks, there always are, but there are teachers here and I have no doubt you can handle a bunch of spotty little kids.' Callum pulled her in for a hug.

'Callum's right, you've got this. You know your stuff and you are a far better speaker than I will ever be,' Ruby encouraged.

'I don't know about that...'

'I promise you, if I didn't think you could do it, I wouldn't have asked you. Don't forget, you have the advantage of this being your old school. Use that to connect with them. And I know you said you didn't want to, but using your attack might help too.'

Frankie nodded once and took a deep breath, her eyes a picture of pure focus – she was ready.

Callum bent down to whisper in her ear. 'Shall we go out for dinner tonight? Celebrate your success?'

Frankie turned to look at him, her face millimetres from his, and smiled.

'That might be a little premature, but I'll take you up on it,' she said, giving him a kiss.

'As much as I hate to interrupt this cosy little romantic interlude, it's time. Are you ready?'

Frankie turned to look at Ruby, took a deep breath and nodded again. Ruby smiled and Frankie watched as Ruby walked confidently into the middle of the stage.

She watched as Ruby waited until the general hubbub had died down, and Frankie tried to draw in as much of Ruby's confidence as possible.

After a moment Ruby spoke, initially thanking the head and the staff then, 'It gives me great pleasure to introduce you to Frankie Currington, an ex-Corstmount student, who will be chatting to you today.'

Without pausing to give it any more thought, Frankie strode out onto the stage amidst a smattering of polite applause.

CHAPTER FORTY-FIVE

L iam stepped into the alcove of the fire door set back in the wall of the music building and placed his rucksack on the floor. Careful to shield it from the view of any passers-by, he tugged open the zips and did his final checks.

He'd had no more than thirty minutes training on how to use the rifle he'd been supplied, but it was a basic point-and-shoot he'd been told – no problem.

The house Liam had picked it up from was completely at odds to the one he had imagined. Instead of a run-down, dark, shabby little terraced house, the address Liam had been given was a detached bungalow on a quiet little road in Corstorphine. The front garden was immaculate and the exterior looked like it had recently been repainted. Liam had checked the address he'd been given three times. He knew the roads in that area all had similar sounding names and he hadn't wanted to get it wrong.

After being ushered inside, Liam had the surreal experience of being shown how to assemble, load and fire the gun while he could hear peals of laughter coming from children in the garden next door.

Confident everything was as it should be, Liam placed the rifle back in the rucksack making sure the stock was at the top to make it easy for him to pull out. He swung the rucksack back onto his shoulder and made his way to the theatre.

As detailed in his plan, Liam entered the theatre a minute or two after Frankie Currington had taken to the stage.

There was fierce whispering from the teachers at the door.

'You're late!'

'Sit down there.'

Liam did as he was told, taking an aisle seat a few rows down. If he'd been on time, he might have been forced to sit in the middle of a row, and that would mean there was a chance of him being stopped before he achieved his mission.

He listened as the main Stacy told her pitying tale of being 'attacked' in an alleyway while she walked home from the city centre one evening. Liam had to stifle a snort – attacked! She was walking home, by herself, in the dark, what did she expect? She was practically asking for it. And, he was pretty sure he'd heard a little moan escape from her lips as she'd felt his erection when he pressed himself against her.

The more Liam listened to her woe-is-me story, the angrier he became. How dare she? She quite clearly enjoyed the experience, because if she hadn't she wouldn't be telling anyone – except perhaps the police. Surely any foid who truly hated the experience would be so utterly humiliated they would never want to tell anyone, much less announce it in such a public way.

He felt the anger well up inside him, like lava inside a volcano ready to erupt and Liam knew it was time. He allowed his fury to flow unfettered, pulled the rifle from the rucksack and stood in one fluid motion.

Before anyone could register what he was doing, Liam stepped out onto the aisle stairs and shouted through the darkness, 'Don't lie, you fucking loved it!'

He raised the gun and in the ensuing melee a small thought pricked Liam's brain, *It really is easy to use.*

CHAPTER FORTY-SIX

'Don't lie, you fucking loved it!'

Frankie had her first cat-caller. Once she'd decided to use her attacks to prove the reality of the situation many women experienced, she'd expected it. If anything she'd expected it earlier. She paused for a second, her flow momentarily disturbed. Ruby had said this would happen and she had given her two ways to deal with it either—

'Gun!'

Frankie's head shot up from where she had been checking her notes as she heard the shout. Suddenly there was screaming and people running, climbing over seats, falling down the stairs.

She locked eyes with the boy halfway down the aisle and immediately registered he did actually have a gun in his hands, and it was aimed directly at her.

She opened her mouth to scream, as she was simultaneously knocked flying from her feet and the air around her exploded with cracks so loud it was as if a bomb had gone off.

The screams grew louder, more blood-curdling, and Frankie's instinct was to run. To run far way and hide from the madness around her.

She struggled and fought to move the mass on top of her. 'Get off, get off!'

The mass fought back, pinning her to the ground. 'Stay down!'

Frankie did as she was told, her breathing heavy and shallow. 'Need to... get off...' Her words barely more than a whisper, but even to her ears she sounded terrified.

A smell of rotten eggs filled the room and Frankie struggled with the assault on her senses.

The deafening screams and cracks continued and with a jolt, Frankie understood what she was hearing – gunshots. Fear swelled from her stomach and every instinct told her to get away.

Frankie could feel the panic attack start to take over, but there was no way to control it in the middle of a war zone.

She started fighting, determined to run and hide. The mass on top of her grunted, not expecting another attempt to get away, and she managed to push him off of her for a moment.

Frankie was scrabbling away from him when he landed like a dead weight beside her.

The cracks stopped, but the screams continued and new voices joined the shouting.

She turned to look.

It was Callum and he was staring at her through eyes that did not see.

The images before Frankie swam, and their edges blurred into one another. Red, there was so much red.

And pain: pain in her chest, in her head, her legs and arms.

Darkness crept in and stars exploded at the edges of her vision seconds before she hit the stage with a thud.

TWELVE PEOPLE DEAD IN SCHOOL SHOOTING MASSACRE

Yesterday armed police attended Corstmount High School after nearby householders reported hearing gunshots. Their response time of just six minutes saved many lives, but sadly they were too late for some of the victims.

It has been reported twelve people have now died, with a further three in hospital being treated primarily for gunshot wounds. Their present condition is unknown. At least one of the victims is known to have died while undergoing surgery.

Police have not yet released the names of any of the victims, contacting next of kin being their number one priority. However, the *Edinburgh Chronicle* has been advised by an unnamed source that at least one of the victims was an off-duty police officer.

There is no news yet of our reporter Frankie Currington who was speaking at the event.

The assailant, named locally as Liam Wallace, was taken into custody before he had the opportunity to take his own life and will face trial. Police Scotland have declined to comment on what charges he will face.

CHAPTER FORTY-SEVEN

A trolly with a squeaky wheel was pushed down the corridor past Frankie's hospital room as she continued to stare at the ceiling.

The police had been to see her earlier that day and told her Callum was dead. Dead because he'd been trying to protect her, dead because she'd pushed him off of her just high enough that a bullet had hit him in the neck and he'd bled out from his carotid artery. Dead and it was her fault.

They had asked her if she knew Liam Wallace, if she had ever met him before – she said no. Except it turned out she *had* because he had been the one to attack her in the alleyway that night; she hadn't recognised him.

The police went on to tell her how they had seized Wallace's computer and even though their investigations were preliminary, it was quite obvious he had been obsessed with her, hated her even. Liam Wallace was responsible for everything that had happened to her over the past few months, he had orchestrated a campaign of hate against her designed to 'put her in her place' and stop her from speaking out about women's rights and feminism.

'He saw you as the head of the snake that needed to be cut off – his words. He thought that if you stopped preaching your "lies" then other women would follow suit. When nothing else worked and he saw you were going to speak at his old school, it was the final straw for him,' said the detective inspector.

Frankie had stared at the officer, bile rising from her stomach. All those people, dead, because she wanted to spout off about feminism? Why had it never occurred to her other people might get injured? Selfish.

'So, what you're saying is, if I hadn't insisted on going ahead with the talk these people wouldn't be dead? Callum wouldn't be dead?' Frankie said eventually.

'This is *not* your fault. If Wallace hadn't fixated on you, then it would have been someone else. His online activity shows the ramblings of a deluded young man.'

'But it was me and there were warnings I didn't listen to.'

She had no more to say after that. Frankie told the officers she was tired and asked if they would come back another time to take her full statement.

Since then she had alternated between sleeping when the morphine took hold and staring into space when it wore off.

Occasionally she would become so overwhelmed by everything that had happened she sobbed uncontrollably. She tried hard not to think about anything, but invariably the memories would sneak into her mind and she would relive the whole thing all over again.

Frankie's thoughts were interrupted by knocking. She turned to see Todd standing in the doorway with a bunch of flowers.

'I would have come earlier, but they wouldn't let me in.'

'It's okay – I'm not really much company.'

'These are for you,' he said, placing the bouquet of peonies on the table over her bed.

'Thank you, my favourite.'

'I know,' he said with a watery smile. 'How are you?'

Frankie raised an eyebrow.

'I mean... you know what I mean,' he said as he sat in the chair by her bed.

'I was lucky. The bullet caught me in the shoulder, a few inches down it would've been my heart, a few inches up and it could have been my head. They've given me morphine on a pump so I can manage the pain, and it makes me sleep so I don't have to think about anything.'

'I'm glad you're okay. Have the police been to see you yet? Tell you what happened?'

'Yeah, they were here earlier. You were right, Todd,' she said as tears welled in her eyes for the umpteenth time.

'What do you mean? Right about what?'

'The shooter was an incel and I was the target. All the attacks have been to get me to stop and if I'd done what they said then all those people would still be alive. Apparently me talking at his old school about women's rights was the last straw for him.' Tears were flowing freely down Frankie's face and she struggled to control her voice, to make herself understood.

Todd froze, his eyes locked on hers. 'I really was right,' he said with undisguised venom, 'and now twelve people are dead with God knows how many more fighting for their lives. People are dead because you were so selfish, so interested in elevating your own *persona* that you had to keep *on* and *on*.' Todd was on his feet and shouting.

'I know, I know. I'm so sorry,' Frankie sobbed. She covered her face with one hand, unable to stand the look he was giving her any further.

'Sorry doesn't bring people back! You made me feel like I was being so unreasonable, you made me feel like shit. You never, ever gave a thought to anyone else, only how things affected *you*. I'm done. I thought, hoped, we could at least be friends, but I don't want or need friends like you.'

'Todd, I—'

'Not interested! You've shown your true colours. Never contact me again, I don't want to know you anymore. My things will be gone from the flat by the time you're discharged.'

A nurse appeared at the door, his mouth open, no doubt to ask what all the noise was about. Todd spoke before he could say a word, 'Don't bother, I'm leaving.' He raised his hand to stop the nurse from speaking.

As Todd left, the nurse rushed to Frankie's bedside and took her hand in his. 'Oh, hen, what's he said that's got you this upset? You're supposed to be resting, not getting all worked up. I'll be having words with him if he shows his face again.'

'It's all my fault,' were the only words Frankie could get out before she broke down completely.

FITNESS TO STAND TRIAL PSYCHIATRIC REPORT FOR LIAM WALLACE

I was asked to prepare this report by the High Court of Justiciary to evaluate Liam Wallace's fitness to stand trial for the murder of twelve people and the attempted murder of three others.

The data used in this report was compiled using notes from several interviews with the client, as well as projective procedures and objective questionnaires. These include: The Thematic Apperception Test and The Minnesota Multiphasic Personality Inventory.

BACKGROUND

Liam Wallace is an 18-year-old male, living with his mother in Edinburgh. His father has been absent since Liam was a young child and, after conversations with his mother, it is apparent there was no other significant male role model in his life. He has no siblings.

By all accounts, Liam led a 'normal' childhood and had a close group of friends with whom he attended Corstmount High School. A series of events approximately 18 months ago, that Liam felt were humiliating, led to Liam removing himself from the friendship group after which he became reclusive, sullen, secretive and rude.

FINDINGS AND OPINION

It is my opinion that Liam is suffering from a form of psychosis, characterised predominantly by delusions, but also by confused and disturbed thought processes.

Liam believes, unequivocally, that there is a secret master plan to prevent him, and his friends online, from enjoying a fulfilling and satisfying sex life. Whilst he says this is the fault of all attractive women, he states with utmost conviction that Frankie Currington is the leader of this movement. He believes it is his duty to rid the world of such women and in shooting a room full of unarmed people he has fulfilled his calling.

After interviewing Liam's mother, old friends, counsellors and prison officers, it is my opinion the cause of Liam's psychosis is severe stress and anxiety brought about by coercive persuasion by person or persons unknown.

Liam's symptoms include: severe mood swings, poor sleep patterns, aggressive behaviour and a series of flashbacks, as well as other more minor symptoms.

RECOMMENDATIONS

It is my opinion that Liam Wallace should be admitted to The State Hospital (Carstairs) in Lanarkshire under The Mental Health (Care and Treatment) (Scotland) Act 2003/2015 for further assessment and treatment before facing trial for murder.

CHAPTER FORTY-EIGHT

They lied to me. This was the thought that ran through Liam's mind as he listened to what his lawyer and therapist were telling him.

@beta2 had promised he would send a lawyer in the event he was arrested, only now it looked like he hadn't expected Liam to survive. He'd also said they'd use a temporary insanity or diminished responsibility defence, 'no problem', but his court-appointed lawyer was telling him neither were applicable in his case. Liam didn't really understand what was going on, but he could grasp the fact things were bad and his friend had abandoned him.

For the last two days he had been talking to a man he'd been told was a forensic psychiatrist, whatever that meant. He'd also been asked to fill out a load of questionnaires. Apparently they were trying to decide if he was insane at the time of the shooting, or if he had other mental health problems that might explain what he had done. The forensic psychologist had decided he needed more tests and should be kept in the loony bin for longer.

Although Liam disagreed entirely with the outcome, he

didn't argue. He knew he was only doing what needed to be done. Frankie Currington needed to be stopped from spreading her lies. Stopping her was only the start, but it was a step towards him and his brothers enjoying a sex life at last. This way meant he wouldn't have to stand trial, yet, and he could live in this cushy little hospital for a while instead.

Every now and then, Liam would flashback to the theatre and it was like he was there all over again. He chuckled to himself as he remembered the puff of blood and brains, and the look of sheer disbelief in the first Stacy's eyes when he shot her. He'd laughed at the time and turned to find his next target.

A strange sensation pricked at Liam's mind and he struggled to recognise it. He remembered seeing a second body at his feet and realised he hadn't meant to shoot his old teacher. He quickly pushed the thought away, if Mr McDonald was there he was obviously with *her* and he needed to be dealt with too.

'Liam? Liam, what are you laughing at?'

'Nothing,' he replied, annoyed his thoughts had been disturbed.

'Right, well, as I was saying. We've put together a treatment plan for you, which we'll start right away. As your lawyer said, the judge has instructed that you be incarcerated here until we've done some more tests. Do you understand?'

'I think so. I'm going to either live here or be in jail forever?'

His lawyer and his therapist gave each other a brief look before his therapist said, 'You'll have to go to trial and be convicted before you go to prison, but yes, you'll stay here until then.'

Later that evening when Liam was back in his room and settled for the night, his thoughts returned to the meeting earlier that day. Had it been worth it? He could see now how his so-called friends had used him, set him up.

Maybe it would have been better if he'd died. He could've shot himself, or aimed his gun at one of the policemen and let them do the job for him. But he'd believed it would be okay, he'd believed what @beta2 had told him and so when the police stormed in, he had calmly laid the gun on the ground, raised his hands in the air and allowed himself to be thrown to the floor and handcuffed while they screamed in his face.

How dare they abandon him after everything he had done for them? After everything he had done in their name? Didn't they understand how much they needed him? He had been prepared to die for the cause but they had told him there was no need and now he had nowhere to turn. Except, maybe...

Liam allowed the thought to roll around in his head. Could he do it to himself? Putting a bullet in his head would have been easy at the time, but there were no guns here. Here it would need to be pills, or a knife to his wrists, both slow and horrible ways to die. Did he have the guts even if he could get hold of either of those things?

With a start, Liam realised these were his choices. Kill himself, or spend the rest of his life miserable and incarcerated. He couldn't decide which was the worse fate.

CHAPTER FORTY-NINE

The taxi pulled up outside Frankie's block of flats. She paid the driver and thanked him as he lifted her suitcase from the boot.

'Sure you don't want me to help you upstairs with it?'

'No, I'm fine, thank you.'

Frankie wanted nothing more than to be alone in the quiet solitude of her own flat. They had been amazing at the hospital, taking care of her, getting her to talk to a counsellor, only letting her parents visit and telling everyone else this was hospital policy despite the fact it wasn't true. Frankie couldn't face a constant flow of people telling her it wasn't her fault when she knew it was – Todd had made that quite clear.

She trudged up the stairs, her left arm in a sling, and dragged her small case behind her. As she stepped inside the front door, she could already feel things were different. Only her coats and scarves hung from the pegs in the hallway.

In the lounge, Frankie stood in the middle of the room and rotated slowly on the spot. There were holes in the space where Todd had removed his belongings. The sofa was gone, dust and crumbs showing the space where it should have been on the carpet. He'd left the armchair she loved – they'd bought it together, but they'd always thought of it as 'hers'. She noticed a folded piece of paper on the dining room table that she'd assumed he would have taken, and saw it had her name on it.

Todd explained what he'd taken and why he'd left what he had. In his cold, emotionless note, he had given her an email address where she could get in contact if she needed to talk to him about the flat, but only the flat. Making it quite clear if she deviated from this there would be consequences.

Frankie screwed up the note, threw it across the room and sat down heavily, her head in her hands. After a few moments, with a surge of determination, and before she could change her mind, she retrieved her laptop from its charging station and opened it at the dining room table.

She composed and sent her resignation letter to Sid. She knew she owed him the respect to go and see him in person, but she couldn't face him, or anyone, at the moment. And if she didn't do it straight away, she knew she might chicken out. She had no idea what she was going to do now, but she knew she couldn't be a reporter anymore. She had lost all desire to be in the public eye, even if only on the fringes.

Next, she calmly deleted each of her social media accounts. There were hundreds of notifications and private messages, but knowing there would be both bad and good in there she ignored them all. Her brain could not handle anymore trolling.

She planned to set up a new email account, only giving the address to her closest friends and family.

That amounts to about five people now, she thought, tearfully. She had no one left apart from her parents and maybe Amy. She could never speak to Ruby again, Todd had made it clear he never wanted to hear from her and Callum was dead.

Before deleting her email account Frankie quickly scrolled through to make sure there was nothing important. She had given the police that email address and added them to the list of people to give her new one to.

After deleting all the spam and marketing, there were only a couple of dozen emails left, which she quickly checked through. She opened the one looking like it was from the police and immediately leapt to her feet, knocking the chair over behind her. She staggered backwards, tripping over the chair as she tried to put distance between herself and the picture on the screen.

The email contained a photograph of Frankie asleep in her hospital bed, but it also showed a sleeved arm, in its hand was a gun and it was pointing at Frankie's head. Beside the photo in large font were the words: NEXT TIME YOU WON'T BE SO LUCKY.

EPILOGUE

He typed in the URL for the Black Knights and Black Pills forum on his web browser. He wasn't sure why, it wasn't a natural environment for him, but he felt drawn to it.

As he scrolled through the posts and read some of the comments he realised there were so many like-minded people here. Men like him who had been cuckolded, who maybe weren't truecels, but had found themselves cast out and browbeaten by a woman.

He had been frustrated when she wouldn't allow him to take care of her. No, not frustrated, she'd emasculated him. Taken away what being a man meant to him. When he thought about it, she was always doing that. She tried to stop him from playing on his Xbox, from going to the pub with his mates, looked down on him because of his job, because he earned less than her.

Never again, vowed Todd. Never again would he put himself in that position. He was the man and this was his world. Was he pleased Frankie had been attacked and all those people had died? No. But he was pleased it had taught her a lesson.

Maybe he could help make other women see how it was supposed to be?

He smiled to himself and clicked on the 'create post' button.

Hi – I'm kinda new to all this, but I wondered if I might be able to help...

THE END

ACKNOWLEDGEMENTS

There are so many people to whom I'm thankful for their help in getting my debut novel published. I am going to try and thank each and every one of them here.

Firstly, my thanks go to the entire Bloodhound Team. I suspect I might be slightly more annoying than your average author since they also actually have to work with me! Betsy, Fred, Tara, Hannah and Abbie you guys all rock!

Special thanks to my friend, Betsy. She has held my hand and guided me through the process of writing a book with honesty and integrity. She lets me know when I've got it right *and* when I've got it wrong and that's exactly what I need – don't ever change, Woman!

My editor Morgen has been amazing and I have learned so much just from editing one novel with her to guide me. To my proofreader, Shirley and my beta-reader Maria – thank you for your diligence and attention to detail.

Thanks to John Marrs, Lesley McEvoy and Graham Bartlett for answering my questions and not making me feel like a total numpty when I asked questions with obvious answers!

My fellow Teletubbies, Patricia Dixon, Keri Beevis and

Nathan Moss, have been nothing short of amazing in their unwavering support while I wrote Open Your Eyes. Thank you for your advice, your guidance, your jokes and for making sure I didn't lose it completely when the writing got tough.

Thank you to my friends who have asked me questions, been excited for me and celebrated every stage of this process with me: Joe, Di, Clare, Pete, Ann-Marie and Jeff – you're all legends!

Huge thanks to my book festival mates for keeping excitement levels high at all times. Ann, Jen, Mik, the two Robs, Danny, Sharon, and anyone else who I've forgotten – sorry! – thank you for the friendship and good times.

Likewise, the support I have received from my family has been everything I could have ever wished for. Thank you, Mum and Dad, for – well, I'm actually at a loss for words here – for everything you have ever done for me and continue to do for me even though I'm now a grown woman! Your support is unwavering and means everything to me.

Special thanks go to Nikki Currington for not only allowing me to name a character after her, but also for allowing me to use her story in my book. The story of Nikki being made redundant because she was pregnant is a true one – although I have used an element of artistic license with some of the details.

My sister, Pamela, went above and beyond when she visited King George V Park in Edinburgh for me. Taking time out of her day to FaceTime and describe everything she could see, just so I could get it right when I was describing it. Thank you – you have no idea just how helpful that was.

I think my ten-year-old niece, Lily, might be the most excited person in the world about my book. Her excitement rubs off on everyone around her and it fills me with excitement and motivation too. Lily – Aunty Heather wrote a book! (But you can't read it just yet!)

I can't let these acknowledgements go by without mentioning my brother-in-law, Craig, and my other niece, and nephew, Teddy and Ivy. I'm sure Teddy and Ivy will be as excited as everyone else once they figure out what it's all about. (As will the bump who will be here by the time my book is published.)

Thank you to all the readers and reviewers who take the time. Without you guys there is little point to all of this – you're all awesome!

My final words are reserved for my amazing husband, Stuart. I do not say it lightly when I say, I could not have done this without him. He has stood by me, held my hand, celebrated with me, laughed with me and told me how proud he is of me often. He has put up with me talking about books for the last fifteen years, he encourages me at all times and even joins me in talking about my characters as if they are real people. I'm not very good at telling people I'm an author, but he never lets an opportunity pass when we meet new people.

My best friend, my soul mate, my prince – thank you for everything. I can't wait to spend the rest of my life with you.

A NOTE FROM THE PUBLISHER

Thank you for reading this book. If you enjoyed it please do consider leaving a review on Amazon to help others find it too.

We hate typos. All of our books have been rigorously edited and proofread, but sometimes mistakes do slip through. If you have spotted a typo, please do let us know and we can get it amended within hours.

info@bloodhoundbooks.com

Printed in Great Britain
by Amazon

83303203R00171